"I'm having child-care problems," Evan confided.

"Gracie's teacher thinks I'm falling down on the job," he continued. "And she's right. I'm screwing up. My kids are climbing out windows and pestering total strangers like you."

"I could pick Gracie up from her school," Filomena offered.

His eyes met hers. She *could* make his life a little easier over the next few weeks—yet he suspected she could make it a lot more complicated, too.

"But you're not going to get to know me sitting in your car in my driveway. Maybe we should discuss this some other time," she said.

He did a quick calculation. "Why don't you come over for dinner tomorrow, and we can see how everyone gets along. I'll broil something."

"Broiled something sounds delicious. See you tomorrow, Evan," she told him, then left.

Damn. He needed a baby-sitter for his kids, not a girlfriend, not a lover, not a babe to star in his fantasies. Not a sophisticated New Yorker who dressed like a gypsy and sat alone in a big house, drinking wine and listening to harpsichord music.

Not a woman named Filomena Albright, who seemed perfectly able to leave him spellbound....

Dear Reader,

The holidays are a magical time. The streets of small towns and big cities alike get cleaned up and dressed up. The music piped into the stores changes from all those sappy, predictable tunes we hear throughout the rest of the year to carols and other holiday classics. We indulge in foods we enjoy at no other time. (In my family, it's my special holiday sugar cookies—which are awfully hard to prepare, but I'm willing to bake them once a year.) And, of course, our children start behaving very, very well....

What better time to revisit THE DADDY SCHOOL?

Evan Myers, the hero of 'Tis the Season, would surely argue that his beloved two brats, Billy and Gracie, are not behaving well at all. Yet their misbehavior brings him magic in the form of Filomena Albright, an exotic, intriguing woman whose life is somewhere else and who has no intention of remaining in Arlington, Connecticut, once the new year rolls around.

Filomena's magic alters Evan's life. Can he and his children work enough magic to keep Filomena from leaving them?

Happy holidays!

Judith Arnold

'Tis the Season
Judith Arnold

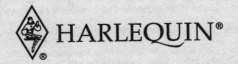

HARLEQUIN®

TORONTO • NEW YORK • LONDON
AMSTERDAM • PARIS • SYDNEY • HAMBURG
STOCKHOLM • ATHENS • TOKYO • MILAN • MADRID
PRAGUE • WARSAW • BUDAPEST • AUCKLAND

ISBN 0-373-70952-8

'TIS THE SEASON

This edition published by arrangement with Harlequin Books S.A.

® and TM are trademarks of the publisher. Trademarks indicated with ® are registered in the United States Patent and Trademark Office, the Canadian Trade Marks Office and in other countries.

Visit us at www.eHarlequin.com

Printed in U.S.A.

This book is dedicated to the Smith College Class of '74
(and especially those very generous Albright women!)

CHAPTER ONE

BILLY DIDN'T HATE Gracie. It was just that she could be a pain in the butt sometimes.

Like when she was whining, she cranked up her voice louder than an ambulance siren and he just wished she would shut the heck up. And she would follow him around when he didn't want her to, and she was always asking him to play stupid games with her, involving dolls and other icky stuff. And she liked to tell on him. Sometimes he told on her, too, but when he did, it was only because he had to, not because he wanted to—if she was doing something dangerous, for instance, or if she spilled popcorn all over the kitchen and Dad yelled at him to clean it up, even though it wasn't his mess. A guy had to defend himself, right?

But he didn't *hate* her. She was his kid sister, so he supposed he loved her, even if she was a pest.

He sure wasn't filled with love when he saw her emerging from the woods into the clearing by the haunted house. This was his special place and he didn't want her knowing about it. He hadn't even told his best friend, Scott, about it. He hadn't told anyone. But now Gracie was here, and she'd probably blab about it all over Arlington.

How she'd managed to follow him without his hearing her was a mystery. He must have been making a lot of noise while he hiked through the woods. In the November cold, the leaves and branches cluttering the ground were so brittle every step he took made a loud crunch, and that must have drowned out the sound of her tramping along after him. Or maybe he hadn't heard her because of the crows, which never disappeared in the winter like other birds and which cawed louder than Gracie's whine. Or maybe he'd missed the sound of her because the wind kept kicking up and rattling the empty tree branches.

In any case, he was pretty startled when he heard her voice, loud and clear: "Whose house is that?"

He spun around and discovered her standing by the edge of the woods, staring past him at the house. Little puffs of vapor came out of her mouth. She had her hands on her hips, and she was wearing a jacket that used to be his a few years ago, blue denim lined with fleecy white stuff. It shouldn't have looked right on her, because it was definitely a boy's jacket. Billy would never wear a jacket that looked good on a girl.

But it looked okay on Gracie.

He turned back to the house. It was constructed of stones—not neat squared-off blocks of fieldstone, but big round stones held together with cement, which gave the building a cold heavy appearance. It had a back porch with a gloomy overhang and a sloping tiled roof. Billy didn't really think it was haunted—he was too old to believe that kind of garbage—but it was cool to pretend.

"It's haunted," he told her, thinking maybe if he scared her she'd leave him alone and go home.

"I don't believe you." For a kid who hadn't even started kindergarten yet, she could be a real wiseass.

"Of course it's haunted. Check it out. It's all dark and spooky."

"So what? I don't believe in ghosts."

"Did I say it was haunted by ghosts?"

That caught her interest. She tilted her head a little and said, "What's it haunted by?"

"Spirits. Invisibile spirits."

"What are spirits?"

"They're kind of like ghosts, only different."

"How can you see them if they're invisible?"

She was definitely too smart. "You don't see them. You *feel* them," he told her.

"I wanna feel one," Gracie announced, marching across the dead grass. It hadn't been mowed all summer and it had gotten pretty long before it died. Now it lay limp and matted like pale brown hair against the ground.

"It's not like you can just go up to a spirit and touch it," Billy warned her as she walked right by him and up the steps to the porch. This was another reason he couldn't hate her. She was so brave. She was a girl, not even five years old, and she was braver than a lot of boys Billy knew.

He hurried up the porch steps after her. The windows overlooking the porch had shutters or something blocking them, and she was too short to see over the shutters. But she was trying, standing on tiptoe, gripping the windowsill and jumping up to get a view.

"Are the spirits inside?"

"Yeah. But they're invisible."

"Pick me up, Billy. I wanna look."

That was one of things he didn't like about her: she could be awfully bossy. "Say please."

She put her hands on her hips again and rolled her eyes at him. "Please," she said, stretching the word out to let him know how unnecessary she thought it was.

Scowling, he wrapped his arms around her belly and hoisted her up. She peeked over the shutters and he let her down. The porch had been painted a dark green a long time ago, and chips of faded paint flaked off when her feet hit the boards. "I can't see anything," she said. "It's too dark."

"You can see better from the side." He led her off the porch and around to the side of the house, where the afternoon sun hit the windows. It was a pretty weak sun, more white than yellow, the kind of sun that promised snow. Billy knew better than to hope for snow, though. It hardly ever snowed in Arlington before December.

The windows were higher off the ground here than on the porch, but there were no shutters and the view was better. He knew; he'd spied through pretty much every window on the first floor, and the windows on this side of the house were the best. The room on the opposite side of the glass was filled with strange shapes draped in white sheets. Billy figured it was furniture covered with cloths to protect it, but the first time he'd seen the draped pieces was when he'd decided to pretend the house was haunted, because the white cloth did look kind of like ghosts. If seeing them didn't scare Gracie, nothing would.

She skipped alongside him to one of the windows, placed her hands on the windowsill and glanced over her shoulder at him to signal that she was ready for a boost. Not a please, not a thank-you—just that bossy look of hers.

Billy sighed and circled his arms around her. If he made a big thing out of her not saying please, she might start whining. Or worse, she might tell Dad about the house, and he'd say they shouldn't be wandering through the woods by themselves and trespassing on someone else's property, and Billy would wind up in trouble.

So he braced his feet and lifted her up. "Oooh!" she said, almost a whisper. "Are those the invisible spirits? They look like ghosts!"

"You can't see the invisible spirits," he reminded her. "They're invisible." She was beginning to get heavy. Her coat was bulky, and it made her heavier.

"They're moving!" Gracie gasped. "Put me down, Billy! Put me down!" She wasn't whiny or even screaming. She sounded as if she was choking on her own breath. "Put me down!"

He lowered her to the ground and she bolted, heading straight for the woods. He knew he ought to go after her, just to make sure she didn't get lost, even though the woods weren't too dense and the distance between the haunted house and their house wasn't that far. But he couldn't chase after her until he looked first. He had to see what was moving.

He inched up to the window. There were all the weird cloth-covered shapes, just as he'd remembered from last time. Dust made the air thick, and with the sun so weak and wintry the room seemed hazy.

Then he saw it. A shadow moving, floating just beyond the doorway, dark and creepy, there and not there.

Whispering a curse that would have gotten him sent to his room for the rest of the day, he charged after Gracie, racing for the woods as fast as he could run.

BY THE TIME Filomena got to the window, no one was there.

She was pretty sure she'd heard footsteps, the hollow thud of someone tramping on the back porch, but when she'd peered outside the porch had been empty. Either the old house was creaking and groaning or her imagination was running wild. Or else someone *had* been outside and had run away.

Whichever it was, she didn't care. The entire experience of being back in the house after so many years was eerie and disorienting. A few extra thuds weren't going to make a difference.

She glided across the small parlor to the window and gazed through the dirt-fogged window at the yard. She used to love romping in that yard—it always captured the afternoon sun, and the lawn would be so much cooler than the air, the grass brushing against her bare soles as she scampered around with her playmates. She hadn't had too many close friends in Arlington, since she'd spent only her summers and holidays here, living the rest of the time at boarding school or else traveling with her parents. The house had seemed much more isolated in those days. Now, newer houses had sprouted all around, right up to the edges of the five-acre estate.

The view from the windows made her smile. Turning, she surveyed the cozy parlor and smiled again. She tugged on one of the drop cloths that shrouded the furniture, freeing a cloud of dust. The piano was under that cloth. After a good five years without a tuning, it was probably a mess. God knew, spiders or rodents might have taken up residence inside it.

But she'd seen no evidence of rodents, and spiders didn't scare her. She lifted the cloth and tossed it onto the floor. Despite all the dust on the topside of the cloth, the wood underneath looked smooth and polished. Taking a deep breath, she slid back the keyboard cover and played a chord. A bit tinny, a bit flat, but not bad.

Her smile grew.

She hadn't been doing much smiling recently. Bad enough that her mother had died. At least she'd died doing something splendidly in character—climbing Mont Blanc. Filomena had flown to France, recovered her body, had it cremated as per her mother's wishes, then transported the ashes to Greece and scattered them into the Aegean Sea. Filomena's father had met her mother in Greece. They'd fallen in love there. When he'd died, her mother had scattered his ashes there and instructed Filomena that when she died she wanted to join him in the magnificent blue sea.

It had been sad—and remarkably expensive—but that was what her mother wanted, and Filomena was not going to ignore her mother's final wish. When it was done, she'd flown back to New York City to grieve. Her grief had taken a stunning turn when she met with her mother's lawyer, who reviewed the estate with her and explained, as gently as he could, that her mother left debts of nearly two hundred thousand dollars. "Climbing in the Alps is an expensive holiday," he pointed out when Filomena had asked how such a thing could be possible. "Traveling through Tibet on the back of a yak doesn't come cheap. Snorkeling at the Great Barrier Reef, sailing to the Galápagos... Your mother lived life to the fullest, Filomena, but she wasn't terribly prudent when it came to her finances."

"But...but my father left her a small fortune," Filomena argued.

"A bit too small for your mother's needs, I'm afraid. At least she didn't fritter it away on junk. I always admired your mother, even when I was warning her about her dwindling resources. Obviously, she didn't listen to my warnings.''

"What am I going to do?" Filomena asked, feeling weak and dizzy. Two hundred thousand dollars? She barely kept herself housed and fed on the income from the modest trust fund her father had set up for her, combined with the research fellowship she received from the university. She was a graduate student, for heaven's sake! How was she going to come up with two hundred thousand dollars to pay her mother's debts?

"There's the house in Arlington," the lawyer reminded her. "I'm not sure what condition it's in, but if you fix it up and sell it, it should bring in enough money to cover her debts and then some.''

It had never occurred to Filomena that this house would someday not be in her family. Even if she hadn't been back in five years, she'd always known that she *could* go back and it would be waiting for her, big and solid and secure. Given how much traveling her parents did, the house in Arlington was the one home Filomena could depend on. Her family might meet in Hilo for Christmas, in Gstaad for New Year's, or her parents might fly her to Fairbanks, Alaska, at the end of the spring term so they could do a little mountain climbing, but she'd always known she had a true home waiting for her in Connecticut.

She'd never been given to swampy sentiment, and she wasn't going to fall apart at the thought of having to sell the house now. It had to be done. Her mother's debts had to be paid.

But it would take at least a month or two to get the house into shape to put on the market. Using that time to fix the place up shouldn't be a problem; no one shopped for a house in the weeks before Christmas, anyway.

She abandoned the piano and yanked the cloth off the wing armchairs facing it. They looked good, their embroidered cushions undamaged. She supposed she would sell most of the furniture along with the house—she certainly had no place for it in the cramped studio apartment she rented in a genteelly slummy neighborhood a few blocks from the Columbia University campus. Some of the pieces might be antiques; she should have an appraiser come in.

But until she did, until she attached a price tag to the place, the house and everything inside it were hers. She could live here through the end of the year, wander the rooms, clean the place and dress it up. Maybe for New Year's Eve she would invite a bunch of her friends up from the city, and they'd have a final bash, bidding farewell to the year and the house at the same time. It was what her mother would have done. Leila Albright had always loved a good party.

Filomena wandered out of the parlor and down the broad hall that ran from the front of the house to the back porch. She twisted the bolt and jerked several times on the knob to get the door open—it was sticky from years of disuse. The back porch had always been a shady haven where she could come to cool off after running around in the sun. She used to sit on the porch with a tall glass of lemonade and a plate of cookies and feel the sweat chill off her arms and feet. It was like hiding on the dark side of the moon.

She shoved on the screen door—shoved three times until it was jarred loose—and stepped out onto the porch. The grass beyond was so long and scraggly, the shrubs so unruly, she was embarrassed. Her mother should have paid a landscaping service to maintain the grounds, at least. But the porch planks beneath her feet felt firm. No sign of termites or dry rot.

Turning back toward the door, she spotted footprints, a faint maze of swirls and wiggles, the sort of elaborate tread found on sneakers. Looking closer, she noticed two different sets of footprints, one pair of swirly treads larger than the other, both sets smaller than her own feet. They led to a window. The film of dirt on the windowsill bore a set of tiny fingerprints.

So she hadn't imagined the thuds. She'd had some young visitors.

Children from the neighborhood? she wondered. Not that the house sat in a neighborhood. The property was too big, the house set far back from the road in front and bordered by a forest in back. Children spying through her windows would not have simply come upon the house while passing by.

She hoped they hadn't committed any acts of vandalism. She observed no damage on the back porch, no broken windows, no spray-painted walls. Descending the steps, she peered into the forest, and saw nothing but leafless trees mixed with pine and spruce above a carpet of dead leaves and browning ivy. She tramped around to the side of the house, where she thought she'd glimpsed some activity through the window. She found more fingerprints on a windowsill—a young child's stubby hands—and below the window, lying in the grass, a small pink barrette in the shape of a butterfly.

All right, then. Children must have been peeking through the windows. No harm in that, she supposed.

That her childhood home would have attracted other

children pleased her in an odd way. Maybe they felt drawn to the house the way she had as a child. Maybe they liked to romp in the sun and cool off on the porch. Maybe they played hide-and-seek under the steps, in the holly bushes and behind the old shed that served as a garage at the end of the gravel driveway. Maybe, like Filomena, they understood the specialness of this grand old house.

She scooped up the barrette, then turned and walked back to the porch, her lungs filling with the raw mid-November air. Behind her the woods whispered in the wind.

Closing her fingers around the barrette, she found herself hoping that the children would come back.

CHAPTER TWO

IF EVAN MYERS'S LIFE were a movie, this would be the scene in which he pounded his fists on a locked door and screamed, "Let me out of here!"

He wasn't in a movie, though. He was in what had to be the most tedious meeting he'd ever endured—and since it had been arranged for his supposed benefit, he couldn't very well rise from his chair, yawn loudly and saunter out of the room. Being the boss meant having to behave himself. After all, the gentlemen making their presentation at the other end of the conference table had traveled all the way from Atlanta just to explain, earnestly and at great length, why Champion Sports ought to stock their cushioned insoles in all its stores. Rudeness wasn't called for.

Did everyone from Georgia talk so slowly? Evan wondered.

They'd brought charts with them. They'd brought slides, too, but Evan had declined to provide an overhead projector, so they were making do with an easel, a pointer and about a hundred meticulous poster-board renderings. The chart on display at the moment allegedly demonstrated that the cushioning of Pep Insoles, when inserted inside standard running shoes, reduced the likelihood of a runner's developing shinsplints by thirty-seven percent.

"Thirty-seven percent?" Evan interjected. If he kept

his mouth shut, the presentation might move along faster, but he couldn't resist. "How do you know it's thirty-seven percent, as opposed to, say, thirty-five percent? Or forty percent?"

Unfortunately, the gentlemen from Atlanta had an answer. In fact, they had a chart. "As you can see," one of them drawled, propping the relevant chart on the easel, "we calculated thirty-seven percent through our performance tests. We tested a group of one hundred recreational runners using the Pep Insoles and a control group of one hundred recreational runners not using them. After both groups had jogged five miles a day for eight weeks on a crushed-asphalt track, we compared the number of shinsplint sufferers who'd been using Pep Insoles with the number in the control group who experienced shinsplints, and this produced the figure we've supplied—thirty-seven percent."

Well, Evan had to give them points for precision.

"But we'd like to emphasize that the reduction in shinsplints is not the primary function of Pep Insoles. As we can see in this chart—" Georgian Number Two flipped through the charts while Georgian Number One drawled on "—the primary function of Pep Insoles is to increase athletic performance. Now here we calculate the vertical jumping ability of basketball players using Pep Insoles as compared with a control group without the insoles. As you can see by the calculations…"

How about the losing-control group? Evan wanted to snap. "This is all fascinating," he broke in, "but I'll tell you what's really got me concerned. You said about a half hour ago that the insoles are being manufactured in Honduras. I want to know if they're being made by ten-year-old kids for a dime a day. Because if they are, I'm not going to stock them, even if they give your average high-school basketball player the air time of a Michael Jordan.''

"We haven't gotten to our labor chart yet," Georgian Number Two told him. "I promise you we'll address that very subject when we get to our discussion on our production facilities.''

"Right now," Georgian Number One added, "we want to complete our discussion of the performance-enhancing abilities of the Pep Insoles. We prefer to give our presentation in order, Mr. Myers. It works better that way.''

It works longer, Evan thought glumly. Next to him, Jennifer kicked him under the table. She was his vice president, and she knew him well enough to recognize apathy when he was suffering a near-fatal case of it.

She'd been the one to set up this meeting; she was the one wowed by the product, the one who wanted to carry it in the Champion stores. He, on the other hand, was the one who had to put together the Tank Moody promo to take advantage of the holiday shopping season, and he ought to be focusing on that right now, not on Pep Insoles. He was also the one who had to make sure inventory was high enough to cover the expected surge in shoppers at this time of year, and to confirm that the clerks at all his stores were maintaining good cheer despite the inevitably frazzled nerves and frayed tempers of the customers. And if that wasn't enough to distract him, he was worried about the kids. They'd been acting strangely ever since they'd come home from a hike through the woods yesterday afternoon.

Once they'd gotten home they'd stayed put and played quietly. During dinner, no bickering, no sniping, no fighting over the salt shaker, no competition to dominate the conversation. Gracie had looked so pale Evan had considered taking her temperature, but she'd insisted she was fine, and her forehead had felt cool to the touch. She and Billy had watched *The Simpsons* sitting side by side on the sofa in the den without tussling over the remote, and they'd gone to bed without a quibble.

There was pre-Christmas good behavior, and there was weird behavior. Billy and Gracie hadn't been exercising pre-Christmas behavior Sunday afternoon. They hadn't appeared to be suppressing their natural hostile instincts or struggling to mind their manners. After Gracie had vanished into her bedroom, Evan had asked Billy if anything unusual had happened to them while they'd been outdoors earlier, but Billy had sworn nothing at all had happened—and then he'd lifted his *Bunnicula* book and started to read.

Without Evan's telling him to turn off the TV and find a book, Billy had started to read. Definitely weird.

One of the Pep reps was elaborating on the comments of a U.S. Olympic track coach who believed the Pep Insoles might improve the performance of hurdlers. Evan sighed—not too audibly, but Jennifer obviously heard him, because she kicked him again. For a compact woman, she packed a wicked kick. Maybe she had Pep Insoles stuffed inside her stylish leather pumps.

He glanced at his watch and grimaced. Four-thirty, and the reps hadn't even gotten to the part that mattered most to him: Were the insoles manufactured by underpaid Honduran children? No way was this meeting going to end in time for him to pick up Gracie at her preschool by five o'clock.

He sighed again, this time not caring if everyone in

the room heard him. "Excuse me," he said, gazing at the Georgian gents and ignoring the anger he could feel radiating from Jennifer. "We're going to have to take a break here. I've got to make a call. Or—" a pleasant idea struck him "—you can keep on going without me." He sent Jennifer a broad grin.

She did not grin back. "I think we'll all take a quick breather," she suggested. Heaven forbid Evan should miss a single scintillating minute of the presentation.

He liked Jennifer. More important, he needed her. She was yin to his yang, or however the saying went. She was the one who found new products, introduced them to Evan and helped him decide whether to stock them in the stores. She was good at her job. And for all he knew, these Pep Insoles might be a fabulous product—although even if they were, he wasn't going to devote precious shelf space to them during the pre-Christmas sales season, when people would be streaming into Champion Sports outlets throughout southern New England hoping to buy little Johnny or Susie or Uncle Mike a nice leather first-baseman's glove, a soccer ball, a pool cue, golf clubs, ice skates, free weights or whatever else might look suitably festive wrapped in red and green paper and planted under a Douglas fir in the family room. Somehow, Evan couldn't imagine little Johnny or Susie or Uncle Mike writing a letter that said, "Dear Santa, I've been really good this year, so please bring me some Pep Insoles for my sneakers."

He nodded to the Pep Insole guys as he passed them on his way to the door. It wasn't locked; he didn't have to pound on it and scream, "Let me out!" Even so, when he crossed the threshold, he felt liberated. He had to stifle the urge to sprint to the elevator and make his escape.

Exercising exemplary self-discipline, he crossed the hall to his office, reached for the phone on his desk and pressed the memory-dial button for Gracie's preschool. After two rings, a familiar voice came on the line: "Children's Garden, may I help you?"

"Molly? It's Evan Myers."

He could almost picture the school's director cringing. "I hope you're not calling to tell me you're going to be late."

"I'm calling to tell you I'm going to be late," he said, seasoning his voice with contrition and brave cheerfulness. "I'm really sorry. These people flew up from Atlanta to pitch their product, and they're running long. I can't get them to shut up. We've got at least another half hour here before we're done."

"Evan." Molly sounded stern. He could understand how she managed to keep a school full of rambunctious toddlers in line. She didn't even have to raise her voice to make him quail in his loafers. "This is the third time in two weeks you've been late."

"I'll pay the late fee, Molly. I'm really—"

"—sorry," she finished for him. "Not good enough. The late fee is supposed to be a deterrent, Evan. It doesn't seem to be deterring you."

He raked a hand through his hair and scrambled for a strategy to soften her up. She was a petite woman, cute and warm and wise in the ways of children—but she was also tough. Very tough.

He decided to make a play for pity. "You know, it's hard being a single father. I've got a business to run, I've got two kids to raise and I'm doing it all by myself."

"You shouldn't be," Molly said simply. "You ought to hire a nanny or a baby-sitter. Or an au pair. Someone to help you out in the afternoons. I know you've got a system of after-school arrangements for your son, but you can't keep leaving Gracie here after hours and expecting us to take up the slack.''

"I know, but—"

"And while I've got you, Evan, Gracie's been very quiet today. Almost withdrawn. She hasn't been herself.''

"I know.'' Even though she didn't have a fever, she could be coming down with something. If he was any kind of father, her health would be his top priority. And it was. But he was stuck in the middle of this god-awful meeting. "All right. I'll send someone over to pick her up,'' he said, guilt devouring him. "I'll send my secretary.''

"Make sure she has a note from you and photo ID,'' Molly reminded him. "I don't like turning Gracie over to someone I don't know.''

"Of course.''

"I mean it, Evan. These jerry-rigged child-care arrangements aren't good for your kids or for you. If you need help, get it.''

"Okay.'' If he were twenty-five years younger, he'd be hanging his head in shame.

"You're a wonderful father,'' Molly added, tossing him a sop before she said goodbye.

One self-abasement down, one to go. He hung up the phone and hurried from his office into the one next door. "Heather, I need an extremely big favor from you,'' he said, reaching for the pad of Champion Sports memo paper on her desk.

Heather was young, gorgeous and endowed with an abundance of attitude. She burned through boyfriends the way Pedro Martinez burned through batters—it seemed as if every guy who went up against her wound up striking out. She alarmed Evan with her high-potency beauty and her sheer nerve, but she was so proficient at her job he was grateful to have her.

"What favor?" she asked, flashing a smile that would fell a weaker man.

"Drive over to the Children's Garden and pick up Gracie for me."

"I hate children," Heather said laconically.

"I'm not asking you to love her. I'm asking you to pick her up. I'm being held hostage by Jennifer and those guys from Pep Insoles, and can't go get Gracie myself."

Heather hesitated, nibbling her lush lower lip. "Picking your daughter up at preschool isn't part of my job description."

"I know it isn't. But flexibility *is* part of your job description. And don't forget, we're getting close to year-end bonus time." He scribbled a note to Molly Saunders-Russo on the memo pad, identifying Heather as his official emissary.

The word *bonus* clinched the deal. "All right," Heather muttered, plucking the note out of his hand. "But this is the last time."

The last time this year, Evan amended silently. Next year another bonus would be at stake. He watched her pull her purse from a desk drawer and saunter past him to the door, her chin held high, her ash-blond hair falling in a perfectly swinging pageboy.

He waited until she was out of sight, then felt the air seep from his lungs. How could it be that he'd come so far, accomplished so much more than anyone would have predicted, building a business and raising two magnificent kids—and yet he felt like a total failure?

All right. He wasn't a failure. He just happened to have a few people exasperated with him right now: Molly at the preschool, Heather, Jennifer. The three women on whom his entire existence depended, he thought glumly.

But he hadn't gotten where he was by surrendering to circumstances. He would tighten the controls on his time at work—as soon as the Christmas retail season was over—and be out the door by ten minutes to five every day, even if it meant taking work home with him in the evenings. He could stick to a rigid schedule from January until June. In the summer the kids had camp, and in the fall Gracie would start kindergarten. Evan could get her into the after-school program Billy was enrolled in.

All he had to do was survive until New Year's Day.

Back in the conference room, the Pep squad were shuffling their collection of posters. Evan hoped they were figuring out which ones were nonessential and dispensing with them. If he sat through this long-winded lecture only to learn that the insoles were manufactured by exploited child laborers, he might just toss one of the representatives through the window. Or both.

"We were discussing the value of Pep Insoles to track performance," one of them began as Evan, Jennifer and Stuart, the head of marketing, resumed their seats at the table. Evan fiddled with a pencil until Jennifer glared at him. He checked his watch again. He paid halfhearted attention as the Pep folks rambled on in their distinctly unpeppy way. He thought about Tank Moody and wondered whether this time would be better than the last time Champion Sports had hired a professional athlete for a special promotion.

Well, of course it would be better. It couldn't possibly be worse. Who was Tank Moody going to run off with?

Jennifer? Given Tank's modest intellectual gifts, she'd never be interested in him. Heather might, though. As far as Evan could tell, Heather cared more about size than IQ.

Not that Evan had any inside information about Tank's size. But sportscasters were always saying that football was a game of inches.

He grinned, then felt Jennifer's suspicious gaze on him, as palpable as a jab in the ribs. Sobering up, he lifted his eyes to the chart on the easel and struck a rapt pose. The guy had launched into a discourse on the similarities between Pep Insoles and shock absorbers. If Jennifer weren't glaring at him, Evan would have started doodling on his notepad.

After about ten minutes on shock absorption, the Pep Insole people finally pulled out a chart concerning their production facilities, which were located in a suburb of Tegucigalpa, and gave a high-minded explanation of why they'd chosen that location. Cheap labor costs had not been their primary consideration, of course; they'd been eager to create jobs in a region suffering from terrible unemployment. Such a lofty rationale might have brought tears to Evan's eyes if he'd believed it.

"We obey the wage and safety laws of the country and hire no one under the age of fourteen," one of the Pep boys said, and Evan began to feel a little better. Fourteen was still way too young for a kid to be working full-time, but different countries had different cultures. At least the company wasn't employing eight-year-old kids. A few years ago Evan might not have felt quite so passionate about the issue of child labor, but a few years ago he hadn't had Billy and Gracie. Fatherhood had given him a whole new perspective on things.

Fatherhood had also honed his senses to an unusual degree. His hearing was keen enough to detect the sound of two sets of footsteps on the carpeted hall outside the conference room—Heather's aggressive stride and a syncopated scamper. Gracie was in the building.

"My daughter's here," he announced, hoping this news would inspire the Georgians to wrap up their presentation.

"Fine. Now here—" Georgian Number Two pulled out another chart, while Georgian Number One continued rambling "—we have a graph illustrating how we've derived the wholesale price for Pep Insoles…"

Annoyed that the men seemed in no hurry to conclude their spiel, Evan rose from his chair. "I'm going to have to let her join us. My secretary can't watch her—she's leaving for the day." Heather, motivated by that year-end bonus, would probably have been willing to stay an extra fifteen minutes to keep Gracie safely occupied in another room, but Evan thought having Gracie join him in the conference room might accomplish what his hint hadn't: bringing the proceedings to a swift end. Before Jennifer could halt him, he moved around the table, opened the door and peered down the hall. "Gracie? We're in here."

His daughter popped out of Heather's office and skipped over to him. Her unbuttoned jacket flapped open and her lunch box clattered as the empty thermos rolled around inside it. Her cheeks were pink from the chilly evening air, and her eyes sparkled. She looked, if not spunky, at least a bit more energetic than she had yesterday.

"Hi, Daddy."

He hunkered down and spread his arms so she could

race into them. Hugging her, he whispered, "I'm stuck in a meeting. Wanna keep me company?"

"Okay."

He straightened up, reached for her hand and led her into the conference room. She gazed around, her tawny hair tousled, her hazel eyes wary. Stuart was spared a hesitant smile—she recognized him because he usually gave her candy when he saw her, and today was no exception. After digging in his pocket, he pulled out a breath mint. Gracie sprinted around the table and took it. "Thank you."

"You're welcome, sugar," he said, chucking her chin. She hated when anyone did that—chucked her chin, pinched her cheek, scruffed her hair—but since he'd just given her a candy, she didn't complain.

Evan resumed his seat and Gracie climbed into his lap. She slammed her lunch box down on the table with a loud clunk, then turned her attention to the Georgians.

They seemed nonplussed by her presence. They stared at her. She stared back. After a moment, they looked away, defeated. Evan's chest swelled with pride at the thought that his young daughter could derail these two gasbags with little more than her dimple-cute face and laser-sharp gaze.

"Well," one of them finally said, "I believe we've covered everything of importance. Do you have any questions?"

"None at all," Evan said brightly, restraining himself from boosting Gracie into the air and hooting triumphantly. "I appreciate your having traveled all this way to discuss your product. I'll want to read the literature you brought with you before we make any decisions."

Next to him, Jennifer bristled but smiled. "I think

we're all very impressed with Pep Insoles,'' she said, shooting Evan a lethal look and then regaining her smile for the reps. "We'll be getting back to you very soon."

"Within the next few weeks," Evan quickly told them, overruling her. They'd made him sweat out this marathon presentation. He'd let them sweat out his decision about whether his chain of stores was going to carry Pep Insoles.

Gracie slid down from Evan's knees, yanked her lunch box off the table and said, "That was a good meeting, Daddy. I liked it a lot."

"I'm glad you did," he said, then winked at Jennifer, who glowered at him and mouthed, *I want to talk to you.* He nodded, then circled the table to shake the reps' hands and feign his utter delight at their having traveled all the way to Arlington, Connecticut, to consume several precious hours of his life. Then he walked out of the conference room with Gracie, abandoning Stuart and Jennifer to perform the closing courtesies.

"We can't leave quite yet," he warned Gracie as they headed toward his office. "Jennifer wants to talk to me."

"I don't like her," Gracie said.

"She works very hard, and she's good for the business."

"Yeah, but she's a grouch. She never smiles. I like Heather."

Evan decided not to inform his daughter that Heather hated children. "Was it fun having her pick you up?" he asked.

Gracie trooped into his office ahead of him. "Yeah. Molly said you need to pick me up on time. It's something you have to work on, she said. We did puppets today. We made them out of socks. Mine came out good, but I left it in school."

"Great." As she jabbered on, Evan watched her for signs that she was incubating some sort of ailment. Her color seemed healthy, though, and her energy level high. "Were you tired in school today?"

"Nope."

"Did you nap?"

"Nope."

He didn't believe her, but that was all right. He lifted his briefcase onto his desk and snapped open the latch. "Did you eat your whole lunch?" he asked.

"Nope. I gave my cookies to Sarah. I didn't want them."

Gracie didn't want her cookies? He took that as an ominous sign.

Jennifer appeared in his doorway, the picture of impeccable professionalism in a tailored suit, shiny stockings and those deadly leather pumps. "What is wrong with you?" she asked crossly, her angular face twisted into a frown.

Gracie's appraisal of Jennifer echoed inside his head, making him smile. "Nothing's wrong with me."

"Those people have an excellent new product."

"Those people are insufferably boring."

"Who cares? They're offering us exclusive rights to sell Pep Insoles in southern New England—"

"And we'll probably accept their offer," Evan said. "But I've got to read all their documents first. And I'll bet the documents will tell me everything that matters. I didn't need these guys schlepping all the way up here to put on their dog-and-pony show for us. If they had to do it, they should have finished by four o'clock, as promised.''

"They talk slowly," Jennifer explained.

"I noticed."

"Don't be such a grouch," Gracie added. Evan wasn't sure whether she was addressing him or Jennifer. He supposed they were both pretty grouchy at the moment.

"I don't want to discuss Pep Insoles until we've got the Tank Moody promo set up," he said.

"It's set up," Jennifer assured him. "Almost."

"'Almost' doesn't count. I don't want anything left to chance, okay? Our last big promo using a professional athlete was a disaster."

Jennifer sighed sympathetically. "This one will go fine. Tank Moody is a gentleman."

Evan shuddered. "Those guys—" he gestured in the direction of the conference room "—were gentlemen, and spending an afternoon with them was torture. I've got to go. We'll do the Tank stuff tomorrow."

"Fine." She handed Evan a thick binder with the Pep Insoles logo on the cover. "You can read this tonight."

Right, he thought. *I'm going to ignore my kids and read 150 pages of statistics on shinsplints and hurdlers.* But he only smiled at Jennifer and stuffed the binder into his briefcase. "Okay, Gracie. Let's boogie."

THEY PICKED UP Billy at his friend Scott's house on their way home. Scott's mother had taken Billy to her place after the boys' Cub Scout meeting. She'd come through for Evan more than once this past fall. He was going to have to get her a nice Christmas present. A bottle of well-aged port. And something from the store—a paddleball set or a volleyball net, something the family would enjoy.

Billy was in a subdued mood. "How was Cub Scouts?" Evan asked, glancing at his son in the rearview mirror.

"It was okay."

"What did you do?"

"Nothing."

"How was school?"

"Boring. We had a sub."

Evan could take a hint. He abandoned all attempts at conversation as he steered around the corner, down the block and up the driveway to his garage.

In the years since Debbie had left, he'd established an effective evening routine. Dinner menus were simple. Evan was a pitifully uncreative cook, but that worked out well because the kids were pitifully unadventurous eaters. They'd eat broiled anything, and he knew how to broil everything. So while they cleaned out their lunch boxes, set the table and emptied a package of salad fixings into a bowl, Evan arranged in a pan what he was going to broil, then broiled it. Yesterday he'd broiled salmon. Tonight it was chicken. Tomorrow it would be lamb chops and the day after, flank steak. If a person was systematic, he could get the job done.

Evan had spent pretty much his entire life mastering that lesson. He'd never been a genius—he had gotten through college on a soccer and baseball scholarship— but he'd wound up earning good grades because he'd figured out systems for studying. It was his flair for systematizing inventory as a summer employee at the Champion Sports store in his hometown of New Haven that had won the attention of the then owner of the two-outlet chain. He'd offered Evan a full-time management job right out of college, and since Evan was engaged to Debbie, he'd grabbed the opportunity.

He'd set to work systematizing the store's operations. "By turning over inventory three days quicker, we'll make five percent more profit," he'd explained, and then showed his boss how to do it. "If we track what's selling in each store, we can inventory different products in different stores. We're selling more hockey gear in Arlington than in New Haven. More beach stuff in New Haven. We shouldn't be stocking the identical inventory in both stores." When his boss suffered a massive heart attack and had to retire, he'd named Evan his successor.

That was nine years ago. Now Champion had seven outlets in Connecticut, two in Rhode Island and one in New Bedford, Massachusetts. No one—least of all Evan—would have predicted that he'd wind up such a success, running a mini-empire by the time he was thirty-one. No one—least of all Evan—would also have predicted that he'd fail so spectacularly in his marriage. He'd thought he'd worked out a system for that, too: listen to Debbie when she wanted to talk, nod when agreement was called for, never complain about the trivial stuff, tune her out when she nagged, make sure she came when they had sex, assure her he loved her...

It hadn't been enough. Somehow the system had let him down.

Maybe all his systems were letting him down. Molly Saunders-Russo, who ran the Children's Garden, seemed to think he was falling short. Had she actually told Gracie that her father needed to work on meeting his responsibilities? Just because he'd been held hostage by those two bozos from Atlanta and couldn't pick his daughter up from her school by closing time...

Glancing over at her, he noticed the sparkle was gone from her eyes. She'd adopted her brother's listlessness. Evan decided to try another conversation as he zapped the potatoes in the microwave. "So, what did you do at Scott's house?" he asked.

"Nothing."

"You know what, Billy?" Evan grinned. "I don't believe you."

Billy scooped forks and knives from the silverware drawer. "We played Nintendo."

"The whole time?

Billy rolled his eyes. He was Evan's boy, through and through. He had the same sandy-colored hair, the same gray eyes and brown lashes, the same lazy style of shrugging, the same contemptuous manner of rolling his eyes. "We told each other ghost stories," Billy said as he distributed the silverware around the table.

Gracie winced. "Billy!" she whined.

"What's the matter, sweetie?" Evan asked. "You don't like ghosts?"

"I don't believe in ghosts," she said, although her voice trembled.

Evan tried to figure out why she seemed so agitated. She was generally fearless, a fact that filled Evan with both pride and terror. Gracie was the sort of kid who would jump off the high board at the YMCA pool if someone dared her to. She had no fears concerning spiders or nasty dogs or monsters under the bed. Surely she didn't believe in ghosts.

Well, that was what she'd just said, wasn't it?

So why was she so pale?

Billy started talking about a film the substitute teacher had shown his class, and Evan's chance to question Gracie slipped away. They ate their broiled chicken, discussing the nuances and subtleties of assorted Disney cartoons, and Gracie relaxed. By the end of the meal, she was jabbering about how she'd much rather be Mulan than Ariel, because Ariel wanted to kiss the prince and kissing was gross.

After dinner, Billy did a page in his spelling workbook while Evan read Gracie *Green Eggs and Ham.* He'd read it to her so many times she had it memorized, and she recited it along with him. Then he got her into a bath. As he washed her hair, he thought about what Molly had said earlier: that he should think about hiring a nanny or an au pair. Was it all right that he—a male adult—was giving his daughter a bath? At what point would this turn from a simple parental chore into something dangerous?

She was his daughter, and she wasn't old enough to wash her own hair yet. Did he have to hire a baby-sitter to wash her hair for her?

Everything he knew about being a father he'd learned on the job. Debbie hadn't taught him much, and Gracie had been only two years old when Debbie had run off. His parents had suggested that he move back to New Haven so they could help, but fortunately he hadn't, because a year later his father was downsized out of his job and wound up taking a consulting position in Washington, D.C. So Evan had learned how to give his daughter a bath all by himself.

She was only four. He probably wasn't traumatizing her by bathing her. But in another year... Could he teach her how to wash her own hair by then?

"Do you think we ought to hire a nanny?" he asked as he helped her out of the tub and wrapped her in a towel.

"A nanny? That's a grandma. Courtney calls her grandma Nanny. Stephen said a nanny was a goat. He and Courtney had a big fight."

"I'll bet," Evan said, rubbing the towel over Gracie's wet hair. "What I meant wasn't a grandmother, but someone who might come here and help out a little. For instance, she could give you your bath."

"I like when you give me a bath. You never get soap in my eyes."

He accepted the compliment with an earnest nod. "Or maybe this nanny could pick you up at the Children's Garden if I got stuck in a meeting."

"You could send Heather. I like her." Gracie reached for her nightgown, a wrinkled heap of pink flannel on the lowered seat of the toilet. She squirmed into it, and when her head popped through the opening, she added, "I think you should marry her."

"Marry Heather?" Evan sat on the floor, leaning against the tiled wall, and shoved his sleeves up above his elbows. Gracie often blurted out peculiar ideas. He still hadn't figured out the way her mind worked, and he probably never would. "Why do you think I should marry Heather?"

"She's so pretty."

"It doesn't really matter how pretty a woman is outside," Evan pointed out. "What matters is if she's pretty inside."

"I bet Heather's pretty inside. If she opened her mouth, you could look inside and see."

He struggled not to laugh. "By pretty inside, I mean, if her thoughts and acts are pretty. If she's a good, kind person. Some people are pretty on the outside and not the inside.'' Debbie, for instance—but he didn't say that. ''Do you think I should get married?''

''Maybe you could find a princess or something and marry her,'' Gracie suggested. ''A princess who likes sports so she could buy lots of stuff at the store. And then maybe we could live in a castle. A big stone castle—'' She cut herself off and handed Evan her towel. ''Uh-uh. I don't want to live in a castle,'' she said, her expression pinched. ''Brush my hair out, Daddy—and don't pull, okay?''

''I never pull.'' So she didn't want to live in a castle, he thought, hauling himself to his feet. He hung her towel over the rack, reached for her hairbrush and carefully brushed the snarls out of her hair, easing the bristles through the damp locks without tugging. He'd assumed most little girls wanted to live in castles, but then, Gracie wasn't like most little girls. ''I don't think I'd want to marry a princess, anyway,'' he told her.

She relaxed. ''You don't have to get married, Daddy. But if you do, you should probably marry Heather.''

''Thanks for the input.'' He and Heather would kill each other in a day, he thought with a smile. Heather was a wonderful secretary, but she was not his idea of promising wife material.

Her hair smooth, Gracie brushed her teeth, then padded barefoot down the hall to bed. Evan tucked her in and turned off her bedside lamp. ''I want my night-light,'' she said.

That surprised him. She'd stopped asking him to leave on her night-light a year ago. But whatever had bothered her yesterday was still nibbling at her.

''Okay,'' he said, clicking on the shell-shaped night-light. It gave the room a faint amber glow. "How's that?"

"Good. I love you, Daddy."

"I love you, too," he murmured, returning to her bed to give her one last kiss. "Sleep tight."

Leaving her door cracked open, he headed down the hall to the den. Billy was sprawled on the rug in front of the TV, watching a sitcom about extraordinarily attractive young singles. "Bedtime, pal," Evan said, because it was easier than telling him to stop watching shows in which three-quarters of the jokes had to do with sex or other bodily functions. He reached for his briefcase, hauled out the binder of Pep Insoles information Jennifer had given him and gave Billy a firm look.

Slowly, grudgingly, Billy hoisted himself off the floor and stretched. He trudged toward the doorway, but Evan caught his shoulder and held him back. "Are you sure everything's okay?" he asked.

"Yeah." Billy stared at the sofa.

"Because you can tell me anything, Billy. If anything's bothering you, if there's anything you want to ask me, that's what I'm here for."

Billy lifted his gaze to Evan. "Everything's okay," he said, sounding less certain than grateful. Everything wasn't okay, but at least he seemed appreciative of his father's attempt to reach him.

"When you want to talk, Billy, let me know."

"It's okay, Dad. Really." He smiled, flashing a gap where one of his front teeth was missing. Evan released him, and he clomped down the hall, his feet too big for his body.

Maybe Billy would open up to Evan, and maybe he wouldn't. Either way, Evan's heart swelled with love and rattled with anxiety. Should he hire help? Find a nanny? Find a wife? Badger his kids until they told him what was bugging them?

Molly had told him he was a wonderful father. But sometimes—far too often—he wasn't so sure.

CHAPTER THREE

THANK GOODNESS the gas company had come through. The house had grown so cold Sunday night that Filomena had gone to bed wearing a nightgown, a turtleneck, a cardigan and knee-high socks, and she'd burrowed under two blankets, one down, one wool. Even with all that she'd awakened shivering before dawn. She could have built a fire in the living-room fireplace—if she had any firewood, which she didn't. So she'd washed in icy water and then dressed, driven down to Dudley Road, bought a jumbo coffee at an upscale café she didn't recall having been there before and started making telephone calls.

By ten that morning she had the gas turned on. That meant not only heat for the house, but a working stove and oven and hot water for bathing. The phone company hooked her up, but although the electrical company had promised she'd have power by the evening, she was still in the dark.

She could survive without electricity. The air in the unheated garage shed was cold enough to keep her milk and fruit from spoiling, and the house could be lit with candles and her mother's blown-glass oil lamp. In fact, she liked the way the candles and the oil lamp gave the place a mystical ambience, all those flickering golden flames creating tiny spheres of shimmering light.

After dinner, she sat in her candlelit living room, sipping a glass of wine and contemplating her surroundings. The furniture was massive, well suited to the massive dimensions of the room. The tables and upholstered pieces were old and faded but in generally good condition. She was amazed her mother had thought to cover everything when she'd closed up the house five years ago. Her mother usually didn't think that far ahead.

If Filomena had been able to afford it, she would have arranged for a professional service to come in and clean the place. But given the debts she'd inherited, she didn't want to waste money on that. Once she had electricity, she would find out if the vacuum cleaner in the upstairs closet still worked. If it did, she could clean the floors herself. Dusting and washing windows certainly fell within her range of abilities. The yard was a mess, but in mid-November she wasn't sure what a landscaper could possibly do to make it look better. Maybe it didn't matter. By the time she put the house on the market in January, the ground might be covered with snow, and the unkempt grass, scattered leaves and overgrown bushes would be concealed.

She took another sip of wine, held it on her tongue and then swallowed, feeling it warm her all the way down to her stomach. She'd found a full rack of Bordeaux in the cellar, thickly layered in dust. Twenty-four bottles, none of them less than ten years old. She wondered what they were worth—enough to pay off some of her mother's debts?

It didn't matter. The house sale would cover the debts. She was going to keep the wine for herself. The bottle she'd opened had aged magnificently, and even if she wasn't quite the connoisseur her father had been, she appreciated a good wine. She could still remember some of the things her father had taught her about wines when she'd been a child. He used to explain about color and balance and bouquet, and then he'd let her take a tiny sip from his glass. Wine had tasted peculiar to her then, but she'd felt naughty and very mature drinking it.

She didn't feel so mature now. Impractical and abandoned was more like it. She was twenty-seven years old, working on a Ph.D. dissertation for a degree that was never going to land her a job—and she was an orphan. *An orphan.* God, that sounded strange.

Actually, it sounded awful.

Her father had been eighty-three when he'd died. She'd grieved for him but taken comfort in knowing he'd lived a long full life. Her mother had been only fifty-five, though. Way too young.

"You died happy, at least," Filomena murmured into the candlelit room. "You died doing what you loved, Mom, didn't you?"

She sighed. If she didn't get electricity soon, if she didn't get to work scrubbing the house from floor to ceiling, if she didn't get her CD player plugged in so she could listen to music while she whipped the place into shape, she was going to sink into a maudlin state. Sitting alone in a dark room, drinking wine and talking to her dead mother? Sheesh.

She needed electricity—and she needed visitors. She needed human contact. After living in Manhattan for the past five years, she found the silence of the house almost terrifying. Dudley Road had been bustling that morning, and she'd savored the din of voices and traffic.

She liked tranquillity and she enjoyed solitude. But still... She wanted visitors.

The children hadn't come back today. She assumed

that because it was Monday they'd been in school all day, but she had hoped maybe they would come prowling around her property after school so she could meet them. She'd even bought a bag of cookies, just in case they'd wanted a snack.

But they hadn't returned.

"Maybe tomorrow," she said out loud, and the possibility made her smile. Thinking about her mother, her debts, the numerous tasks and chores that awaited her was depressing. But thinking about the children who'd left their little fingerprints and footprints on her house lifted her spirits.

She hoped with all her heart they'd visit her house again.

"WHAT ARE YOU DOING?" Gracie squealed.

"Shh!" Billy waved her off, then tiptoed through the hall to the top of the stairs. Down in the kitchen, it was poker night. Dad and a bunch of guys played every Tuesday night, always at the Myers house because Dad claimed he had baby-sitting problems. Billy was glad the game was at his house. If Dad had gone to someone else's house and left a baby-sitter behind, she might actually pay attention when Billy made his escape.

He hovered near the stairway, listening to the sounds of the men's voices. They were talking about the New England Patriots, debating whether the team had a shot at the Super Bowl this year. Billy wanted to shout, "Of course they do!" but he kept his mouth shut.

Dad and his buddies were fine. They were drinking beer, rattling their chips—Billy believed they played for maybe a nickel a game, something really cheap—and they sure weren't thinking about him. Which was a good thing.

He tiptoed back down the hall. Gracie blocked his bedroom door. She was wearing her nightgown and her fluffy slippers with Minnie Mouse sewn onto the toes. "What are you doing?" she whispered.

"I'm going out."

"You can't go out!" Amazing how loud her whisper sounded.

"Shh." He ducked into his bedroom.

She followed him in, her hands on her hips and her head tilted to the side. "Where are you going?"

"The haunted house."

"You can't go there, Billy! It's haunted!"

"It is not. Anyway, you told me you don't believe in ghosts."

"It's got spirits in it. I saw a spirit. You did, too."

Well, yeah, he *had* seen a spirit in the big stone house. And that really bothered him. It bothered them both. Him more than Gracie, because she wasn't too good at hanging on to an idea from one day to the next. But he hadn't stopped thinking about the ghost, or spirit, or whatever it was he'd seen moving in the house on Sunday. Wondering about it was driving him crazy. He had to go back and figure out what was in there.

He couldn't go during the day, because by the time Dad picked him up from Scott's house or the after-school program, it was time for dinner, and then he had to read or do a page from a workbook or something. So there was no way he could hike over to the stone house to see if it was really haunted.

He could do it tonight, though, because of the poker game. His dad wouldn't notice he was gone. He'd just run through the woods, peek in the window, come up with an explanation for what it was he and Gracie had seen on Sunday and then come home. Dad would never even know.

"How are you going to get out?" Gracie asked as he pulled a hooded sweatshirt over his head. He couldn't go downstairs and get his jacket. He hoped it wasn't too cold outside.

"Through the window."

She darted past him to his window. The screen was easy to unhook—he'd already done it—and it opened onto the roof of the garage. From there, he could reach the oak tree and shimmy down. He'd climbed the oak tree lots of times, and he'd been able to swing from one of the limbs onto the garage roof, so he knew he'd be able to get back in once his mission was accomplished.

Gracie seemed excited and a little frightened. He hoped she wouldn't race downstairs and tell on him the minute he was out the window. If she did tell...well, he'd sure be in trouble. Grounded for life, probably. "You're not going to tell, are you?" he asked, making sure his sneakers were laced tight.

She shook her head. Her eyes were so wide they looked like they were going to pop out of her face. "What if there *is* a ghost?" she wanted to know. "What if you don't come home? What should I tell Daddy?"

"There's no ghost. Whatever is in the house, I'll figure it out and tell you." That promise ought to keep her from tattling on him. "And I'll come home. Why wouldn't I come home?"

"Because if there's a ghost, it might kill you."

"We don't believe in ghosts. Right, Gracie?"

She thought about that for a minute, then nodded uncertainly. ''Right.''

''Okay. See ya.'' He shoved the window as high as it would go and then maneuvered himself over the sill. The garage roof was right beneath his feet. This was so easy he wanted to laugh.

Climbing down the tree was easy, too. He jumped the last few feet to the ground and glanced through the sliding glass door in the family room. He could see across the family room into the kitchen, where Dad and his friends were playing cards around the table. Dad had his back to Billy.

Convinced that his father was too caught up in the game to notice him missing, Billy turned and started into the woods. The three-quarter moon shed a lot of light, and the path was visible. He'd gone to the stone house enough times to know his way.

About halfway there, he started hearing footsteps behind him. Or imagining them, probably. It was dark, and even though he pretended to be tough for Gracie, he had to admit he was, well, not scared but a little nervous. He knew there wasn't a ghost in the house—but *something* had been in there. He'd seen it move, and it had scared the heck out of him on Sunday. He really wished he could have gone back to check the place out during the day, when there was still some sunlight.

But he couldn't stand not knowing what he'd seen. Day or night, he had to go back for another look.

He took a few more steps and halted. Definitely someone was following him.

Sucking in a big breath, he curled his hands into fists, just in case he had to fight off a monster or something, and turned around.

Gracie stood on the path in her pink nightgown and her Minnie Mouse slippers, with her denim jacket—*his* denim jacket—pulled around her shoulders. She stomped toward him, snapping twigs and trampling on leaves and breathing heavily. "What are you doing?" he asked. He could hear the impatience in his voice.

"I thought I should come, too."

"You climbed out the window? Gracie, you are so stupid! You could've gotten hurt! I can't believe how stupid you are!"

Her mouth started twitching like she was going to burst into tears. "I'm not stupid!" she wailed. "Take it back!"

She *was* stupid. No way would he get caught if he was doing this himself, but with her along... How was she going to get back into the house? Maybe she could climb down the tree, but she was too little to climb back up. He was going to have to hoist her or something.

"You've spoiled everything," he said, even though he knew that would set her off. He was just so mad.

"I did not!" She charged up the path, pushing past him. "If there's a ghost, I wanna see it, and you can't stop me."

She was right about that—he couldn't stop her. If he sent her back to the house, she'd wind up ringing the doorbell, and then Dad would know and come after him and he'd be in big trouble. He had no choice but to let her accompany him. It made him even angrier that she'd twisted things around to get her way. He knew a couple of swear words—the fifth graders used them all the time on the bus, and he'd heard his dad use the s-word a few times when he thought Billy wasn't around. He whispered it under his breath and caught up to Gracie. If he was going to wind up in trouble anyhow, he might as well swear.

The woods weren't too thick. They spread behind the houses on the side of the street where his house was, down a little dip and then up a rise to the clearing where the stone house stood. He supposed the house was on another street, but there were no other houses near it, so Billy guessed it was set back from the road by a long driveway. He'd tried to find the street on his bicycle once, but he'd come to a major road and there'd been too much traffic, so he'd turned around and biked home. But even if the stone house was hard to reach by the roads, it really wasn't that far away if you just hiked through the woods.

He and Gracie reached the clearing and paused by the forest's edge, in the shadows. The house looked dark. It looked spooky, too, the porch overhang casting a black shadow, the roof steep. Gracie slipped her hand into his and he didn't pull away. He would never admit he needed to hold her hand as much as she needed to hold his, but it helped to know he wasn't alone, even if she was just a kid.

"Come on," he whispered. "And don't make a sound." He tugged her toward the house. She wasn't so brave anymore; he practically had to drag her around to the side of the house. But she didn't talk or whine or complain. Her slippers hardly made any noise on the grass.

Nearing the side window, he positioned her against the wall, not too close to the window. "I'll look first," he whispered. "You stay out of sight."

She nodded. Her eyes appeared ready to pop again.

Shrugging to make his shoulders feel bigger, he let go of her hand and crept up to the window, hunching slightly so he wouldn't be visible. When he reached the window, he straightened slowly until he could peek inside. What he saw made him gasp.

Candles. Four of them, maybe five, flickering on a table where there used to be just a big white sheet. More candles were visible through the doorway in another room, creating little dancing shadows on the floor. And music! He could barely hear it through the thick glass, but it sounded weird and tinkly.

He sank back down below the edge of the window and ran over to Gracie. "Did you see the spirit?" she asked.

He shook his head. "But there're candles all over the place."

"Candles?"

"Yeah. And they're lit."

"Like on a birthday cake?"

"No, like in candlesticks. On tables and stuff."

"I wanna see!"

"Shh." He glanced toward the window, thinking. If he didn't believe in ghosts—which he didn't—then the candles must have been lit by a person. Which meant someone was inside the house. Which meant that if the person inside saw them spying through the window, that person could do something bad, like chase them or call the police, or maybe even pull a gun on them and shoot them. Billy just didn't know.

Gracie started revving up. "I wanna see," she said in the whiniest whisper he'd ever heard. "You saw the candles. I wanna see them, too. I bet the spirit lit them. I wanna see!"

"I think we should go home," Billy said, feeling very old and responsible.

"That's no fair! I wanna see! If you make me go home without seeing the candles, I'm gonna tell Daddy."

She would, too. She'd go right ahead and get herself in trouble over this if it meant she could get Billy in trouble, also.

Sighing, he weighed his options. He hadn't seen anyone through the window, so maybe if Gracie took a quick look, she wouldn't see anyone, either. And with the music, maybe they wouldn't be heard. And if, just if, there *was* a ghost in the house, they were as good as dead, anyway—which was probably better than getting in trouble with Dad.

"Okay," he muttered. They moved together toward the window, Billy hunching down as they neared it. Once they were under the window, he wrapped his arms around Gracie's middle and straightened, lifting her as high as he could.

She gripped the windowsill and gazed inside. She didn't squirm, didn't speak, didn't try to scramble higher. She didn't even seem to breathe.

And then, all of a sudden, she blasted out a scream loud enough to explode his eardrums. She shoved away from the windowsill so hard he fell backward, losing his footing and sprawling on the ground with her on top of him, still screeching like a maniac.

"Shut up!" he shouted, trying to wriggle out from under her. "Shut up, Gracie!"

"Aaaiiieee!" She clung to him and howled.

"Shut up!"

Through her wailing he heard the creak of a window opening, and then another voice. A woman's voice. "Hey, there! What's going on?"

"Get off of me," he grunted, figuring if Gracie wasn't

going to shut up, at least she didn't have to be sitting on his stomach, pinning him to the ground, with her mouth so close to his ear her howling was making him deaf. He wanted her off him, and he wanted to see whoever was talking to them. He peeled Gracie's fingers away from his sweatshirt and heaved her to one side. She jumped to her feet and started running in circles, yelping and flailing her arms as if she was being attacked by wasps.

He ignored her and turned to the window. It was brightly lit now, with real light, not just candlelight. The woman standing in the window was just a silhouette. But she was a real human being, not a ghost.

"I'm sorry," he mumbled. "We were just looking. My sister's an idiot."

"I am not! I am not!" Gracie shrieked, bouncing up and down and zigzagging around the yard. "It's a ghost! It's a witch!"

The woman laughed. "I'm not a witch. Meet me around by the back porch and you'll see for yourself." She turned from the window and walked away.

Billy snagged Gracie on one of her sprints around the yard. "It's just a lady, you moron," he told her, giving her a small shake to get her attention. "She's meeting us at the back porch."

"She's a witch. She's gonna eat us," Gracie whimpered.

"Don't be stupid. She's not gonna eat us. She wouldn't wanna eat you, anyhow. You'd probably make her puke."

"You're mean!" Gracie shouted, yanking her arm free and scampering to the back porch. She must have decided she'd be better off with a witch than with her own brother.

He used the s-word again. Leave it to Gracie to act like such a jerk.

By the time he reached the rear of the house, a porch light was on, spreading a bright yellow glow across the porch and down the steps. The woman stood on the top step, and Billy could see how, at a glance, Gracie might have taken her for a witch. She was wearing a sweater so long it came down nearly to her knees, and a skirt that came down to her ankles, and black boots. Her hair was long, dark and kind of ripply, and huge earrings that resembled lots of little silver coins woven together dangled from her ears. Around her neck hung a necklace on a black cord. The pendant was shaped like the moon, a silver crescent on top of a circle, as big around as the lid on a jar of mustard.

But staring up at her face, he knew she wasn't a witch. An angel would be more like it. She was really, really pretty.

"I'm Fil," she said. "Who are you?"

"Fill?" Gracie scowled. "What kind of name is that?"

"It's short for Filomena. What's your name?"

"Filomena?" Gracie echoed. Billy, too, was amazed by the name. He'd never heard a name like that before. It sounded like an angel's name.

"That's right. What's your name?"

"Gracie. That's my brother, Billy. He's an idiot."

"Hello, Gracie. Hello, Billy," the lady said gently. "It's kind of late for you to be out, isn't it? It's past eight-thirty. And you, Gracie, you're in your pajamas! You must be cold! Why don't you come inside and warm up?"

"Don't go in," Billy warned, reaching out and grabbing Gracie's arm. The lady might look like an angel, but Billy knew better than to go anywhere with a stranger. "We're just going home," he said, even though she was so pretty he didn't want to leave her.

She gazed around. "How did you get here?"

"Through the woods," Gracie told her.

"In the dark?"

"It's easy," Gracie bragged, although Billy was thinking his sister would have gotten totally lost if she hadn't been following him. "We live on the other side of the woods."

Filomena stared into the trees, then shook her head as if she wasn't quite sure she believed this. "Maybe I ought to drive you home. Your parents will be worried."

"Our mommy is gone," Gracie explained, "and our daddy is playing poker." From screaming and acting like a ninny, she'd turned into a regular chatterbox.

"He could still be worried," Filomena insisted. "Let me drive you home—or at least phone him and tell him you're safe."

"No," Billy said quickly. If she called Dad and told him where they were, they'd be in such deep trouble they'd never be able to climb out of it. "We can get home ourselves. Thanks anyway."

"I'm not going to let you go tramping through those dark woods," Filomena said. "Gracie, you're wearing bedroom slippers. And oh, they're beautiful. That's Minnie Mouse, isn't it? I love Minnie Mouse."

Gracie grinned. Swell. In another minute she'd be following the strange-named lady into the house. "We'll be fine," he insisted, because he knew how dangerous going into her house might be. They'd had classes in school about this stuff—not trusting strangers, not going places with them and that kind of thing. Dad had also lectured him and Gracie about safety with strangers. "We don't want a ride home. We can't go in your car anyhow."

Filomena mulled that over, then nodded. "Well, then, I'll walk you through the woods, just to make sure you get home safely."

"We can get home okay."

She scooted toward the door, her skirt swirling around her. "Let me just blow out the candles and get a flashlight. Oh, and you know what? I think I have something of yours, Gracie." Before Billy could stop her, she was in the house.

Billy and Gracie exchanged a glance. "She's beautiful," Gracie murmured.

"Five minutes ago you thought she was a witch."

"I think she's a fairy godmother."

"What does she have of yours?"

Gracie shrugged.

Billy stifled a groan. If she had something of Gracie's, maybe she was going to do something awful, like make them pay to get it back. Or burn it in a voodoo ritual—he'd seen some kind of ceremony in a movie Scott's parents had rented last summer. It involved a big bonfire and lots of weird singing and dancing, and people wearing face paint. "We are in *so* much trouble," he muttered. "If she walks us home—" if she didn't hex them with the voodoo ritual "—Dad's gonna kill us."

"Not if we go in through the window."

"How are we gonna go in through the window if she's with us?"

Gracie didn't have an answer for that. And anyway, Filomena was already back, carrying a flashlight and a scarf. She heaved the door shut behind her, flicked on the flashlight and came down the porch steps. "You look cold, Gracie,'' she said, wrapping the scarf around her. It was too big, and it went three times around Gracie's neck and shoulders and dangled down to her knees.

Gracie's smile was so gigantic it practically split her face in two.

''Are you going to trip on it? Maybe I should carry you so you don't trip.''

''Okay. What do you have of mine?''

''I don't know if it's yours…'' Filomena dug into a pocket of her skirt and pulled out something small and pink.

''My butterfly clip! Where did you find it? I thought I lost it in my room, 'cuz my room is kind of messy.''

''I found it outside the window you were peeking into tonight.'' Filomena handed the barrette to Gracie. ''I guess you've been peeking into that window before, hmm?''

Oh, boy, were they in trouble. Billy wasn't sure, but he'd bet there were laws against people peeking into windows. And now she had evidence—Gracie's stupid butterfly hair clip. She could take the clip to the police and have them thrown in prison for looking through her window. If only Gracie hadn't kept following him around, none of this would have happened. It was all her fault he was going to wind up spending the rest of his life in jail.

''There you go,'' Filomena said, pressing the barrette into Gracie's hand and then lifting Gracie into her arms. ''Hold on tight. And don't drop the barrette.''

Billy bit his lip. He didn't like the idea of a stranger carrying Gracie, no matter how nice the stranger acted. But he figured he could tackle her if she tried to do anything evil. He knew his way through the woods better than she did, with or without her flashlight.

They started down the path, Billy one step ahead of Filomena, who had Gracie arranged so her butt rested in the bend of Filomena's elbow and her arms were wrapped around Filomena's neck. The beam from the flashlight speared ahead of Billy on the trail, illuminating roots and rocks. He had to admit walking the path like this was a lot easier than counting on the moonlight to reach all the way through the branches to light the ground.

After a few minutes they arrived at his backyard. "This is our house," he said quietly. "Thanks. You can go home now."

Still holding Gracie, who was all snuggled up in her arms with her head resting on her shoulder, Filomena studied the rear of the house. "I'd like to say hello to your father."

"Uh, no, that's okay. I mean, he's playing poker now. He wouldn't want to meet you."

She pressed her lips together and shook her head. "I think it would be better if I met him. So he won't be worried that you were with me."

"Well, he doesn't have to know about that," Billy explained.

"If I were your father, I'd want to know."

"He's just playing poker, anyway," Billy argued. He wished she would just leave so they could sneak into the house before they got caught. "Really, it's okay. You should go back to your house and light your candles, okay? I mean—"

At that instant, the sliding door shot open and his father came charging out, looking half-insane, his eyes flashing and his hair a mess. "Oh, my God! Are they okay? What happened? Are my kids okay?" He froze a few steps from the lady, his breath puffing in the cold air and his panic slowly fading, replaced by a frown as his gaze shifted from Billy—who was obviously just fine—to Gracie, snuggling up against Filomena, to Filomena herself.

His frown deepening, he asked, "What the hell is going on?"

CHAPTER FOUR

HE WASN'T SURE what had prompted him to leave the game and check on the kids. Maybe it was that the lack of noise upstairs had seemed unnatural. Maybe it was that when he'd stood at the foot of the stairs, he'd felt a chilly draft blowing down from Billy's room. Maybe it was that Gracie's door had been standing wide-open. When he'd tucked her in fifteen minutes ago, he'd left her door open just a crack, the way she liked it.

"Hey, Evan, are you in?" Murphy called to him from the kitchen.

"Not this hand," Evan shouted over his shoulder, already halfway up the stairs. He barged into Billy's room and saw the window up, the screen unhooked from its frame. Leaning out, he saw no sign of Billy.

He abandoned Billy's room for Gracie's. Her blanket was rumpled, her night-light on, her favorite stuffed animal—Pokey the elephant—propped on her pillow. She was gone.

Exerting superhuman self-control, he refrained from screaming, cursing or punching a hole through the wall. Inhaling and exhaling in an even tempo—this took some effort—he left Gracie's room. From the kitchen rose the sound of laughter. Apparently Tom had attempted to bluff his way through the hand, and the others were ribbing him about it. It amazed Evan that Tom could be a private investigator, a profession that presumably required a flair for bluffing, but he couldn't bluff his way through a hand of five-card draw.

Evan's friends seemed a universe apart from him, their laughter an incomprehensible language. He staggered down the stairs, searched the family room, crossed to the glass slider, turned on the patio lights and surveyed the backyard. Empty. No children. *No children.*

"Evan?" Levi called from the kitchen. "Are you going to join us?"

"My children are gone," he shouted—only, the words emerged as barely a whisper.

"What?" Levi appeared in the doorway, tall and craggy and bemused. "Something's wrong with your kids?"

"They're gone." Evan stood in the middle of the family room, his heart pounding so fiercely that he was surprised his sweater wasn't fluttering with each beat. "They climbed through Billy's window and ran away."

Murphy pushed past Levi and joined Evan in the family room. "Your kids ran away? You're joking, aren't you."

Evan shook his head.

"Should we call the police? When my kids got in trouble—"

"Forget the police," Levi broke in, gesturing toward the windows overlooking the backyard. "I think Evan's kids changed their minds about running away."

Evan spun around and saw Billy coming across the dead grass, followed by an unfamiliar woman carrying Gracie and shining a flashlight. Billy was leading the way.

Evan absorbed the scene, then shoved open the slider

and hurled himself outside, wanting to weep, wanting to throttle the kids, wanting to sink to his knees and thank God for bringing them back safe, and then ask God to wreak vengeance on their miserable little souls for having come so close to giving him a heart attack.

He stared at them. Billy met his gaze for less than a second, then glanced away. Wrapped in a thick colorful muffler of some sort, Gracie peeked at him from her perch in the woman's arms, evidently trying to gauge his mood.

He started babbling, asking if they were okay, asking what the hell was going on, tossing in a few profanities for good measure. When no one answered, he paused to catch his breath and directed his attention to the woman.

He'd never seen her before. If he had, he would have remembered. She appeared mysterious and exotic and altogether riveting. Black hair flowed halfway down her back, framing a face of huge dark eyes, chiseled cheeks and full lips. Her skin was tawny in the diffuse light from the outdoor fixture, and her clothing struck him as arty, too big and bulky for her slender build. Her jewelry—flamboyant earrings and a moon-shaped necklace—was oversize. Her feet were encased in clunky boots.

He wondered what she would look like without all that oversize apparel hiding her. An image—a very erotic one—of her in lacy lingerie flashed across his mind, and he chased it away. Now was not the time to entertain adolescent fantasies about the stranger holding his daughter.

"Who are you?" he asked.

She smiled and extended her right hand, practically blinding him with the flashlight. "Oops!" She clicked it off and handed it to Billy, then presented her hand to Evan again. "Filomena Albright."

Filomena Albright? Quite a mouthful, he thought as he shook her hand. "Evan Myers," he introduced himself. "What are my kids doing with you? Why are you holding Gracie? Gracie, why are you running around outside in your nightgown?"

"I'm not running around," Gracie corrected him. "Fil is carrying me."

"That's very nice of her, and she's probably going to send me a bill from her chiropractor once she assesses the damage to her back from hauling you around." He reached for Gracie and eased her out of Filomena Albright's embrace. Gracie immediately lowered her head to Evan's shoulder. It was way past her bedtime. She was probably exhausted. "How did you wind up with my kids?" he asked Filomena. He was beginning to calm down; his voice was no longer edged with hysteria.

"They showed up in my yard," she explained. "I'm not sure why, but I thought they needed to be brought home."

"They should never have left home in the first place." He glared at Billy, who glanced everywhere but at Evan. "I can't believe you climbed out your window."

Billy peered up at the open window above the garage roof—one more place he could look to avoid meeting his father's gaze. "The screen snaps in and out real easy," he mumbled.

"Too easily. Why did you do that? What the hell were you thinking? You could have fallen off the roof and gotten killed!"

"It's not that far to the ground. And anyway, the oak tree is right there."

"I'm having that tree chopped down tomorrow," Evan snapped, although of course he wasn't going to do that. It was a beautiful tree, older than Evan and the house combined. It deserved to live.

Which was more than he could say for his children at the moment. "Okay," he murmured, then sighed, trying to keep his rage from erupting. "I don't know what's going on, but..." He caught Filomena's eye and managed a feeble smile. "I've got to get the kids inside. Would you mind coming in for a minute? Maybe you can help me make sense of this whole thing."

"All right." Something in the woman's smile befuddled him even more than the situation with his kids did. Her smile was dazzling, intoxicating. It overwhelmed him as the thought of his kids climbing through an upstairs window overwhelmed him. It made him just as breathless, but in a different way. It made his heart pound, not with fear but with something else.

Too much adrenaline. Too much anger, too much relief that the kids were home safe. What he was feeling right now had nothing to do with Filomena Albright.

She took her flashlight back from Billy and gave his shoulder a nudge, steering him toward the back door. Evan was grateful for her protective gentleness toward his children. If he'd been the one to give Billy a nudge, he'd probably have shoved the boy hard enough to flatten him.

Gracie was growing heavier on his shoulder. He twisted his head to look at her and found her fast asleep.

They entered the family room, and Evan used his free hand to close the door. "Upstairs," he ordered Billy. "Now."

Billy headed straight for the stairway, not daring to argue.

Turning to Filomena, Evan murmured, "I'm going to take Gracie upstairs, too. Please don't go away. I'll be right back."

"No problem." She smiled again. His heartbeat kicked up another notch. He blamed it on the physical strain of carrying his daughter's dead weight.

Following Billy up the stairs, he tried to sort out his thoughts. He didn't know any Albrights in the neighborhood, and he knew most of his neighbors. Where had she and the kids come from, anyway? One minute the backyard had been empty, and the next they'd materialized as if teleported there. Why hadn't they come to the front door? Had Billy intended to enter the house the way he'd exited, through the window?

Evan paused at Billy's door. Billy was seated on his bed, wrenching off his shoes. "This was bad, Billy," he said grimly.

"I know."

"It's late, and you've got school in the morning. So wash up, brush your teeth and go to sleep. We'll talk about this tomorrow."

"Yeah." Billy still wouldn't look at him.

Sighing, Evan lugged Gracie to her own room, unwrapped the muffler from her, slid her jacket down her arms and off and tucked her blanket around her. She looked so sweet and angelic when she was asleep. Evan snorted. There wasn't a single sweet, angelic cell in her body.

He returned to Billy's room. "Stop acting like you're on death row," he said.

Billy glanced up at him, his expression defiant and

sheepish at the same time. "We were just checking to make sure her house wasn't haunted, that's all," he said.

Well, that certainly clarified the situation, Evan thought wryly. He shook his head. "Climbing out the window was an idiotic thing to do. Going out alone at night was dangerous. Do you get the idea, Billy? What you did was really, really stupid."

"Yeah."

"And there's no such thing as a haunted house."

"Well...well, when we saw it Sunday we thought we saw a ghost. We were only going back to check. And she had candles going in the house tonight, so Gracie thought maybe it was a witch inside, and she kind of freaked out."

Candles or no, Evan couldn't imagine anyone ever mistaking Filomena Albright for a witch. "I kind of freaked out, too," he said, "when I found you and Gracie gone. You scared the hell out of me. I don't like having the hell scared out of me, Billy. You shouldn't like it, either. Your life will be much easier if you never, ever scare the hell out of me again."

"Okay." Billy was trying very hard not to cry. Evan could see him biting his lip and forcing his eyes open to keep the tears from accumulating. His little-boy stoicism made Evan want to cry, also.

Instead, he entered the room and lowered himself to sit on the bed next to his son. "I love you, Billy."

"I love you, too," Billy said, his gaze on his knees.

Evan gave Billy a harder hug than he'd intended, the remnants of his fear making him want to cling to his son forever, to protect him from open windows and ghosts and all the demons that inspired him to take crazy risks. But no father could protect his child completely from danger. He could only hug, and yell, and make sure his child knew how much he was loved.

Evan left the room, closing the door behind him, and descended the stairs. The voices of Evan's friends emerged from the kitchen in a rumble, but Filomena Albright remained in the family room, studying the framed portraits of the kids on display on the mantel.

"I think this is yours," he said, presenting her with the muffler.

"Thank you." She took it and smiled again. It was an amazing smile, full of energy and vitality, full of soul. He felt bewitched by it.

"Can I offer you a drink?" he asked. "Or an apology?"

"Don't apologize. Your children are adorable. I was hoping they'd come back."

"Come back?"

"They've been to my house before."

"They've been visiting you?" Why didn't he know this? How much of their lives was he in the dark about?

"No, they didn't visit me. They were just snooping around the house, I think. Peeking through the windows. I found your daughter's barrette near one, and their footprints. It's an intriguing house. I guess they were drawn to it."

He struggled to assimilate this information, plus what he'd gleaned from Billy. "According to my son, your house is haunted."

"Haunted?" She tossed back her head and let loose with a rich, throaty laugh that was even more enchanting than her smile. Maybe Gracie was right. Maybe Filomena Albright was a witch.

"They didn't say anything to me about my house being haunted," she told him. "But the house was empty for five years. I suppose it might have seemed a little spooky to them."

Five years? Had they been going to her house for five years? That was impossible! Gracie wasn't even five years old.

Evan felt, if possible, more overwhelmed, more confused. He was sure everything would make sense if only Filomena Albright wasn't standing so close to him, looking so utterly gorgeous.

"Evan!" Murphy called from the kitchen. "Is everything all right, or should I phone the police?"

"No police," he shouted back, then smiled at her and explained, "My buddies. I guess they deserve an explanation." He deserved an explanation, too. Maybe Filomena would offer one.

Touching his hand to her elbow, he ushered her into the kitchen. The guys were standing around the table, clutching their beers, eyeing Evan curiously—and Filomena even more curiously. "This is Filomena Albright," he said, discovering that the name rolled rather pleasantly off his tongue. "This is Dennis Murphy, Tom Bland, Levi Holt and Brett Stockton."

They stared at Filomena as though she were an alien who'd just dropped in from another planet.

"Most people call me Fil," she said.

"Fil?" Evan nodded, then gestured toward a chair. "Please, have a seat. I'll get you something—a cup of tea, maybe? Coffee? Beer?"

"No, really, I'm fine." The men shuffled around the table, presenting her with a chair and smiling bashfully, quizzically. Evan recalled a scene in a movie he'd watched recently with Gracie, the Disney version of

Snow White and the Seven Dwarfs. In the scene, the dwarfs all made a fuss over beautiful Snow White. His kitchen had only five "dwarfs," and their physiques ran from average to tall, but they exhibited that same deference, awkward and eager to please the lovely young stranger in their midst.

"I'm interrupting your game," she said, noting the piles of chips and playing cards on the table.

"That's okay," Tom said. "I was losing, anyway."

Filomena smiled. The guys laughed, except for Evan, who wished they'd all go away so he could learn more about her, her haunted house and how she'd wound up with his kids on a Tuesday night.

"We could deal you in," Brett offered.

Still smiling, she shook her head. "Really, Mr…" She gazed questioningly at Evan. Apparently she'd forgotten his name.

"Evan Myers."

"Evan Myers," she echoed. "I should be going. You're busy here and I've got things to do, too. I only wanted to make sure your children got home safely."

"I want to make sure *you* get home safely. Let me drive you." He immediately felt less addled. Driving her home was the right thing to do, and it would give him a few minutes alone with her, an opportunity to find out exactly what had occurred at her house.

"I can walk," she insisted, rising from the chair. "It's just through the woods."

"No, I'll drive you." He caught Murphy's eye.

Murphy motioned with his head toward the door. "Go ahead. We'll stand guard over the monsters until you get back."

Evan sent Murphy a grateful nod. Murphy was the father of twins a year older than Billy. They were a pair of hellions—which, of course, meant that Billy and Gracie idolized them. If Murphy could handle his own children, he could surely handle Billy and Gracie for the brief time it would take Evan to drive Filomena to her place.

He led her through the mudroom door and into the garage, where he turned on the light so she could see her way around the bicycles and skateboards, the roller skates and hockey sticks, the Velcro dartboard, the footballs, the soccer balls, the whiffle balls and the basketballs that cluttered the perimeter. He admitted to going a bit overboard when it came to supplying his kids with sports gear. But athletic equipment was his business, after all.

Filomena said nothing as she took in the abundance of jock stuff. He opened the passenger door of his Saab for her, then closed it behind her once she was settled in the seat. After pressing the switch to raise the garage door, he got in behind the wheel and revved the engine.

Now that he had her alone, he wasn't sure how to start a conversation. Ordinarily, he had no trouble talking to women, even women he found attractive. He didn't date much—he had neither the time nor the energy—but when he did, he never felt particularly out of his depth.

He felt way out of his depth with this woman. She wasn't glamorous or sophisticated, at least not that he could tell. Yet there was something about her, something in the contours of her smile, in the alluring darkness of her eyes. Something that could make Gracie fear her as a witch one minute and cuddle in the curve of her arms the next. Something that entranced Evan.

"You'll have to tell me where you live," he reminded her as he backed out of the driveway.

"Poplar Ridge Road."

"And your house is just the other side of the woods from ours?" He tried to work out the geography in his mind. Poplar Ridge Road wound in a big curve a distance from his own street.

"As the crow flies," she said. Her voice was like velvet, soft but textured. "You really shouldn't have abandoned your card game. I could have cut right back through the woods and been home in ten minutes."

I wanted to abandon my card game, he almost said. He turned left at the foot of the driveway, stealing a glimpse of her as he scanned the road for traffic. She wasn't looking at him, and just as well. He wasn't at his best right now. His jaw was scratchy with an end-of-the-day growth of beard, and his hair was probably mussed from his having charged through the house in a mad state when he'd discovered the kids were missing. He'd changed clothes as soon as he'd gotten home from work, trading his tailored business attire for faded jeans, an old V-neck sweater and sneakers. The night was chilly, but he hadn't bothered with a jacket. The car heated up well.

As he drove to the end of his block, he tried to think of a conversational gambit, then gave up. He had legitimate questions, pressing concerns, and he didn't want to waste what little time he had with her on small talk. "I need to know what happened tonight," he said. He also needed to know what was happening right now in his car, but he didn't expect her to explain that. She might not even be aware that anything was happening. It might not be happening to her.

"I was sitting in my living room, listening to some harpsichord music on the stereo and sipping a glass of wine, when I noticed your children spying through my window," she said, making it sound like the most normal, mundane event in the world.

"Spying through your window? Like Peeping Toms? I don't believe it." He sighed and shook his head. "I mean, I *do* believe it. I just don't like it. I don't know what got into them, doing something like that."

"The house is big and old and kind of odd. I guess they discovered it while it was still empty, and it intrigued them."

The way its current resident intrigued their father, he thought, deeply unsettled by just how much she intrigued him. "You recently moved in, then?"

"Sunday morning," she said.

The kids had been out exploring Sunday afternoon, he recalled. And they'd come home and acted strange. "Were you in the house Sunday afternoon?"

"Yes, why?"

"I think my kids were there then. They must have seen you and taken you for a ghost or something."

"Tonight they took me for a witch," she said. "At least, Gracie did."

He glanced her way and found her smiling. "You don't find that insulting?"

"Now that they've met me, they don't seem to think I'm a witch anymore." She settled back in the seat and gazed at him. Even when he was watching the road, he could feel her eyes on him. What did she see? he wondered. A scruffy man at the end of a long day? A harried dad? A neglectful poker player? The kind of parent who raised Peeping Toms?

"I'm really sorry they bothered you," he said, stopping at the corner and turning to her.

She dismissed his apology with a laugh. "I'm not sorry

and they didn't bother me. It's lonely all by myself in that house. I was delighted that they came to visit. I just wish they had come at a reasonable hour.''

"Really? You want them to visit?''

"Is that a problem?'' she asked, her smile fading.

"No, not at all.'' At least, he didn't *think* it was a problem. He hardly knew this woman, though. He shouldn't automatically trust her enough to let his children visit her. "Where did you move here from?'' he asked casually, steering around the corner.

"Manhattan.''

She must be one of the rich city folks who bought vacation retreats in the Arlington area. They mostly settled west of town, not in Evan's hilly north-side neighborhood, but why else would an attractive young woman buy a house in Arlington?

Actually, he could think of lots of reasons. For example, maybe she had a husband who'd been transferred to the area. "Are you married?'' he asked, then realized what a tactless question that was. He hastened to remedy any offense she might have taken. "I'm just wondering why you left New York City to move into a haunted house. If you've got family here or something…''

Her mood seemed to change, her smile losing its alluring radiance. "No family, but I did grow up in the house.''

That would explain it, he supposed. "I'm sorry if you thought I was being nosy, but…well, I just worry about the kids, that's all.''

"I understand.'' But her smile didn't return.

He turned onto Poplar Ridge Road. "You'll have to tell me which house.''

"It's up a way. You can't see it from the street.''

They drove in silence. His apology couldn't erase the low-level tension that hummed in the car. He wasn't sure why he felt so contrite—it wasn't just because of his kids or because he'd inquired about her marital status. He suspected it had something to do with the fact that as soon as he'd calmed down enough to look at her when she'd first appeared in his backyard, he'd practically stripped her naked in his imagination.

In and of itself, that wouldn't be a crime. He was a man, single and unattached. He was allowed to appreciate an attractive woman, allowed even to fantasize about her. But Filomena Albright wasn't simply an attractive woman. She had an aura about her. Maybe it was her elaborate earrings, or her long, flowing hair. Maybe it was the sight of her with Gracie in her arms—like a powerful savior who'd rescued his fragile pajama-clad daughter from the evil shadows of the forest.

There was nothing fragile about Gracie, of course. But he'd been taken by the way Filomena had looked holding her: strong yet protective. More than a savior—an Amazon goddess, a magical spirit, a warrior endowed with mythical powers.

Evan was not given to flights of fancy. He couldn't begin to guess why Filomena inspired him to imagine such things.

"There," she said, pointing toward a barely visible driveway, its entrance flanked by two short stone columns. He turned onto the gravel driveway, pebbles crunching beneath his tires. His headlights guided him up the curving drive until suddenly the house loomed before him.

It was huge. He wouldn't call it a palace—there was nothing elegant about it—but the house had a rugged grandeur. Its walls were constructed of randomly shaped stones, its double door arched, its windows filled with light. The cast-iron lamps hanging on either side of the door illuminated not just the porch but the shaggy front lawn and untrimmed shrubs. The driveway ended in a circle near an overgrown path of slate leading to the broad front steps. Astonished, Evan shut off the engine and gawked. "This is your house?"

"Yes."

"Wow." He craned his neck to admire the roof, whose patterned tiles sloped sharply above the third story. "I never knew there was a house hiding back here. How old is it?"

"Around a hundred years, I think."

"Wow." No one would have built a house like this today. It would have required too much labor, and the land it sat on—a huge parcel, given the length of the driveway—would have been zoned into smaller lots. "I guess I can understand why my kids were curious about the place."

"Do you think it looks haunted?"

He eyed her. Her smile had returned, warm and tantalizing. "It looks like the sort of house that would be haunted by a woman named Filomena."

Her eyebrows flicked upward. "Oh?"

"Unusual name. Unusual house." *Unusual woman,* he wanted to add, but he had no way of knowing whether she was unusual. He only sensed it. "And my house is really just through the woods?" he asked, scrutinizing the expanse of forest behind the house.

"There's a path. It wasn't too clear to me, but Billy had no trouble following it even in the dark."

He turned his gaze back to the house. He couldn't

imagine Filomena rattling around in it by herself. She'd said it was her childhood home. Had she endured an odd childhood? Or an average one in an odd house?

He tried to picture her the way she'd been before Sunday, in Manhattan. He envisioned her as an artist, living a bohemian life in SoHo or TriBeCa, or whatever Manhattan neighborhood was funky-chic these days. He envisioned her in long skirts and flamboyant earrings, drinking espresso and discussing the latest gallery showings with adoring men clad in black. What he couldn't envision was her becoming friends with a divorced father of two in Arlington, Connecticut.

Yet he wanted to become friends with her, at least until he could figure out why his nerves seemed to sizzle from her nearness, why her gaze seemed to suck him in. What he felt in her presence wasn't anything as simple as healthy male lust. Sure, he appreciated her beauty, but that wasn't it.

She made him anxious. She fascinated him. She knocked him off balance.

Or maybe he reacted strangely to her because he was strung out over his kids' stunt. Maybe it had nothing to do with Filomena Albright herself.

"So what brought you back to Arlington? Were you homesick?"

She shook her head. Her hair glided around her face, smooth and glossy. "I inherited the house. I've got to spruce it up and sell it."

"Oh." Someone must have died, then. "My condolences."

"Thank you." Her eyes shimmered and her smile looked brave and shaky. Once again he felt undermined by her. If she was going to collapse in a fit of grief-stricken weeping, what would he do? Hug her? Comfort her? Pass her one of the fast-food napkins he kept stored in the console between the seats, handy for mopping up the kids' messes?

Fortunately, she didn't fall apart. She blinked a few times and her smile grew less forced. "I figured I'd stay here in Arlington through New Year's Day, enjoy the house and get it into shape, then put it on the market in January."

She was going to be in town until January? His brain abruptly shifted gears. She would be in town until the holiday retail season was over and his schedule calmed down. She would be just a short walk through the woods from his house during the next few weeks, when his life was going to be chaotic, when his daughter's preschool teacher believed he would need help in the form of a baby-sitter so he wouldn't keep picking Gracie up late. Filomena thought his children were adorable, and Gracie had trusted her enough to rest her head on her shoulder, and—

What the hell was he thinking? He didn't even know this woman!

But he was thinking it anyway. Because she scrambled his thoughts. Because she wore the moon around her neck. Because he'd believed his children were gone—the absolute worst nightmare a father could experience—and she'd rescued him from that nightmare by bringing his children back to him.

"We need to talk," he said.

Her smile grew inquisitive and her eyes glowed like onyx, a hint of gold in their depths.

"I'm probably crazy, but—" He clamped his mouth shut to stop thinking aloud. He couldn't discuss his thoughts with her until he knew what those thoughts actually were, and until he was convinced that they weren't the ravings of a lunatic.

"You're probably crazy, but...?" she prompted him.

He smiled and studied the dashboard, hoping his mind would clarify itself if he wasn't distracted by her beauty. "Maybe we'd better talk tomorrow. May I phone you?" he asked.

"You can't leave me hanging like that," she protested. "Why are you probably crazy?"

He turned back to her. God, she had a glorious smile. He couldn't look at it without smiling himself. "I'm probably crazy because my kids made me that way," he joked. "But I was just thinking..." There was no *probably* about it. He was *definitely* crazy.

"Yes?" It was a murmur of encouragement.

"I'm having child-care problems."

"Evan, just because your kids snuck out of the house doesn't mean you're a bad father," she reassured him, reaching across the console and patting his hand. Her touch surprised him. He hadn't been expecting it, and although he knew she'd meant to comfort him, he didn't feel the least bit comforted. Her fingers were warm and slender. Had she really been strong enough to haul thirty-eight pounds of living, breathing Gracie all the way home? "Didn't you ever do anything naughty when you were a kid?"

"I did much naughtier things than what Billy and Gracie did," he conceded, doing his best to ignore the lingering sensation of her hand on his. "If my kids do half the stuff I did as a kid, I'll kill them. But I was thinking about child care as in day care. I've got them both in programs, but it's a hectic time of year for my business.

Gracie's preschool teacher thinks I'm falling down on the job.''

"Are you?''

He met her probing gaze. Although still smiling, she seemed almost solemn, as if his paternal insecurities actually meant something to her. "I don't know. Sometimes I pick up Gracie late from preschool. I just can't get there on time.'' He drew in a breath. "This can't possibly interest you.''

"It does. Gracie is a such a little cutie.''

"She's a demon.''

"A cute one.'' Filomena smiled gently. "She said her mother was gone…?''

Evan frowned. How had Gracie happened to have mentioned that? "I'm divorced. I have custody. I'm not sure where my ex-wife is living right now, but she's not a part of their life.''

"Ah.'' Filomena continued to study him, her expression enigmatic. "So you can't pick Gracie up from preschool on time.''

"I've been making arrangements, kind of ad hoc, but…'' He sighed. "The preschool director is right. I'm screwing up. My kids are climbing out windows and pestering total strangers.''

"I could pick Gracie up from her school, if that's what you're asking.''

His eyes met hers. Why did he want to trust her? He hoped it wasn't simply because she could make his life a little easier over the next few weeks. She *could* make it easier—but he suspected she could make it a lot more complicated, too. "Okay,'' he said with a grudging smile. "I guess that was what I was asking.''

"I don't think it would be a problem. What about Billy?"

"Look." Logic fought its way to the forefront of his brain. "I hardly even know you, and—"

"And you're not going to get to know me sitting in your car in my driveway while your poker pals are waiting for you back at your house. Maybe we should discuss this some other time."

"Good idea." He did a quick calculation, then nodded. "Why don't you come over for dinner tomorrow, and we can see how everyone gets along. And if we think it's viable, we can work something out. I'd want to pay you for your time, of course."

"Dinner sounds like a good idea," she agreed, ignoring his remark about paying her. "What time should I come?"

"How about six-thirty? I think we can get organized by then. I'll broil something."

"Broiled something sounds delicious," she said, her grin shaping dimples in her cheeks. "I'll see you tomorrow, Evan."

"Great."

She pushed open her door and swung her booted feet out. Her skirt swirled around her as she stood, and he felt a blast of cold that he knew came from the open door, although he couldn't shake the suspicion that her departure had caused it. When she'd been sitting beside him in the car, she'd emitted a warmth—or maybe it was that her nearness made him warm, because she was beautiful and womanly and...

Damn. He needed a baby-sitter for his kids, not a girl-friend, not a lover, not a babe to star in his fantasies. Not a sophisticated New Yorker who dressed like a Gypsy and sat alone in a big house, drinking wine and listening to harpsichord music.

Not a woman named Filomena Albright, who seemed perfectly able to leave him spellbound.

CHAPTER FIVE

FILOMENA FINALLY SETTLED on black denim jeans and a textured white tunic. She'd taken an absurdly long time choosing her outfit because she hadn't been sure exactly what she was dressing for. A dinner party? A family meal? A job interview?

A couple of hours in the company of Evan Myers?

Sighing, she ran a brush through her hair. The mirror above the dresser in her old bedroom had a warp in it, making the outline of her bosom wiggle when she moved. Not that it mattered. Her hair was also wiggly, mysterious waves overtaking it in all the wrong places. None of the three different pairs of earrings she'd tried on looked right to her, although she'd resigned herself to the third pair, which featured colorful clusters of beads. Twin lines rose from the bridge of her nose, punctuating her frown.

She was anxious and edgy, which bothered her because she had no reason to be. Evan was offering her a wonderful opportunity—a chance to get out of the house for an hour or two every day, to keep an eye on his children until he got home—and she ought to be pleased about it. If she didn't have something to occupy her time besides cleaning the house, inventorying its contents and shuffling through her research notes, she'd go crazy. Playing with Evan's kids, who seemed charming if somewhat spunky, would be a perfect distraction.

And she'd even earn a few dollars, which she could certainly use.

In the mirror, she noticed the lines in her forehead deepening. She didn't want to think about receiving money from Evan, and that was a bad sign. He'd invited her for dinner to discuss a job. The evening would re-volve around nothing more than that job. He didn't care if her outfit was attractive or her earrings brightened her complexion, as long as she was willing to pick up Gracie at her preschool and keep an eye on her and Billy until Daddy got home from work.

A job, she reminded herself as she descended the stairs, digging through her purse for her keys. Tonight was about nothing more than a chance to assess whether she and the Myers children were compatible.

Yet when she thought about the way Evan had looked at her, his deep-set silver-gray eyes glinting with fear for his children and fascination with her, the air in his car simmering with an inexplicable warmth when they'd been seated side by side last night, driving through the dark streets of Arlington... Could there possibly be something more going on than just a father's attempt to arrange child care for his two children?

If there was, Filomena would be wise to avoid it. She was going to remain in Arlington only long enough to get the house into marketable shape. Her life was in New York City, in Columbia University's library collections and seminar rooms. After she finished her doctorate, she would try to find a faculty position somewhere, and spend her summers traveling, hiking and exploring the world the way her father had. He'd been a professor of classics when he'd met Filomena's mother on the worn marble steps leading to the Parthenon one Athens summer. By the time Filomena was four, her father had retired from his university position, but she'd always thought his career had been ideal—teaching nine months of the year and replenishing his intellect and imagination the other three months. That was the life she wanted for herself.

The temporary job Evan was offering wouldn't pay for any trips to the Parthenon, but Filomena had been a self-supporting graduate student long enough to know what it meant to scrimp and budget. She ought to be grateful he'd mentioned paying her at all. Accepting compensation from him would define their relationship as strictly employer-employee.

"Employer," she whispered, hovering near the cellar door. "Employee. That's what this is about."

But speaking it aloud didn't stop her from detouring downstairs to get a bottle of her father's well-aged Bordeaux. Even in employer-employee situations, when a person invited another person to dinner the guest was supposed to bring the host a gift of wine, right?

She arrived at Evan's house only a few minutes late, and muttering only a few vague imprecations at the Buick sedan for which she'd signed a three-month lease. It was a big, staid car, the kind her aunt and uncle in Sun City, Arizona, would drive. But it got her where she was going. The lease terms had been reasonable, and if western Connecticut saw snow during the weeks she was in Arlington, the weight and traction of the car would keep her on the road.

Lights illuminated the driveway and the front door of the Myers house. It was as interesting architecturally as hers, a sprawl of rooms that had probably been considered shockingly modern in the sixties. The roof was angular, the windows broad, the walls constructed of cedar and fieldstone. The house was lanky and loose-limbed. Like Evan.

She shouldn't be thinking about his loose-limbed lankiness. She shouldn't be thinking about his long straight sandy hair, his sharp jaw, his enigmatic smile or his seductive eyes, glittering gray ringed with black. If all went well tonight, he would hire her. That, not his athletic physique and his sharply etched features, was what she needed to focus on.

She parked in the driveway and hesitated before reaching for the wine bottle, then decided that since she'd brought it with her, she might as well give it to him and hope he viewed the gift as nothing more than a courteous gesture. Strolling up the walk to the front door, she lectured herself to remember the purpose of the evening— and the purpose of her stay in Arlington. On the small front porch, she took a deep breath, filling her lungs with the crisp, tart scent of late-autumn air, and rang the bell.

The door swung open, and her entire pep talk evaporated from her mind as she took in the sight of him. Evan Myers was a phenomenally attractive man.

At the moment he seemed a bit frazzled. His hair was as disheveled as it had been last night, silky strands straying across the side part, and his dress shirt, unbuttoned at the collar and rolled up at the sleeves, was wrinkled. Like last night, his jaw was shaded by a day's growth of beard, which gave him a rugged look at odds with his cozy suburban surroundings. He was wiping his hands on a dish towel and grinning.

"Come on in," he welcomed her.

She stepped into the entry, willing her pulse rate to

subside. She knew she'd make a fine part-time baby-sitter
for his children, so she shouldn't be nervous about the
job-interview aspect of her visit. She also knew that nothing other than the job-interview aspect would occur tonight, so she had no reason to be nervous on any other
account, either.

She handed him the wine. "I hope this goes with whatever you're serving," she said, sounding much calmer
than she felt. "Broiled something, wasn't it?"

He accepted the bottle with a surprised smile.
"Thanks. I—"

"Is she here?" a shrill voice resounded from another
room. "Is Fil here, Daddy?"

Before he could answer, Filomena heard the patter of
footsteps. In less than three seconds, Gracie appeared at
the end of the entry hall, Billy right behind her. Gracie
charged straight past her father to plant herself in front
of Filomena, but Billy held back, as if he didn't want her
to think he was too eager to see her.

Filomena appreciated the arrival of the children, two
living, breathing reminders of what this dinner was all
about. "Hi, Gracie," she said, hunkering down so she
was eye level with the girl. Gracie wore a cute outfit—
stretch leggings and a shirt in a matching pattern of white
stars on a dark-green background—and her hair was
pinned back from her face with the pink butterfly barrette
Filomena had found on the ground near her window last
Sunday. Gracie probably hadn't chosen it deliberately,
but Filomena was delighted that she was wearing it.

Billy remained lurking at the end of the hallway,
watching her through solemn gray eyes so like his father's. In fact, Billy looked exactly as Evan must have
looked a quarter of a century ago, before the bones of

his face had taken a manly shape. Billy had the same blond-brown hair, the same stubborn chin, the same expression—slightly wary but definitely interested.

"We made a puppet show in school today," Gracie said, taking over the hostess chores. "We made the puppets out of socks and today we made a puppet show. My puppet was the best." She grabbed Filomena's hand and led her into the kitchen. "We're gonna eat now. We were waiting for you."

"I'm sorry—I'm a little late," she said, glancing over her shoulder at Evan.

He smiled and shook his head to let her know she had nothing to apologize for. "Tell Filomena some more about the puppet show," he said. "I've still got a few things to get together."

The kitchen seemed larger without Evan's poker friends filling it. The Tiffany-style lamp over the kitchen table gave the dining area a warm, cozy feel, while the bright spotlights in the cooking area created an aura of efficiency in that part of the room.

Gracie reflected efficiency more than cozy warmth. "You're gonna sit here," she said, yanking out a chair and dragging Filomena over to it. "Next to me."

"Let her take her coat off first," Evan suggested with a laugh as he rinsed a tomato at the sink. "Billy, can you get her coat?"

Billy hurried around the table, displacing Gracie with a little more enthusiasm than necessary. "I'll hang up your coat," he said, as if the idea had originated with him.

"Thank you, Billy," Filomena said, removing the heavy suede jacket and handing it to him. When he left the room, she noticed Gracie pouting on the far side of the table, evidently unhappy that Billy had gotten to be Filomena's hero. She smiled and beckoned the little girl over. "Now, tell me some more about your puppet show," she said.

Gracie's pout vanished, replaced by a bright grin. "It was great. There were 'splosions and everything in it. There was this monster, and the puppets had to kill him, and…"

She narrated a grisly scenario, overflowing with mayhem—lots of "'splosions" and other preschool-level gore—that concluded with the triumph of all the puppets over the evil monster. By the time Gracie was done, Evan had arranged dinner on the table: a platter of sliced beef, a bowl of baked potatoes, one of green beans and a plate of tomato wedges. Colorful plastic cups filled with milk stood at the children's places, and stemware goblets stood at Filomena's place and Evan's, which was directly across the table from her. With a festive pop, he opened the wine she'd brought and poured some into the glasses.

"Wine, Daddy? You're gonna drink wine?" Billy asked incredulously.

"Why shouldn't I drink wine?" he countered. "I like wine."

"You never drink it. You always drink beer."

"I don't *always* drink beer," he argued, shooting Filomena a quick grin. "I like wine. I just don't like drinking it by myself. You two are way too young to drink it with me. That's why I don't drink it very often." He set the bottle on the table and lowered himself into his chair. "Tonight, I have someone to drink the wine with, and I intend to enjoy it. In fact—" he raised his glass "—I think we should drink a toast."

The children both hoisted their milk cups high. "A

toast! A toast!'' they bellowed, leading Filomena to assume they'd seen toasts on TV shows or in a movie.

"You have to lift your glass," Gracie told Filomena.

Smiling, she obeyed Gracie's instructions and turned to Evan. He gazed straight into her eyes, sending her a message that she couldn't decipher. All she knew was that it was personal, just between her and him, and even if his children were the reason he'd asked her to dinner, this one moment, this one look, had nothing to do with them. She held her breath, wondering what he was going to toast to.

"Here," he said, "is to the two finest kids in the world."

"That's us!" Gracie added, as if there might be some question which kids he meant.

Smiling at how wrong she'd been about that one moment and that one look, Filomena touched her wineglass to Evan's and sipped. He tasted the wine and his eyebrows arched. "Wow. This is the good stuff."

She chuckled. "I'm afraid so."

"Don't be afraid. I'm supposed to say something, right? Like, 'It's complex but round, with a finish of...' what?"

"Booze," Billy suggested.

"Okay. A finish of booze."

"That about describes it," Filomena said, laughing.

Evan passed her the platter of meat. Once she'd taken some, he forked a portion onto each of his children's plates. He also helped them with the beans and the potatoes, cutting Gracie's potato open for her, adding a pat of butter and mashing it into the soft white center. He cut her meat into small pieces for her, too, before taking any food for himself.

Filomena watched him, wondering at his patience. Admittedly, she had little evidence to go on, but he seemed like a good father, one who took the time to prepare a nutritious meal for his children after a full day of work, one who assisted them and drank toasts to them and laughed when they teased him. They seemed like healthy, happy kids.

So why was their mother out of the picture? What kind of woman would have abandoned not just her children but Evan? The world was not exactly overrun with kind, devoted, strikingly handsome men. What terrible thing could he have done? How could he have chosen as his wife and the mother of his children the sort of woman who would walk away from all this?

Filomena wished there was a way to ask him. But really, it wasn't her business. He wanted a baby-sitter, not a relationship. When he'd gazed at her over the rim of his wineglass, his grand message had probably been nothing more complicated than *Hey, there's another adult at the table. I don't have to drink wine by myself.*

"This meat tastes funny," Gracie announced.

"It's broiled flank steak," Evan assured her.

"It tastes funny. Billy, does yours taste funny?"

"It tastes different," he agreed.

Filomena forked a piece of meat into her mouth. "It tastes delicious," she said. It really did.

"I marinated it," Evan told Gracie.

She glared at him suspiciously. "What does that mean?"

"I soaked the meat in something before I broiled it."

"Daddy broils everything," Billy informed Filomena.

"What did you soak it in?" Gracie persisted.

"Salad dressing."

"Eeeuw!" she shrieked.

"Gross!" Billy chimed in, although he was giggling. "Salad dressing is for salad!"

"Well, Heather told me that if you marinate a flank steak in that noncreamy French dressing, it makes the meat taste better."

"It's very good," Filomena assured him.

"Heather is Daddy's secretary," Gracie said. "She's beautiful. I think Daddy should marry her."

"Heather hates me," Billy muttered.

"She does not," Evan said. "She hates children in general, but other than that, she doesn't hate you."

"I think she's the most beautiful lady in the world," Gracie said, a swooning lilt in her voice.

"You're not supposed to say that in front of another lady," Billy told her.

Filomena took a sip of wine to keep from erupting in laughter at the children's exuberant tactlessness. But one corner of her brain toyed with the possibility that Evan agreed with his daughter about his secretary's assets— agreed enough to have acted on them. Was he having an affair with his beautiful secretary? Was that what had driven his wife away? But if he had been having an affair, why wouldn't his wife just kick him out and keep the children?

Maybe Heather the secretary hadn't entered his life until after his wife had left. In any case, Heather's existence as the most beautiful lady in the world would likely keep Evan from pursuing anything personal with Filomena. Which was exactly as it should be. She couldn't have a relationship with him. She didn't want one.

Billy distracted her by launching into a description of a scientific demonstration his teacher had performed in class that day, involving boiling water and a balloon. The project proved that hot air took up more space than cold air, a fact that Gracie absolutely refused to believe. "How can it take up more space? Does that mean if the house is hot the walls are gonna 'splode?"

"Walls are stronger than air," Billy explained in a condescending tone.

"Not in a hurricane. Right, Daddy? Walls blow down in hurricanes."

"There's a difference between air pressure and wind," Evan said, sending Filomena a questioning look. Did he expect her to teach his children science? She could handle basic questions, but science had never been her strong suit.

Even so, it was fun to hear the children debate the expansion of hot air. They were obviously intelligent and curious about the world.

She still had a fair amount of food in front of her when Gracie started to squirm and play with the green beans left on her plate. Billy had done a marginally better job of finishing his dinner—his potato skin was an empty shell on his plate, a single bean lying beside it. "Would you guys like to be excused?" Evan asked.

The children sprang out of their chairs, mumbling, "'Scuse me," and rubbing their napkins across their faces. Before Filomena could speak, they were gone, their voices trailing back into the kitchen as they bickered over who was going to hold the TV's remote control.

Evan waited until the air stopped vibrating with their echoing shouts, then refilled his and Filomena's wine-glasses and leaned back in his chair. He regarded her with a smile that was not quite gentle. Perhaps he was trying to put her at ease, but his eyes were too intense, too questioning, reminding her that she was in his house for a reason, and that reason wasn't to sip wine with a gorgeous man.

"I like your children," she said.

"They're on their best behavior at the moment. They're both grounded for the week because of last night. I think they're trying not to do anything that might make me sentence them to hard time."

"You didn't take away their TV privileges," she noted, glancing over her shoulder in the direction they'd disappeared.

"Actually, I did. But tonight I'll let them watch because it'll keep them out of our hair." He took another sip and smiled again. He didn't strike her as a true oenophile, but he clearly was enjoying the wine. Or maybe his smile meant he was enjoying her company. She would like to believe that. But she knew she shouldn't.

She drank a bit of her wine. She had so many questions to ask him, most of them unaskable—like, how close he and Heather were, why his wife had left him, whether lots of women went all fluttery inside when he aimed his bedroom eyes at them. Whether his children had been born so wonderful, or had become wonderful because he was such a fine father. Whether he'd truly invited her over to discuss a job.

She kept her mouth shut. It was a tactic she'd learned from her mother, who had always done the exact opposite, asking too many questions, talking too much, making assumptions. Leila Albright's forwardness had led to some of her most exciting adventures, but she'd lived profligately. Not just in her finances, but in her personal engagements; she had always spent every last scrap of herself, saving nothing. She'd declare that Filomena ought to loosen up, or lose a few pounds, or gain a few, or stop burying herself in books, or do better in school, or date more, or not date whomever she'd been dating at the moment Leila had happened to open her mouth. The good part was that Filomena had never had to doubt her mother's honesty. But sometimes, Leila would have been better off shutting her mouth and listening.

Filled with questions, Filomena shut her mouth and listened, waiting for Evan to speak.

Eventually, he did. He took another leisurely sip of wine and said, "Here's my situation. I run a chain of sporting-goods stores. The weeks between now and Christmas are the busiest time of the year for the stores. I'm supposed to pick Gracie up at preschool before five o'clock, but I just can't do it at this time of year. We've got a big promotion revving up and all the holiday chaos. I simply can't get to the preschool by five."

Filomena nodded. She could easily solve his problem for him, but she exercised patience and kept listening.

"Billy is in an after-school program at the Elm Street School most days. Monday afternoons he has Cub Scouts, and his friend Scott's mother picks him up from the troop meeting. But the other days, he has to be picked up by five-thirty. Even that's been a little tricky for me. And with this Tank Moody promotion, it's going to get harder and harder."

"Tank Moody?"

"Yeah. The football player who's going to be appearing at our stores over the next few weeks, signing autographs and hopefully bringing in customers. I..." He hesitated, then sighed. "I did a promotion with a pro athlete once before and it was a disaster. So I've really got to keep a close watch on it this time. I don't want it to blow up in my face.''

"This man's actual name is Tank Moody?" Filomena couldn't get past that. The only professional athletes whose names she knew were tennis players, gymnasts and icons like Babe Ruth.

Evan appeared bemused. "You've never heard of Tank Moody?"

Filomena shook her head.

He shrugged. "Well, so much for that promotion. I guess we won't be luring you into the store."

"What's the name of your store?"

"Champion Sports. We're on Hauser Street."

"I remember that store! You own it?"

"I own a majority stake. I took the helm nine years ago."

She grinned, a joyous memory washing over her. "My father bought me my first bicycle there. We went on my fifth birthday, and he was so patient. I considered every single bicycle in the store, even the big adult-size ones. I fell in love with a yellow bike with red flames painted on it. It looked so wicked. I was heartbroken when I finally outgrew that bike.''

"Did you buy your next bike at Champion?" Evan asked, grinning.

"I honestly don't remember. Somehow, the first time you buy a bike is the most memorable.''

Filomena felt his gaze on her. She suspected he was thinking about other first times, about memorable times. "Anyway," he said after a long moment, "I should probably do the whole child-care thing properly, hire a nanny through an agency or ask for recommendations or something. But I just got a sense about you last night..." He sighed and shook his head. "Maybe I'm nuts, but I think you'd be great with the kids. If you're willing, of course."

"I'm quite willing. It would work perfectly into my schedule."

He set his glass on the table and nodded. "Can you tell me what your schedule is?"

"Cleaning the house, doing repairs, getting the place ready to sell." She thought for a minute, then added, "Working a bit on my thesis."

"Your thesis?"

"I'm a Ph.D. candidate in English literature at Columbia University."

"Oh." He seemed impressed. Maybe a bit overimpressed. "You're going to be Dr. Albright?"

"If my thesis is accepted and I pass my orals."

"Wow." He reached for his glass, as if the thought of her earning a doctorate drove him to drink. "What's your thesis on?"

"Freddy the Pig," she said.

"What?"

"Freddy the Pig. He was a character in a series of children's books by Walter Brooks. The stories are all allegories, commentaries on society and politics. They're wonderful. I bet Billy would love them. He's, what, eight years old?"

"Good guess."

"Then he's probably old enough for them. I'll bring one over for him to read. Does he do much reading?"

"Not enough," Evan complained. "He's working his way through the Bunnicula books right now."

"Wonderful!" Filomena cheered. "My broader research revolves around the use of anthropomorphic animals in children's literature.''

''Anthropomorphic animals.'' He seemed to be counting the syllables.

''Animals depicted as having human attributes. The Bunnicula books are full of animals with human intelligence, human neuroses and fears. The Freddy the Pig books have that same sensibility. These books help children to understand the human condition without shocking or depressing them, because everything is presented one step removed, with animals standing in for humans.'' She clamped her mouth shut, afraid she sounded pedantic.

Evan didn't seem to mind. ''If you know so much about children's books, I guess you must know something about children.''

''I guess I must.'' She smiled.

''So you'll be a good baby-sitter.''

''I should think so.''

He tapped his fingers some more. ''If you're working on a Ph.D., I'm going to have to rethink my pay scale. I mean, *Dr.* Filomena Albright...''

''I'm not a doctor yet,'' she reminded him, then stifled herself. She had no idea what he'd been planning to pay her. But even though the subject of compensation made her uncomfortable, she shouldn't give him the idea that he could underpay her.

''I'd been figuring about fifty dollars a week. Some days you'd be working only one hour, some days two or two and a half, so it would all balance out. But if you think that's too little...''

She'd actually been expecting him to offer less.

''I guess sixty dollars would be fairer,'' he decided, negotiating the offer upward without her having to say a word. "Cash, off the books. We're talking about an informal arrangement here."

"All right," she said.

"Are you sure? Billy and Gracie can be a handful," he warned.

She smiled slyly. "Hmm. Maybe I should ask for more money."

"Go ahead," he invited her. "How much do you think would be fair?"

"Sixty dollars a week is fine. Really, Evan, it's..." *Too much,* she wanted to say. Too much to be paid for the pleasure of getting out of the house for a couple of hours every day, of having the chance to introduce two new children to the glories of Freddy the Pig and Stuart Little and all the other anthropomorphic animals she'd been hanging out with in graduate school. Too much to be paid for the opportunity to see Evan, to talk to him, to admire his lean physique and his beautiful eyes. "It's fine," she finished.

"When can you start?"

She shrugged. "Whenever you need me."

"I needed you last week. Is tomorrow too soon?"

"No—but maybe you ought to talk to the children first. They might not like me."

"Oh, sure." He snorted. "I could see that right away. They really hate you. Sticking them with you will be part of their punishment for running away last night."

"I'm not kidding, Evan—"

"You'll start tomorrow. If they've got a problem with the arrangement, we'll deal with it." He shoved away from the table. "I'll need your phone number. And I'll need to write a letter you can present to Molly Saunders-Russo—she's the director of Gracie's preschool—and

Maryanne Becker, the director of Billy's after-school program. They'll want something in writing stating you have my permission to pick up my kids. And you'll have to have photo ID with you, a driver's license or something, so they'll know you're who you say you are.'' He rose from the table and crossed to a small desk built into one of the counters. When he returned to the table, he held a pad and pen. ''If you could write your address and phone number, I'll go run up some letters on my computer. And I'll get you information on the kids' pediatrician, and written permission to take them to see her if there's a problem....'' He was thinking out loud, apparently composing his letters in his mind as he set the pen and pad down before Filomena. She was impressed by his conscientiousness, and equally impressed by his graceful way of moving, his economical gestures, his lithe motions. She was impressed by the way his shirt stretched smooth over his shoulders, the way his slacks emphasized the length of his legs.

Fortunately, he wouldn't be around when she was watching his children. Because, loath though she was to admit it, she would rather be watching him.

HE EMERGED from his study ten minutes later, carrying several letters, a printout of emergency information—his office phone number, the pediatrician's phone number, health-insurance policy numbers, Scott's mother's number—and a check for twenty-four dollars to cover payment for Thursday and Friday. The kitchen was empty, but he heard her voice mingling with Billy's and Gracie's in the family room.

He halted by the table and stared at the dishes, the leftovers, the two empty wine goblets. He wondered whether the wine had actually been as delicious as he'd thought, or had just tasted that good because he'd been drinking it with her.

Even though she was going to be working for him, he couldn't shake the understanding that she had the upper hand in their dealings. Not because she was bossy or domineering, but because...

Because looking at her turned him on. Hearing her velvet-rich voice turned him on. Gazing at the long, thick tumble of her hair and imagining his fingers buried in it, imagining her eyes closing and her mouth opening for his kiss...

He had to be insane, hiring her to watch his kids. The phrase *asking for trouble* whispered through his brain.

But *not* hiring her would be asking for trouble, too. The streets of Arlington were not exactly teeming with baby-sitters who liked his children and wanted to spend a little time with them every day. If he didn't hire Filomena—a woman who seemed to have patience, a good sense of humor and a particular expertise in children's literature, of all things—who else was there? It might take him weeks to find someone else, and by then the holiday shopping season would be over.

If he put some serious effort into it, he could probably convince himself he was hiring Filomena with the noblest of motives. It would be best for his children. Molly at the Children's Garden would get off his back, and so would Heather—who'd been absolutely right when she'd said picking up Gracie wasn't a part of her job. With Filomena to bridge the gap between the end of the kids' programs and Evan's arrival home in the evening, he wouldn't have to keep asking favors of people, feeling indebted to them.

Really, hiring her was the right thing to do, and her hair and her lips and her large, dark eyes had nothing to do with anything.

Even so, he couldn't deny that he was glad she'd worn slacks tonight. Not that they revealed more than her long skirt had yesterday, but at least he could get a sense of her proportions. Her hips were trimmer than he'd thought, her bosom fuller. And he was some kind of jerk for thinking about her bosom.

He followed the cheerful sound of competing voices into the family room, where the TV was off and Filomena was seated on the floor, a deck of cards spread before her. Billy sat facing her, his elbows on his knees and his chin resting in his palms as he observed her hands moving over the cards. "She's reading Billy's fortune, Daddy!" Gracie announced, jumping to her feet and then settling back on the floor next to Filomena.

Filomena sent him a hopeful look. "You don't mind, do you?"

"Only if you tell him he's doomed to a life of pain and misery," Evan said, moving toward the couch uncertainly. Was he supposed to eavesdrop? Did he want to? Did he want Filomena brainwashing his kids with New Age mumbo jumbo?

"Don't worry," Filomena said, turning from him. She studied the cards. "His future looks very promising."

"Am I gonna play for the Giants or the Patriots?" Billy asked her.

Recalling that she'd never heard of Tank Moody, Evan enlightened her. "Those are football teams."

"I know," she said, a smile flickering about her mouth. "Billy, the cards can't tell anything as specific as that. The question is, do you have the discipline and the focus to make your dreams come true? That's what we're searching for here."

"I've got lots of discipline," Billy said. "Daddy disciplines me all the time."

Evan rolled his eyes. Filomena laughed.

He settled onto the couch and watched as she worked her magic with the children. Whether or not the magic was in the cards he didn't know, and after a while he didn't care. What *was* magic, as far as he was concerned, was that she'd gotten them so interested in what she was doing that they'd turned off the television, and she had them both sitting quietly and calmly with her, listening to everything she said, answering her quiet questions earnestly. When she pointed out to Billy that a certain card combination indicated that he could be impetuous and he needed to develop the habit of thinking before he acted, Evan grinned. He'd bet the cards indicated no such thing. She was just playing a little head game with Billy, giving him useful advice while pretending everything she said was actually coming from the cards.

His smile deepened. She was good. She wasn't just beautiful, she wasn't just intelligent, she wasn't just the right person at the right time. Cards or no, she was magic. A witch, a ghost, a spirit. A woman.

She was magic.

CHAPTER SIX

"EVAN, I'D LIKE YOU to meet Tank Moody," Heather announced as she led a giant hulk of a man into Evan's office. Evan stood six feet tall in his socks, but Tank dwarfed him by at least six inches and outweighed him by at least eighty pounds of granite-hard muscle. As he rose to shake hands with the linebacker—whose beefy grip swallowed Evan's hand the way Evan's swallowed Gracie's—he realized that if Tank was this intimidating in a stylishly tailored suit, he'd be even more daunting in his uniform, with all those pads adding bulk to his massive frame.

His size might have been scary, but his face wasn't. A boyish grin displayed even white teeth—a nice advertisement for the effectiveness of mouth guards, Evan thought—and his cheeks were prepubescent smooth. He was, in fact, only a few years younger than Evan. Obviously, running around a football field and ramming into colossal opponents didn't age a man as much as running a business and butting heads with a couple of kids did.

Then again, maybe getting paid a few million dollars a year plus bonuses was what kept Tank youthful.

"It's a pleasure," Evan said, managing not to wince as Tank's fingers pulverized his. In truth, having the bones in his hand mangled was arguably the highlight of his day so far.

When he'd dropped Gracie off at the Children's Garden that morning, he'd spent several minutes at the front desk with Molly, explaining his new child-care arrangements. He'd thought she would praise him for his initiative, for having acted responsibly and gotten the help he needed—and for having the foresight to prepare written documentation identifying Filomena as the person who would be picking Gracie up each day.

But rather than praise him, Molly had surprised him by saying, "I think you would benefit from some Daddy School classes."

"What?" He'd had no idea what Daddy School classes were, but the suggestion had insulted him.

"Daddy School. You seem a little overwhelmed these days, Evan, and—"

"I'm not overwhelmed. I hired this woman, Filomena Albright—" he jabbed a finger at the letter he'd written for the school's files "—to pick up Gracie at five." If he *was* overwhelmed, it would have been Filomena, not his children, who overwhelmed him. All night long, after she'd read both Billy's and Gracie's cards and then taken her leave, he'd been overwhelmed by thoughts of her long hair, her fortune-telling, her educational pursuits— a Ph.D. in talking animals?—her wide mouth and arching cheekbones and her dark, dark eyes. Having Filomena in his life for the next few weeks was going to tax him in all sorts of ways. The least he'd expected was Molly's approval of what he'd done for his children.

Instead, Molly had told him he needed to take lessons in how to be a father. "I'm not teaching a session this fall—with the new baby, it's a bit too much for me," she'd explained, gesturing lovingly at her infant asleep in a stroller in one corner of her office. "But my colleague Allison Winslow is teaching a class. I think you'd find it useful.''

"I don't need classes in fathering," he'd said indignantly.

"Everyone can improve at anything with a few classes. You might pick up some pointers."

"I don't need pointers."

"Yesterday, Gracie shared with all of us how she and her brother climbed out a second-floor window of your house and snuck through the woods at night. Now, I know you're doing a good job, Evan, but…" Molly had peered up at him, her smile so warm and sympathetic he'd wanted to kick something. "Everyone could use a few pointers sometimes."

"I don't need classes," he'd argued stubbornly.

"Talk to Dennis Murphy. You play poker with him, don't you?"

One of those small-world things. Arlington was a city, but it was close-knit and intimate, filled with intersecting circles. About a year after Murphy, the lawyer who took care of Champion Sports's and Evan's legal business, had invited Evan to join his regular poker game, Evan had learned that Murphy was also the brother-in-law of the director of Gracie's preschool. "What should I talk to Murphy about?" Evan had asked.

"The Daddy School. He's taken a few classes."

"He has?" *His children are wilder than mine,* Evan had wanted to add. *He couldn't have learned that much.*

"You'll find it fun. And useful. And now that you've got some child care lined up, you could sneak out for an hour on Monday evenings. That's when Allison's teaching them—Mondays at seven-thirty, at the YMCA."

"Thanks," he'd muttered. He'd left Molly with the

letter about Filomena and departed from the school, grumbling. He didn't need parental training. He was a great father. Outstanding. Top of the class—if he were in a class, which he wasn't.

Anything he needed to learn about child care that he didn't already know, he'd learn from Filomena. He was paying her sixty bucks a week, wasn't he? And she was a regular Dr. Doolittle when it came to children's literature. He didn't need any Daddy School classes.

Heather's voice dragged him back to the present, to his office, to the towering football player facing him across his desk. "So he's scheduled to appear at the New Haven store from eleven to one," she was saying. "You should be leaving here by ten to give yourselves plenty of time to get a bite to eat and all."

"Mmm," Tank said, eyeing Heather up and down. "I wouldn't mind biting into something tasty right about now."

Evan gritted his teeth and prepared to defend Heather's honor. Heather ignored Tank's insinuation, however, and continued addressing Evan about his day. "Jennifer won't be able to meet you there. She's teleconferencing with the Rhode Island stores about carrying Pep Insoles."

"I told her we weren't going to deal with Pep Insoles until the new year."

"She's gotten inquiries from the athletic departments at a couple of the colleges in Providence. She wants our stores to have the product in stock."

"Fine." Evan didn't want to quarrel with Jennifer about insoles. He didn't even want to think about them. He had all of ten minutes to clear his desk of messages before he was going to have to escort Tank Moody to New Haven.

If he'd been in a saner state of mind, he would have arranged for someone else to drive Tank to the New Haven store. But the whole promotion had him on edge because of what had happened last time. It wouldn't happen again—it couldn't—but he wanted to stay on top of it, to monitor every detail, to make sure there were no surprises, no mistakes, no oversights, nothing that could trip him up and leave him bruised.

Tank was still beaming at him, as if waiting to be entertained. Evan considered warning the guy that his mood resembled a cross between a Möbius strip and a cross-hitch knot—twisted and tangled and generally unfathomable. But he thought better of it. *Get through the promotion,* he lectured himself. *Forget about that Daddy School nonsense. And for God's sake, forget about how magnificent Filomena Albright is.*

He asked Heather to take Tank around the offices and introduce him to everyone. As soon as they were gone, he tackled the pile of notes demanding his attention. Heather would bring Tank back when they had to leave for New Haven. She was better at keeping track of time than he was. And meanwhile, her beauty would probably so dazzle Tank that he'd be half gaga and easy to manage once they got back to Evan's office.

He paced himself well, and was hanging up the phone from the last call he had to make just as Heather returned with Tank. Donning his jacket and straightening his tie, he sent Tank the warmest smile he could manage, then pocketed his keys and nodded toward the door. "Ready to hit the road?"

"Sure," Tank drawled. "I've got my driver downstairs."

"Your driver?" Why hadn't he been told about this?

"Is that a problem?"

"No. Not at all." At least, Evan hoped it wasn't a problem. If Tank's driver was some brawny sidekick, a hanger-on or bodyguard of some sort, well, Evan supposed professional athletes were entitled to spend their millions however they wanted. He only hoped the fellow knew how to drive.

They took the elevator downstairs, Evan wedging himself into one corner to make the majority of the space available to Tank, who needed it. He searched his mind for small talk—if he wasn't going to be driving, he'd probably be expected to engage Tank in friendly chitchat during the forty-minute drive down to New Haven. What could they talk about? The current football season? Tank's team didn't have a spectacular record this year, so that might not be a good subject. The sights? Once they left Arlington, there wouldn't be much to comment on, just small towns and stretches of forest lining the roads.

The holidays. That would be a safe topic. Evan would ask Tank how he planned to spend Christmas, what he hoped Santa would bring him, that kind of thing. They could talk a bit about Champion Sports, too. He could find out what kind of equipment professional athletes respected most, which brands of cleats they preferred when they weren't being paid to endorse one particular brand, which pads protected them best. Evan was pretty sure he'd survive the trip with Tank.

His certainty flagged slightly when they emerged from the building. There, waiting at the curb in front of the store's main entry, was a shiny black stretch limo. "That's yours?" Evan asked.

"I'm a big man," Tank pointed out unnecessarily. "I like my comfort."

"Okay." Evan had been in a stretch limo only once before—on his wedding day. Not what he wanted to think about while cruising through Connecticut with Tank.

The driver, in a dapper black suit that, combined with the limo, made Evan think of funerals, emerged from behind the wheel to open the door for them. Tank climbed in first, limber despite his bulk, and Evan followed him into the spacious passenger area. It featured wall-to-wall red carpeting, paneled walls, a small TV and a cooler chest filled with sports drinks. Evan was relieved that it wasn't stocked with liquor.

He took the backward-facing seat, leaving the forward-facing one for Tank to sprawl out on. The driver closed the door with an expensive-sounding click, then returned to the driver's seat and started the engine. It hummed, a murmur as quiet and gentle as Gracie's breath when she was asleep.

"It's nice traveling in style," Evan commented.

"It's nice being so effin' rich," Tank responded.

Well, yes, there was that. "I assume you won't be using that kind of language around the customers at the store," Evan said hopefully.

Tank laughed. "Relax, Evan. I'm cool."

"Okay." He gazed at the splendor surrounding him— the chrome fittings, the elaborate console that controlled the stereo and television. "The driver knows where we're going?"

"He knows everything."

"He must be handy to have around."

"So what all do you expect is going to go wrong?" Tank asked, his dark eyes zeroing in on Evan.

"Nothing," Evan insisted, sitting straighter. "Nothing at all. Why do you think I think something is going to go wrong?"

"You're wrapped tighter than an Ace bandage on a sprain. Seems to me you've got something on your mind."

Evan sighed. He wasn't going to tell Tank about the last time he'd done a promotion with a pro athlete—a baseball player that time. He wasn't going to discuss how Debbie had insisted on meeting the guy, inviting him to their house, attending his appearances at the stores and then running off with him, leaving behind a note explaining that she wanted glamour and excitement and a life in the major leagues. When she and Evan had dated in college, he'd played varsity soccer and baseball, but he'd never planned to play sports professionally. He played because he was good, the games were fun and the college was giving him much-needed scholarship money. He'd enjoyed Debbie's enthusiasm for his games, her groupie devotion to his teams, but he'd been clear with her from the start that the life of a professional athlete didn't interest him. He didn't want all the traveling, all the stress, all the worry about how long his body would hold up. He'd been good enough to play at the college level, but he never would have been a big success as a pro, and he'd had no regrets about putting his jock days behind him and growing up.

Debbie had said she'd understood—and maybe she'd even meant it at the time. They'd been young, infatuated with each other. They'd laughed at the same jokes, enjoyed the same movies, had phenomenal sex. Evan had truly believed he'd found his life partner.

But she'd grown restless in their marriage. He'd assumed that was because Billy had arrived in their lives less than two years after they'd tied the knot. Evan had tried his best to shoulder his share of the parenting chores. He'd changed diapers, taken Billy for walks, sung lullabies off-key, but Billy hadn't complained. Evan had loved being a father, and he would have gladly spent even more time with Billy if he could have. But he'd been putting in long hours trying to build Champion Sports into the regional powerhouse it now was.

He'd thought Debbie would snap out of her doldrums. Instead, she'd had Gracie and sunk even deeper into the blahs. Evan had tried surprising her, coming home with a baby-sitter and sweeping her out for dinner at Reynaud, the classiest restaurant in town. On their fifth anniversary he'd bought her a diamond pendant. Diamonds were glamorous, weren't they?

Evidently, she'd preferred baseball diamonds to the kind you could wear on a gold chain around your neck. So when she'd seen an opportunity, she'd grabbed it and ran.

Tank was right. Evan was wrapped as tight as an Ace bandage right now. Debbie was gone, but he couldn't control his reflexes. He couldn't control the dread that gnawed at him, the memories of how a professional athlete could destroy his world simply by being rich and cool and glamorous enough to ride around town in a stretch limo piloted by a driver who knew everything.

And if that wasn't enough, he had other things on his mind. He was coming off a sleepless night—a night during which his mind had churned with inappropriate ideas about Filomena Albright—and a morning during which Molly Saunders-Russo had more or less told him she thought he was an inadequate father. "Do you have any children?" he asked Tank.

Tank chuckled. "None that I know of." He leaned back against the leather upholstery, obviously quite at home in the limo. "I suppose if I had a child, his mother would be sure to keep me in the loop, given my deep pockets and all."

"I suppose."

"So, you got kids?"

"Two. A son and a daughter." If Tank hadn't asked, Evan would have moved on to other things—the weather, Christmas, athletic equipment. But Tank *had* asked, and since the subject was bugging Evan, he figured he might as well beat it into submission. "My daughter's preschool teacher told me I need to take classes in how to be a father."

"Oh, man. That sounds bad."

"Yeah, it does, doesn't it?" Evan grinned, pleased by how easy Tank was to talk to. "The thing is, I'm a fantastic father. I'm raising the kids myself, and they're terrific. Not perfect, but pretty damned close."

"Never get into trouble, do they?"

"Oh, they get into trouble, but…" He sighed again. "I don't know. Maybe she's right. Maybe if I love them as much as I think I do, I'd be willing to take these classes and become a better father."

"What does their mother say?"

"She's gone," Evan said tersely.

"Oh, man. Ladies. Can't live with 'em, can't live without 'em. Thing is, I'd rather live without 'em. Just bring 'em in for special occasions, if you know what I mean, and then send them on their way. Having a driver comes in real handy if that's what you want to do," he added, gesturing toward his chauffeur.

"I suppose it does."

"So this teacher thinks you ought to take some classes, huh? Is she cute?"

"She's married," Evan told him.

"Yeah, but is she cute?"

Evan glared at Tank, who chuckled as if to imply he was joking. At least, Evan hoped that was what he was implying. "What difference does it make if she's cute?"

Tank shrugged. "Maybe there'd be some cute ladies at the classes."

"It's a Daddy School. Why would there be any women in the class? Women aren't daddies."

"Well, I'm thinking maybe the instructor'll be a lady. In fact, I'm thinking it's *got* to be a lady. Who else is gonna teach men how to be daddies?"

"Other daddies, maybe."

"Now *that* sounds like a losing proposition." Tank reached into the cooler chest and pulled out a bottle, then gestured for Evan to help himself. Evan declined with a shake of his head. "Seems to me," Tank said, yanking the cap off, "ladies are the experts when it comes to raising kids. Dads do their part to create the kid, but the ladies are the experts. My mama raised me, and I must say she did a damned fine job. That's why I love ladies so much—because the first person I ever loved was a lady." He lifted the bottle as though in a toast to his mother and all the other ladies he loved, then took a swig.

Evan mulled over Tank's observations about the Daddy School and found his resentment melting away. Maybe Tank had the right attitude: not that Evan might meet cute ladies by attending class, but that he could give it a try and not take it so seriously. His poker buddy Murphy seemed to have survived the ordeal, although it seemed pretty clear to Evan that he hadn't learned how to turn his two rambunctious kids into quiet, well-behaved youngsters.

Evan didn't want Billy and Gracie to turn into quiet, well-behaved youngsters. All he wanted was for them never to climb on a roof again. If the Daddy School taught a father how to guarantee that his kids would stay safe and act sensibly, the class might be worth it.

FILOMENA FOUND the Children's Garden preschool without too much trouble. Driving down Dudley Street, she'd noticed quite a few new stores and businesses, as well as older businesses she remembered from her stays in Arlington years ago. Although Thanksgiving was still a week away, most of the shops were already decorated with Christmas lights, wreaths and smiling Santas waving in windows framed with garlands of holly and tinsel.

She almost laughed out loud when she saw a house with a neon hand glowing in the window, and the sign Readings, Predictions, Tarot. Madame Roussard, Licensed Palmist. She remembered the time—she'd been around nine or ten—when her mother had brought her to visit Madame Roussard. They'd both had their tarot cards read. Filomena couldn't remember what her mother's cards had predicted, but her own reading had promised a life of passion. Filomena's father had dismissed the whole thing as utter nonsense and a waste of money, but Filomena and her mother had had a grand time listening to Madame Roussard describe their futures and then going out for ice-cream sundaes.

As a teenager, Filomena had learned tarot and regular-card reading, but she'd never told her father. She'd wanted him to think she was as wise and dignified as he was. She hadn't told her mother, either, because her mother tended to take the cards just a bit too seriously. Heaven knew, if her mother had found out Filomena was studying tarot, she might have urged her to quit college and set up a quaint little storefront like Madame Roussard's, where she could issue prophecies at twenty dollars a pop.

The preschool was less than half a block from Madame Roussard's, and its parking lot was half-full when Filomena pulled in. Bright lights illuminated the asphalt and the front door. She parked, hugged her suede jacket tightly around her and scampered inside, out of the blustery breeze.

A pretty young woman sat at a desk just inside the door. "Hi," Filomena said, approaching the desk. "You must be Molly."

The woman shook her head. "I'm Cara. Molly's left for the day. Can I help you?"

Molly had left? Who was this woman? Would she release Gracie to Filomena? Her first day as a baby-sitter, and already she sensed a disaster brewing. "I'm here to pick up Gracie Myers. My name is Filomena Albright."

Cara swiveled away from Filomena, opened a file drawer and flipped through the files until she found the one she was looking for. She pulled it out, opened it and skimmed a document inside. Then she slid the file back into the drawer and smiled at Filomena. "I'll need to see some photo ID," she said.

As if Filomena were trying to board a plane or visit a prison inmate. Was the woman going to frisk her, too?

Sighing, she pulled out her wallet and opened it to her driver's license.

Cara studied the ugly little photo on the license and nodded again, apparently convinced that Filomena was who she claimed to be. "Gracie's in the back room. Just go down the hall. You'll see her."

Filomena tucked her wallet back into her purse and started down the hall, her wool skirt floating around her legs. She loved wearing skirts, long ones that gave her the freedom to sit any way she wanted. Skirts flowed. They billowed. They danced even when she wasn't dancing. And on cold days like today, she could wear tights under them, so she was just as warm as she would have been in slacks.

One side of the hallway was lined with cubbies, filled with puffy, colorful jackets and parkas and bright plastic lunch boxes. The cubbies were set low into the wall, designed for child-size people to reach the hooks and shelves. High-pitched voices pealed in the room at the end of the hall. Filomena realized she'd never been in a preschool before—at least not since she'd been a preschooler herself.

In New York City, none of her friends had young children. Some of her cousins had started families, but they lived all across the country and she rarely saw them. If she'd been a less confident person, she'd question whether she'd had any right to accept Evan's job offer. What did she know about children?

She knew she liked them. She knew they were honest more often than not, they saw the world through unbiased eyes, they were a hundred percent potential and zero percent cynicism. She knew they could believe in witches and ghosts and talking animals in books.

And she *was* confident. She'd climbed mountains. She'd sailed down the Amazon in a flat-bottomed wooden boat. She'd hiked to the bottom of the Grand Canyon and back up again, carrying everything she'd needed on her back. If she could do that, she could handle kids.

The hall opened into a spacious room filled with tiny chairs and stepladders and play areas. Only about six children were present, although their shrill voices were loud enough to give the impression that the room was packed with noisy youngsters. An older woman was with them, overseeing a game of duck-duck-goose that seemed to entail more shrieking laughter than skill and strategy.

Gracie leaped to her feet and broke from the circle when she spotted Filomena. "Fil!" she bellowed, clearly happy to see her. Filomena realized she was happy to see Gracie, too. She instinctively opened her arms and Gracie ran into them, giving her an enthusiastic hug.

"It's time to go home," she said.

"I know." Of course Gracie knew. She knew much more about preschool than Filomena did. With a self-assurance that bordered on arrogance, she strutted through the room, leading Filomena back to the hall. At one of the cubbies she stopped to get her coat and lunch box. Filomena bent over to assist her with her zipper, but she backed away from Filomena and closed it by herself, then shot Filomena a smug look.

Filomena smiled back. "All set? Let's go."

In the car, she checked her old road map of Arlington to make sure the Elm Street School was where she thought it was. Gracie sat behind her, buckled into the booster seat Evan had given Filomena last night. The little girl bubbled with energy, yammering about who did what to whom, who swapped cookies at lunch, who spilled the apple juice at snack time, who made the worst painting during art. "He just dumped all the colors on his paper and the whole thing came out brown," Gracie reported, as stern as a conservative art critic. "It was so ugly. It wasn't a good brown at all. It looked like mustard."

"Mustard is yellow," Filomena pointed out as she eased into the rush-hour traffic on Dudley.

"Dirty mustard. Mustard with mud mixed in it. It was so ugly! I can't believe he did that!"

Gracie's indignation lasted until they picked up Billy at his after-school program. Strapped into the back seat next to his sister, he outshouted her, describing all the stupidity he'd had to encounter that day. "This kid Joey Hemmenway? He always belches in class. Sometimes it's funny, but he did it today when the principal was standing in the doorway, and the principal got upset and Joey had to leave the room. I mean, he is so stupid! Belching in front of the teacher is stupid enough, but in front of the principal?"

"What could he have been thinking?" Filomena said sympathetically.

"He's really disgusting," Billy continued. "He calls people 'mucus-head.'"

"That's disgusting," Filomena agreed.

"What's mucus?" Gracie wanted to know.

Filomena gave Billy a chance to answer his sister's question, but he gallantly deferred to Filomena. "It's the fluid that lubricates the inside of your nostrils," she said delicately.

"Like snot?" Gracie asked.

Filomena choked on a laugh. "Yes, Gracie. Like snot."

They arrived at Evan's house and she parked carefully on one side of the driveway, leaving enough room for him to drive past into the garage. The key he'd given her felt strange in her hand—or, more accurately, her hand felt strange holding it. It was a normal, ordinary key, but it wasn't hers. It wasn't a neighbor's or a friend's. It was Evan's, the key to his house, and she was going to be entering his house as if it were hers, as if she belonged there.

For the next few weeks she *did* belong there. In time, she was sure she would no longer feel like a trespasser.

The children seemed to know what to do in the kitchen. They removed their jackets and tossed them onto chairs—Filomena told them to hang their jackets in the closet, and they did, with only minor grousing. When they returned to the kitchen, Billy got to work cleaning out his and Gracie's lunch boxes. Filomena turned to Gracie. "What does your dad usually do when you get home?" she asked.

"He makes dinner," Gracie informed her, crossing to the refrigerator. "I help. There's leftover chicken."

"I *hate* leftovers," Billy said dramatically.

"Well, is there anything else in there?" Filomena asked, peering over Gracie's head at the refrigerator's contents. "Maybe I could get something else started for him."

"There's hamburgers," Gracie said, pulling a package of ground beef from a shelf. "You could broil hamburgers."

"We could make something more interesting than hamburgers." Filomena checked the package—one pound, and it looked pretty lean. "What else does your father make with ground beef?"

Gracie and Billy gazed at her, both obviously perplexed. "He makes hamburgers," Billy said. "He broils them."

"He broils everything," Gracie added.

"Oh, come on." Filomena laughed. "He doesn't broil spaghetti, does he?"

Gracie and Billy exchanged a look and shrugged.

"Let's cook something more exciting than hamburgers. How about..." Filomena turned back to the refrigerator and surveyed its contents. Tomatoes, green peppers—she could make stuffed peppers if Evan had any rice and tomato sauce. She closed the refrigerator and moved to the cabinets, then opened them one at a time until she found the area where he stored food. When she located a box of instant rice, she tried not to curl her lip. Instant rice lacked texture and taste, but it would work in stuffed peppers.

"What are you going to make?" Gracie asked anxiously.

"Stuffed peppers."

"Is it broiled?" she asked. "Daddy broils everything."

"We like broiled things," Billy concurred.

"You'll like this, too. And it's lots of fun to make. Billy, you can scrape the seeds out of the peppers. Gracie, you can help me make the rice."

The children seemed apprehensive. Filomena kept them too busy to complain or tell her how very much they liked broiled things. Billy did a painstakingly complete job on the peppers once Filomena had cut out the stems. Not a single seed remained when he was done with them. The instant rice cooked as quickly as the box promised, and Filomena let both Gracie and Billy take turns stirring the rice and seasonings into the meat. They had so much fun stuffing the meat into the peppers, they didn't even notice when Filomena set the oven to the "bake" setting, instead of the "broil" setting.

She'd just slid the tray of peppers into the oven when the sound of jingling keys reached them from the mudroom. "Daddy!" Gracie yelled, jumping down from the chair on which she'd been kneeling. She raced out of the kitchen, Billy at her heels.

Filomena smiled, refusing to take their abandonment personally. Evan was their father—obviously a devoted, loving father, given how eager they were to greet him. Once again she wondered why his wife had left him and their children, and why no other woman had staked a claim on his heart.

The children were chattering loudly, dragging Evan into the kitchen. "It's not broiled," Billy was saying, half a warning and half a cheer.

And then her gaze met Evan's, and the kids and their clamor seemed to vanish.

Only for an instant. Only for the briefest blink of time, she gazed into his glowing silver eyes and felt as if he were her man coming home to her, tired but content, wanting only to be where she was, where she waited for him.

He did look tired, she recognized as reality rushed back in, the spell broken as the children continued to yap about the stuffed peppers and their contributions to the meal. "I got the seeds out," Billy boasted. "All Gracie did was measure the rice. I did the hard part."

"Measuring the rice was hard!"

"Anyone can measure rice. Getting the seeds out—"

"Okay, guys," Evan cut them off. "I'm sure you both did plenty. Now, why don't you scram for a few minutes so Filomena can explain what's going on."

"Fil," Gracie corrected him as she headed out of the kitchen. "She likes to be called Fil."

The children were gone. The room grew peaceful, silence wrapping around her and Evan until she felt uncomfortable in its intimacy. She turned to the oven and lowered the door to check on the peppers. Evan remained where he stood, on the other side of the counter near the table, the warrior returning home after a day of battle, tie loosened, leather briefcase in hand.

"I didn't hire you to cook for us," he said quietly. He didn't sound angry. More bewildered, and a bit concerned.

"I know," she said, still facing the oven. She was afraid that if she turned around, she'd experience that same strange sensation she'd felt when he'd first entered the room—only, now they were alone, without the children to shatter the mood. She didn't want to feel as if anything beyond employer-employee existed between her and Evan. It was foolish, pointless, her imagination performing cartwheels. Nothing more.

"I thought preparing a meal would be a fun way to keep the kids busy," she explained.

"Apparently it worked. Billy got the seeds out."

She couldn't tell from his voice whether he was annoyed. It occurred to her that if he was, he'd be fully within his rights. Mustering her courage, she turned back to him. "I'm sorry. It was presumptuous of me to fix dinner. I guess you prefer things broiled."

He smiled. He had the most complex smile she'd ever

seen, part amusement, part bemusement. Part happiness, part caution. Pleased yet self-protective, open but not too open. "We eat things broiled because broiled is the only way I know how to cook food," he explained. "Stuffed peppers sounds pretty elaborate—and I wouldn't place bets either way whether the kids are going to eat them."

She suffered a pang of regret. "I should have just prepared hamburgers," she said. "Then you could have broiled them and the kids would have eaten them and—"

"Thank you," he cut her off, sounding so sincere she believed his gratitude was real. "If you can perform miracles in the oven, you can probably perform miracles on the children. Can you do me one favor, though?"

"Anything." His thanks notwithstanding, she felt guilty about having meddled in his meal plans.

"Stay for dinner and make them eat it."

She wanted to protest that he didn't have to feed her. He was paying her to do a job, and she'd already skirted close to blowing it. The last thing he ought to be doing was rewarding her by including her in his family's dinner for a second night in a row.

But when she analyzed his invitation, she realized he really was asking a favor of her. Since the kids had helped her prepare the meal, they'd be more likely to eat it if she was present. They'd be less likely to complain that it wasn't what they were used to.

Besides, Evan looked exhausted. She couldn't imagine him coming home after a draining day and having to prepare dinner himself, and deal with Billy and Gracie. Maybe he wanted her there just because he didn't have the strength to take on his rambunctious children right now. He might simply be asking her for help.

"All right," she said. She did want to help. Not because he was paying her, not because she felt guilty, but because he was Evan and for that one simmering moment she'd felt so strongly connected to him, she couldn't bear to leave him when he needed her.

Right now, he needed her. She knew it as well as she knew the shade of her back porch, the scent of her candles, the messages the queen of spades and the five of hearts carried in a plain old deck of playing cards. Evan Myers needed her.

"I'll stay," she said.

CHAPTER SEVEN

GRACIE NIBBLED at the meat and rice, poked the shell of the green pepper with the tines of her fork and pronounced the meal delicious. Billy actually ate a few bites of his pepper and most of his meat, although he carefully separated all the grains of rice from it.

Evan didn't care if they didn't finish their meals. It wasn't as if they were going to starve to death. And anyway, he had more important things on his mind than whether his kids cleaned their plates. As soon as he realized they were spending more time pushing their food around than consuming it, he excused them from the table and they bolted out of the kitchen, arguing over who was going to hold the remote control while they watched TV.

When they were gone, he was left alone with Filomena—who shouldn't have been the most important thing on his mind. But she was.

He'd had an unusual day—a surprisingly good one, considering how it had started. Tank Moody had done a fabulous job in New Haven. He'd been ingratiating and funny with the customers. He'd posed for snapshots with fans, flirted with gray-haired ladies, discussed sports with paunchy men and emptied the store's entire stock of Tank Moody jerseys and footballs, all of which he autographed with patience and good humor. He'd stayed at the store forty-five minutes longer than he'd been scheduled to, just because people kept coming in and wanting his autograph. Evan hadn't had to do anything except keep Tank's glass of ice water filled and help the store manager and clerks maintain order among the hordes of fans.

They'd journeyed back to Arlington in the limo, and Tank had dropped him off with a promise to meet him next week for the promotion in New London. Evan had returned to his office to find no major catastrophes awaiting him. Jennifer had badgered him a bit about Pep Insoles, and he'd warned her that if she didn't bug off, he'd make her do the New London promotion with Tank. The threat worked; she'd avoided mentioning insoles for the rest of the afternoon.

He'd telephoned his friend Murphy and asked him about the Daddy School. "It's great," Murphy said—which wasn't really what he'd hoped to hear. "I don't remember much about it, except that it's thanks to the Daddy School that I'm married to Molly's sister."

"What the hell does that mean?"

"Gail and I went to the Daddy School classes together. I think Molly coerced us into going because she was playing matchmaker."

"How did that make you a better father?"

"It didn't. I was already the best damned father in Arlington."

Evan hadn't exactly been persuaded that the Daddy School would do him any good. He wasn't looking for a wife. Even if he were...

His gaze zeroed in on Filomena.

No, he wasn't looking for a wife—but it sure had been nice to walk into his house and have a woman waiting there for him. It had been nice to be greeted by his children and the enticing aroma of something delicious roasting in the oven. It had been nice to come home to a warm, well-lit, welcoming place, and to have an adult sitting across the table from him while he ate.

"This is really good," he said, scooping another stuffed pepper from the platter. His third, but he didn't care if he was making a pig of himself. The kids might be satisfied with broiled something for dinner every night, but he appreciated variety.

"The children hated it," she said pensively.

"The children have no taste," he said, then smiled because she seemed worried. "Really. This is a treat for me. I don't expect you to be cooking dinner for us every night."

"I'm sure the kids will consider that good news," she said. He detected the hint of a smile on her lips.

"Tell me about your day," he said. He was tired of thinking about his own obligations, his overbooked schedule, his stresses and strains. More than just having another adult to gaze at over dinner, he wanted another adult to talk to—or better yet, to listen to. He wanted to be reminded that an entire world existed beyond Champion Sports and the Children's Garden preschool, the Elm Street after-school program and an occasional night of poker.

"My day?" She set her fork down and regarded him with apparent surprise, her eyebrows arched and her head tilted.

The dark luster of her hair tempted him. If the table had been smaller, he might have given in to the urge to reach across it and touch her hair, to weave his fingers through the lushness of it. Lucky for her the table blocked him—and luckier that he had enough common sense to know touching her was out of the question.

"Your day," he repeated.

"Well...I swept my back porch."

He wasn't sure if she was joking. Her mouth was solemn, but her eyes sparkled. "That must have been exciting," he said dryly.

"It was depressing," she confessed. "The paint is flaking off. I've got to repaint the porch before I put the house up for sale. But it's nearly winter."

"It's not too cold," he told her. "How big is the porch? You might be able to do it over the weekend."

"How could I possibly hire someone so fast? In New York, you have to book contractors months in advance. I'm sure that's true here, too."

"Contractors? Can't you just paint the porch yourself?"

She seemed dubious. "I wouldn't begin to know how."

"It's not brain surgery, Fil. You scrape off the loose old paint, sand the wood down a little, then slap on a fresh coat."

"You make it sound easy." She shrugged. "Some of us know how to cook. Others know how to paint porches."

"And in the long run, cooking is probably a more important skill," he conceded with a laugh. "You want me to paint your porch for you? I could probably get it done over the weekend if it's not too big."

"It's small, but no," she said. "I couldn't ask that of you."

"You didn't ask. I offered."

"And I said no, Evan." She actually seemed kind of stunned. "You work so hard all week—you don't even have time to pick your daughter up from her preschool. You can't spend your weekend painting my porch.''

"The kids could help," he said, the idea popping into his head as he spoke it. "Why not? We can turn it into a family activity. And you can keep them occupied while I do the hard parts.''

"Wouldn't you rather do something fun with them? Take them to a movie or something?''

"I'm so sick of G-rated movies," he groaned melodramatically. "No, I wouldn't rather take them to a movie. If *you* want to take them to a movie while I paint your porch, that would be great.''

"Evan." Apparently she thought he was joking.

He wasn't. Painting the porch would be an easy job, unless the porch was twenty-by-forty, with rotting boards and an intricate ornamental railing. Sitting through one more full-length cartoon, or one more movie about an underdog sports team with a crabby coach, or one more science-fiction extravaganza with enhanced sound effects, was likely to send him screaming for Thorazine. Filomena obviously didn't know what taking children to the movies was like. "Not only are the movies lousy," he explained, "but someone invariably spills a soda or drops an open box of candy that costs more than the gross national product of Peru, so all the candies roll away, and the theater is filled with squealing, whimpering kids. And the floor is sticky.''

"From the spilled soda and candy," Filomena guessed, her smile ripening. "Are the movies really that lousy?''

"I don't know. You like books about talking pigs. You might enjoy movies about dancing candlesticks and Darth Vader's childhood.''

"You sound a little burned-out," she observed gently.

"A little?" He snorted, then settled back in his chair and mulled over her statement. "Maybe that's why Molly thinks I need the Daddy School."

"The Daddy School?"

He sighed. He didn't want to whine—but damn, it was so nice talking to her. Even about mundane subjects like back porches and fatherhood. *Especially* about subjects like that. "Molly is the director of Gracie's preschool. You probably met her when you picked Gracie up."

"She'd already left," Filomena told him. "I met a woman named Cara."

"Okay." He nodded. Gracie had been enrolled in the Children's Garden practically since the day Debbie had split. Evan knew everyone who worked at the place. "Cara probably thinks I need the Daddy School, too."

"What is the Daddy School?"

"Classes on how to be a father. A *better* father," he corrected himself, studying Filomena, measuring her reaction. Deep down, he wanted to hear her say she considered the idea of *his* needing such classes preposterous, even though she was in no position to judge how good a father he was.

"When are the classes held?"

He hadn't expected her to focus on the practicalities of his attending the Daddy School. But why shouldn't she? She was his new baby-sitter, his kids' temporary part-time nanny. She probably recognized that his attending these classes would depend on some child-care arrangements. "Monday evenings. If I decide to go, I'll figure something out."

"Something?" Her eyebrows rose.

"I'll hire a baby-sitter." He sighed again and brushed

back a lock of hair that was tickling his forehead. The logistics of his taking classes weren't as important as his ability to talk to Filomena about them. Hell, he'd be a better father if he could talk to her every evening over dinner, after the kids were gone from the table. He'd be a better father if he could gaze into her hypnotically pretty eyes and fantasize about running his hands through her hair.

She turned him on. She wasn't just the perfect baby-sitter at a time in his life when he'd been so desperate even a flawed baby-sitter would have been acceptable. She was also beautiful. Womanly. Mysterious, with her alluring eyes and her enigmatic smile, the curves of her body hidden beneath shapeless skirts and baggy sweaters. From the moment he'd first seen her, he'd desired more from her than she was offering, more than he had any right to want.

He probably didn't even have the right to want her companionship during his evening meal. He reminded himself that she was going to be departing from Arlington as soon as the new year arrived. In less than two months, she'd be out of his life and the children's, as well. He couldn't get involved with her. It wouldn't be fair for the kids to think she was anything more than a baby-sitter when she already had her return trip to New York planned.

"...because I wouldn't mind staying with the kids," she was saying.

He dragged his attention back to her. "Excuse me?"

"I said, if you want to go to these classes, I can stay Monday evenings."

"I can't ask you to do that."

"You didn't ask." Her smile widened as she returned his words to him. "I offered."

He was getting himself into trouble here. He'd already offered to paint her porch, and now she was offering to watch his kids beyond the time they'd agreed on when he'd hired her. If he felt guilty asking his secretary, Heather, for a personal favor, he felt even more guilty contemplating the possibility of swapping favors with Filomena—because unlike Heather, Filomena attracted him the way a target attracted a heat-seeking missile. All he wanted from Heather was an efficiently run office. What he wanted from Filomena was—

Don't even think it, he cautioned himself.

She was still smiling at him. Still gazing at him, her expression curious but inviting. Once again he had to suppress the urge to leap over the table and haul her into his arms.

Oh, yeah. He was in big trouble.

"So, what time should I come over on Saturday to paint your porch?" he asked.

THIS WAS GOING to be cool, Billy thought—spending the whole day at Filomena's house. Actually going inside, looking around, checking for…well, not ghosts, because he didn't believe in them, but spirits. He was convinced spirits lived in that big old place. Maybe, if he was really quiet and patient, he'd see one.

The only problem was, Gracie was going to be there, too, and she didn't know how to be quiet or patient. If spirits lived in the house, she would scare them away. She was just too loud.

Dad pulled into the circular driveway at the front of Filomena's and stopped the car. The front porch was stone and it didn't need painting. The windows had wooden shutters on them, but Billy didn't think his father was going to paint them, because he didn't have a ladder with him, and what was the point of painting the first-floor shutters if you weren't going to paint the upstairs shutters? That would be like washing one sock of a pair and not the other—which Billy had done, but never on purpose; just when one sock got lost under his bed or something.

Dad was dressed in layers. He was always telling Billy and Gracie to dress in layers, but he himself never did, except when he was going to be doing outdoor activities, like raking the leaves or snow-blowing the driveway or skiing. Or painting a porch. He had on a long-sleeved thermal shirt, a plaid wool shirt over it, a jacket over that and old jeans that were worn to nearly white on the knees. Billy thought his own cargo pants were much better than jeans, because they had all those extra pockets where you could put things.

Filomena swung open the front door while Dad was getting together some tools and stuff he'd tossed into the car under the hatchback. She had on loose-fitting overalls and a turtleneck sweater that was so thick Billy figured she must have dressed in layers, too. Her hair was pulled back into a braid that made it look like a black rope hanging down her back. "Isn't it a gorgeous day?" she said, smiling so wide Billy felt her smile like a naked lightbulb inside his chest, hot and bright.

She was right. It was a really nice day, the sky blue the way it rarely was in late November, and the air dry and sharp. It was the kind of day you'd want to go apple picking, although it was too late in the fall for apples. He hoped his father would let him play in the woods a little—without Gracie tagging along. She could really ruin a guy's time in the woods.

Filomena turned from him and Gracie to his father. Billy noticed that the way she looked at Dad wasn't the way she looked at him and Gracie. Her smile for Dad was different. It was a little softer or something. When Dad looked at her he seemed different, too—less sure of himself, but kind of hopeful, as if he thought she might give him a slice of pie.

For some reason, the way they stared at each other made Billy feel good and bad at once, like something could go really right or really wrong between them.

"I've got the paint and brushes out back," she said. "And I've got some old sheets you can use as drop cloths if you need them. My mother had everything inside the house covered with drop cloths."

Billy remembered all those white cloths. They'd resembled ghosts lounging on the furniture.

"And I was thinking—" she finally turned to Billy and Gracie "—maybe the kids could help me bake some cookies."

"Yeah!" Gracie shrieked. She shrieked just as loudly when she was happy as when she was angry. He wished she had a volume dial so he could turn it down.

He didn't want to help bake cookies. He'd eat them, sure, but he didn't want to hang out in the kitchen with Gracie and Filomena. It wasn't that he had anything against baking—it could be fun, especially if you were baking something like cookies, where there might be a bowl to lick, or icing or chips or sprinkles. But he'd been grounded all week because he'd climbed out his window, and to have to spend Saturday cooped up inside with Gracie... "Can I help you, Daddy?" he asked.

His father grinned as if he thought Billy had chosen to help paint the porch because he wanted to, not because he was trying to avoid getting stuck in the kitchen with his baby sister. "Sure. Follow me."

Billy trooped around the house with his father. He knew where the back porch was; he'd climbed on it and tried to peek through the windows, and the Sunday afternoon Gracie had followed him there she'd tried to peek through the windows, too. Whatever had been blocking them on the inside was gone, and Billy could now see the kitchen through them. It wasn't like his kitchen, or his friends'. The oven wasn't built into a wall but stood on the floor, and the cabinets had glass in the doors so you could see right through them, and all the appliances—the stove, the refrigerator, the dishwasher—were white. The floor was a black-and-white checkerboard of tiles, and a long table stood in the middle of the room, with tall wooden chairs around it.

Billy bet the room smelled like apples. Or maybe he was just imagining everything smelling like apples because it was that kind of day.

"So what are we supposed to do?" he asked.

His father tossed him a pair of work gloves. "These'll probably be too big on you, but I want you to protect your hands," he said. "What we're going to do is take these scrapers—" he handed Billy a flat-edged tool that looked like a short-handled spatula "—and rub them along the boards like this." He put on a pair of canvas-and-leather gloves, knelt down on the porch and ran the edge of the tool down the board. It peeled loose chips of paint off the wood.

"We're scraping off the paint?"

"Not all of it. Just whatever is loose enough to come

off. You don't have to use much pressure. Why don't you give it a try?''

Billy slid his hands into the gloves. They were way too big, and they held the shape of the hands that had been in them before. Dad's hands, probably. Billy's fingers felt as if he'd slid them inside warm, round tubes, and the gloves swam around his palms. But he could still hold the scraper tool.

He knelt down on the porch and rubbed the scraper along a board. Some of the paint flaked right off. Some of it stuck on hard. "Like that?"

"Exactly like that," Dad said. "But you know what? Why don't we do this systematically. Start right at the edge—" he pointed to one side of the porch "—and work your way across. Then when you've got a bit done, I'll follow with the sandpaper."

"What are you gonna do with the sandpaper?"

"Just smooth it down a little more. That'll help the paint to go on nice and even."

"How do you know this stuff?" Billy asked, running his scraper along the board and discovering it was actually fun. A lot more fun than baking would have been.

"I know *everything,*" Dad said, but Billy could tell from the way he made his voice sound all deep and serious that he was joking.

The back door opened and Filomena peered out. "Are chocolate-chip cookies acceptable to everyone?" she asked through the screen.

"Sounds good to me. What do you think, Billy?"

"Sounds good to me, too," he said.

"That's two votes for chocolate chip," Dad reported to Filomena. Billy glanced up to see them gazing at each other that way again, sharing one of those smiles that seemed to shut out Billy and the porch and the entire universe. It was as if everything stopped when they smiled at each other, the crows shutting up, the breeze dying down, Billy's own breath snagging in his throat, unable to escape. Then Filomena closed the door and his father sighed.

Billy resumed scraping the boards. His father picked up a square of sandpaper, extended it past the end of the porch and pulled down on it, tearing off a neat strip. Then he crossed the porch to where Billy was working, got on his knees and began sanding the part where Billy had scraped off the big stuff. The sandpaper made a hissing sound.

Something was going on between Dad and Filomena, something more than her baby-sitting for Gracie and him. Billy had sort of sensed it during the two dinners she'd had at their house, the way Dad let him and Gracie leave the table and watch TV even though they were grounded, the way Dad's voice changed when he talked to Filomena—soft and tender, without any anger or laughter in it. It was the voice Dad used when he was having important discussions with Billy, when he was telling Billy he loved him.

"Do you ever miss Mom?" Billy asked. The question just sort of popped out. Billy hadn't even realized he was thinking of his mother. He'd thought he was just thinking of Dad and Filomena.

Dad didn't answer right away. He didn't even look at Billy. He just rubbed the sandpaper along the boards. "No," he finally said, then thought some more and added, "I miss having someone to share the work with— the chores, the responsibilities, the shopping. And I miss having someone to share the good things with, too. When you score a soccer goal, or you get everything right on a spelling test, or when Gracie does something special.''

''Gracie never does anything special,'' Billy muttered. That got his dad to look at him. He grinned to show he was just kidding.

Dad smiled but didn't play along. He rubbed the sandpaper hard on the boards, in a constant *shh-shh* rhythm. ''Sometimes I'm just so proud of you and Gracie, and I want to share my pride with someone. If your mother were still around, I'd be able to share it with her. But other than that, no. I don't miss her.'' He sanded for a minute. ''Do you?''

''No,'' Billy said. One of his gloves had gotten kind of bunched up, and he had to use his teeth to adjust it, because with the gloves so much longer than his fingers, his hands were too clumsy for anything except using the scraper. When he resumed scraping, he tried to picture his mother. She'd left over two years ago, and he remembered her, but not too clearly. Sometimes it felt like she'd never been in his life at all.

''How come she left?'' he asked.

His dad gave him a sharp look, and Billy wondered whether he was going to ask why he was even talking about her. Billy himself wondered about that. All he knew was that something in the way his dad and Filomena kept looking at each other had gotten his mind stuck on the subject.

After a moment, his dad glanced away. ''She left because she thought she found something better.''

''Better than us?''

''She was mistaken, Billy. There is nothing in the world better than raising you and Gracie. *Nothing*.''

Billy glanced at him. He was rubbing the sandpaper

on the porch so hard he was beginning to sweat, even though the air was cold. After a moment he pulled off his jacket, tossed it onto the railing and then went back to sanding.

Billy was glad his father thought there was nothing better than raising Gracie and him. He was really, really glad his father loved him, even if his father worked too hard sometimes and seemed too tired and got mad at him when he wanted to stay up late and grounded him when he did something bad. If a kid was going to be stuck with only one parent, his dad was a good one to have.

It was still probably a lot better to have two parents, though. "If Mom came back, would you forgive her?" he asked.

Evan stopped sanding, leaned back and thought for a minute. "Yeah, I'd forgive her. Forgiveness is important. It heals the heart."

"So, you'd let her come home and be our mommy?"

"She'll always be your mommy, Billy. But if you're asking me if I'd take her back as my wife, no."

"I thought you just said you'd forgive her."

Dad gave him a funny smile. "I think I've already forgiven her, Billy. You can't live your whole life being bitter and hurt. It's much better to let go of all that. But no, I wouldn't want her to be my wife again. I guess you could say I found something better, too."

"What?" Billy asked, not sure if he was ready to hear his father's answer.

"I've found that it's better not to be married than to be married to someone who would make the choices your mother made. Marriage is a great thing, Billy—but it can be a terrible thing if the people are wrong for each other, or if they haven't grown up enough to know what they want." He pulled off a glove and ran his hand through Billy's hair. "I'm sorry you and Gracie had to learn these things so young. I'm sorry your mom left us. But I'm not sorry I'm here and I've got you kids and we're a family. You and Gracie are the best things in my life. Better than your mom ever was."

Dad's words made Billy feel warm inside, not the way Filomena's smile had made him feel warm, but a deeper heat in his gut and along his spine, in his toes and his fingers, which were sweating inside the gloves. "I guess this would be a good time to ask for a raise in my allowance," Billy said.

His father threw back his head and laughed. Then he shoved his glove onto his hand again and checked out the area Billy had finished scraping. "You want a raise, you'd better work a little harder," he advised. "I'm doing the hard part here and I've practically caught up to you."

Laughing along with his father, Billy moved down the porch and started scraping a new section. For a kid who was grounded, who couldn't get together with his friend Scott today the way he would have liked, or hop on his bike for a spin through the neighborhood, or talk Dad into taking him and some friends to the high-school football game, but who, instead, was stuck scraping paint off his new baby-sitter's porch, he was feeling really good. He was feeling even better because Dad hadn't asked him why he'd wanted to talk about his mother.

It was a good thing he hadn't asked, because if he had, Billy wouldn't have known what to say.

THE COOKIES were delicious—warm and soft, the chips still gooey from the oven's heat. After the kids had eaten a few, Filomena gave them a deck of cards and told them to play in a small sitting room off the living room. Evan had the distinct impression she'd sent them away so she could be alone with him, just the way he'd sent them off to watch television so he could linger over dinner with her.

"I hate to say this," she murmured, staring through the back door while Evan filched another cookie from the plate, "but the porch looks worse than when you started."

"It's fine. It just needs to be swept, and then I'll slap down the first coat of paint."

"How many coats will it need?"

"Two ought to do it. The weather is supposed to hold, so the second coat can go on tomorrow."

"I'll paint that coat. You've already done so much...."

"Yeah," he said with a laugh. "I made it look worse." He wanted to wrap her braid around his hand and give it a tug. He wanted to wrap his arms around her, to see how much of what he saw was bulky clothing and how much was her. He wanted...

He wanted things he shouldn't want. He wanted things that couldn't be. Yet what he wanted must be pretty damned obvious if a perceptive eight-year-old boy could figure it out. Billy's questions hadn't just materialized out of the autumn air. They'd come from something specific, something he sensed. Something that kept springing to life between Evan and Filomena, pushing up like new green grass out of the cold November ground. The timing was all wrong, but those tender spears wouldn't stop growing.

He'd known he wanted her when he'd offered to paint

her porch. He'd known it when he'd found her in his
home after work. He knew it whenever she left his house
and it suddenly seemed a little darker, a little emptier.
He'd probably known it the very first time he'd seen her
standing in his backyard at night, with Gracie in her arms.
He hadn't recognized the feeling for what it was right
away, but he knew it now.

He wanted Filomena Albright the way he hadn't
wanted a woman in a long, long time.

She turned from the door and her smile faded as she
scrutinized Evan's face. He'd rolled up the sleeves of his
wool flannel shirt when he'd come into the warm kitchen
and shoved up the sleeves of his thermal shirt. But when
she looked at him, her eyes so large and dark, he felt
overheated.

"I was wondering," he said, then cleared his throat
because his voice sounded scratchier than the sandpaper.

"Yes?"

"Whether you had plans for Thanksgiving." Because
she was all alone in Arlington—that was why he was
asking her. Because his parents were in Washington,
D.C., and he wasn't going to be able to spend the holiday
with them, and because three people seemed at least one
too few for a Thanksgiving dinner. Because there was a
faint smudge of flour on her chin, and for some reason
it made him want her even more.

"Actually, I— No," she said, almost but not quite
smiling.

"I'm not planning anything fancy. I was figuring I'd
just broil a turkey—"

That made her laugh. "Turkeys aren't broiled, Evan."

"They're not?" He scowled. "Uh-oh."

She laughed harder. "You just want me to cook for you."

"Well, after eating these cookies and the stuffed peppers you made the other night..." He smiled and shook his head. "I don't want you to cook for me. I want..." *to touch you. To rub my thumb over your chin and wipe away flour, and feel how smooth your skin is.* "Your company," he concluded.

"Evan." She crossed to the table and brushed some invisible crumbs from its surface into her cupped palm. "It's a very sweet invitation, but..." She fell silent.

"But?"

"Daddy?" Billy barged into the room, all spiky energy. "Gracie fell asleep on the couch and I'm bored. Can I go play in the woods?"

"She fell asleep?" He glanced at his watch. Two o'clock. She still needed her nap most days.

"So can I go play in the woods?"

Evan turned to stare out the windows. The afternoon sun was bright. "Are you wearing your watch?" he asked Billy. Billy nodded vigorously. "Okay. Be back here by three."

"Okay!" He bolted out the back door as if he expected Evan to change his mind. The screen door clapped against the door frame, and Filomena gave it an extra tug to close it all the way.

Silence circled them, silence and the rich aroma of the cookies. Evan gazed at Filomena, trying to remember where they'd been before Billy had interrupted them. He'd been contemplating the flour on her chin. He'd been admiring the glittering darkness of her eyes.

She'd been telling him she didn't want to have Thanksgiving dinner with him. And she was probably right. He shouldn't push it. He should defer to her superior wisdom and accept her decision gracefully.

"So how come you don't want to eat broiled turkey with us?" he asked, forcing a smile to mute the disappointment in his voice.

"I didn't say I didn't want to spend Thanksgiving with you, Evan. It's just that..." She sighed. "I don't want to become dependent on you."

Dependent on him? Hell, he was the one dependent on her. She'd brought his children back to him the night they'd climbed out Billy's window, and she'd provided him with the perfect solution to his child-care dilemma, and she'd made the past couple of evenings at his house more pleasant than any workday evenings in recent memory.

What on earth could she become dependent on him about? Surely the money he was paying her wasn't going to make a huge difference in her life, given that she owned this gorgeous minimansion and was working on a Ph.D. She was a classy lady. She earned the salary he was paying her, and she deserved every penny of it, but she wasn't going to become dependent on him over it.

"You mean, because I'm painting your porch? That's nothing, Fil. That's what neighbors do for each other."

She shook her head. Having already cleaned the nonexistent crumbs off the table, she concentrated on sponging nonexistent drops of water from the counter by the sink. "I'm all alone," she said, her voice so low he had to strain to hear her. "Both my parents are gone, I've got no sisters or brothers... But you and Billy and Gracie have made me feel like I'm not alone."

"What's wrong with that?"

"Nothing. It's just..." She set down the sponge and

spun around to face him. Her eyes were dry, her mouth curved in one of those smiles he couldn't read. "I'm leaving in January."

"I know."

"I mean, maybe I'm assuming things I shouldn't, but…"

"No, you're not." He was assuming the very same things. An electric thrill sparked his nerve endings at the thought that she was assuming what he was assuming.

"So nothing is really going on here."

Like hell. "Just friendship," he lied.

"And a job."

"And a job," he agreed.

They stared at each other for a long minute. Then he took a step toward her, and another, until he standing next to the sink, facing her. She smelled of baking scents and something more, something subtle and feminine. Her eyes were wide, almost defiant, as she gazed up at him.

He reached out and rubbed his thumb over her chin. Her skin was like velvet, downy and warm. "You've got flour on your face," he explained. "It's been driving me crazy."

"Oh." She didn't laugh. Didn't back away. Didn't flinch as he stroked his thumb over her chin again, tracing the line of her jaw, the indentation under her lower lip. "Just friendship and a job," she reminded him in a near whisper.

"Right," he murmured, then lowered his mouth to hers.

It was foolish, he knew. Risky and brainless. She was leaving in January, and she was the kids' baby-sitter, and he was a guy who'd failed spectacularly at marriage, and there was really no room for an involvement here, no room at all. But her mouth was so soft beneath his, soft and welcoming, and if he hadn't kissed her, he would have gone nuts. So all right, sue him for being irresponsible and selfish and wanting just one kiss from a woman who'd been haunting him since the first time he'd seen her with her hair flowing wild and a silver-moon pendant resting between her breasts. Charge him with gross stupidity. Call him dimwitted, hormone-driven, bewitched. Definitely bewitched.

Her lips moved, glided against his, pressed lightly. Energy zapped through his body, tensing his muscles, coiling in his groin. He slid his hand under her braid, under the ribbed turtleneck collar of her sweater to the warm skin at her nape. She drew a shaky breath and lifted her hands to his shoulders, sending another shock through his body.

He brought his other hand to her waist, wanting to draw her tight against him—except, for God's sake, it would be embarrassing for her to realize how much one kiss could arouse him. He could explain to her that it wasn't just the kiss that turned him on—it was *her,* her smile, her eyes, her dependability, her affection for his children. Or else it was magic. Because they hadn't even done more than brush mouths, and he was already imagining making love to her, more than imagining it. More than wanting it. *Craving* it.

Her hands tightened on his shoulders and he realized, through a blur of brain-numbing lust, that she was pushing him away. He jerked his head back, furious with himself for having done what she clearly didn't want him to do. If she quit baby-sitting for the kids, it would be his fault. Yeah, he needed Daddy School classes. He was the worst father in the world, jeopardizing a magnificent child-care arrangement just because he'd been unable to resist kissing Filomena.

"I'm sorry," he muttered, staring at the deep porcelain sink to avoid looking at her.

She cupped her hand under his chin and steered his face back to hers. "No," she said, shaking her head for emphasis. "You're not sorry. Neither am I."

Her cheeks were flushed, her eyes slightly glassy, her lips damp. All from that one little kiss? Had it staggered her as much as it had him?

"It can't happen again," she added, sounding rueful.

"Okay." Not okay, but what choice did he have?

She took a step backward and sighed. "Do you think…do you think we can still manage Thanksgiving together?"

"Sure." A hell of a lot better than he could manage it alone, given that she seemed to know a great deal more about how to cook a turkey than he did. They'd have the kids between them for Thanksgiving, though, so the temptation to kiss would be thwarted. And now that he'd kissed her once, maybe he would build up an immunity to her, the way a person built up an immunity to certain diseases by being exposed to them. For all he knew, his blood might already be bubbling with Filomena antibodies. She would never be able to enchant him again.

Sure.

"I'm going to go paint your porch," he said, because at the moment it seemed like the only way to avoid her spell. A dose of biting November air, the sharp chemical smell of the paint, some muscle-flexing labor—he'd stick with that until the antibodies kicked in and the fever broke.

CHAPTER EIGHT

"IS THAT TURKEY big enough?" Gracie asked dubiously.

Filomena checked the tag. Eleven and a half pounds. "It's big enough," she assured Gracie. "And it's better to get a smaller turkey. The smaller ones taste better. They're younger and juicier. Like you."

"I'm not juicy!" Gracie protested with a giggle.

Filomena lowered the turkey into the shopping cart, then turned to see Billy approaching from one of the aisles, carrying four cans of cranberry sauce, one balanced atop another, his chin propped on the uppermost can to keep the stack from collapsing. *"Four?"* she blurted out. "How much are you guys planning to eat?"

"Lots," Gracie answered for both of them.

Filomena had taken the kids to the supermarket Monday evening while Evan was at his Daddy School class. The outing would keep them occupied, and she didn't want to wait until Wednesday to buy her Thanksgiving supplies, because the aisles would be jammed with frenzied last-minute shoppers then. Even Monday evening, the store was busier than normal.

All right, so she'd buy four cans of cranberry sauce. Evan was going to pay for the groceries, anyway. He'd insisted on it, saying it was the least he could do once she'd insisted on cooking the meal. No way was she going to let him prepare it. If she did, they'd wind up with broiled turkey.

She'd also insisted on hosting the meal. She had so many wonderful memories of Thanksgiving dinners at her parents' old stone house. She used to come home from school for the holiday weekend, and her parents would be in Arlington along with friends of theirs, fascinating people—academic colleagues of her father's, artistic, bohemian friends of her mother's, one year the guide who'd accompanied them on a white-water expedition on the Snake River, another year a New Zealand couple they'd met in Sydney, Australia. Every bedroom would be occupied, and all the guests would mix and mingle. Filomena's mother would serve a magnificent feast, her father would uncork his best wines, and they would all give thanks for the privilege and joy of being together.

This year would be her last opportunity to have Thanksgiving in the house. She would use the heavy linen tablecloth and napkins her mother had stored in the sideboard, the elegant candlesticks, the china. Her meal wouldn't be as grand as her mother's used to be—she was nowhere near as talented in the kitchen—but at least she would be able to give thanks for a fine hearty meal shared with friends.

Friends. She didn't like using that word to refer to the Myers family. The children were her wards, and Evan...

Damn it. He never should have kissed her. She never should have let him. Because ever since Saturday afternoon, she'd discovered she could no longer think of him as a friend, an employer, a dad.

She thought of him only as a *man.* A tall, virile and unbearably *male* man. Just one kiss had been enough to obliterate the professional aspect of their relationship and the easy camaraderie of it. She still accepted his money for watching his children, and she still enjoyed his company, but...

Oh, that kiss.

It lingered in her body, dormant, but flaring up every now and then; it stirred a need so powerful it hurt. It throbbed in her memory like a life pulse; it visited her in her sleep. It made her want more than she could have. If Evan knew how irrationally she'd reacted to one little kiss, he probably wouldn't let her near his kids anymore.

"Okay, do we have everything?" she asked brightly, surveying the contents of the shopping cart. "Cans of pumpkin? Apples? Whole-wheat bread?"

"I don't like whole-wheat bread," Gracie whined.

"It's for the stuffing. Trust me, you'll love it. Butter? Garlic?"

"I don't like garlic," Billy said.

"You'll hardly even notice it," she promised. "I think that's everything. Let's go."

A half hour later, the groceries were wedged into her refrigerator and she and the kids were back at Evan's house. He wasn't yet home from his Daddy School class, so she organized Billy to read a chapter of *Freddy the Detective* and filled the tub in the upstairs bathroom with warm water for Gracie's bath.

Filomena had never given a child a bath before. But she assured herself that if she could hike to the bottom of the Grand Canyon and back up again, she could probably handle giving Gracie a bath—especially since Gracie was so willing to offer guidance. "Don't make it too hot," she warned. "And don't make it too cold, or I'll get goose bubbles."

"Goose bumps?"

"Yeah. This is good," Gracie said, dipping her hand into the water accumulating in the tub. "Don't make it too high or I'll *dround.* And I need my toys..." She gathered a plastic sailboat and a plastic frog from the ledge of the tub. "And my washcloth..." She unhooked it from a bar attached to the wall and tossed it into the water. "That's it, Fil. That's enough water." Without a moment's modesty, she peeled off her clothes, struggling only a little with her pullover shirt. "My nightgown is in my bedroom, prob'ly somewhere on my bed, okay? You better go get it, 'cause I'll need it when I come out." She climbed into the tub and sat with a gentle splash.

Filomena hoped it was all right to leave the child alone in the tub for the time it took to fetch the nightgown. She raced down the hall, located the garment under the wrinkled blanket on Gracie's unmade bed and raced back to the bathroom, to find Gracie propelling her boat contentedly through the water. "Daddy gives me the best shampoos," she announced. "You have to do it without getting any shampoo in my eyes."

"I'll do my best," Filomena promised, shoving up the sleeves of her sweater and kneeling on the hard tile floor next to the tub.

"You can talk to me, too."

Filomena lifted the bottle of baby shampoo from the side of the tub. "What do you want to talk about?"

"I don't know."

"Well, what do you talk to your dad about when he's shampooing your hair?"

"We talk about whether he should get married," Gracie said. "I can't decide whether he should marry a princess or a jock—because you know, he loves sports. Sports is his job.''

''Are those his only two choices?'' Filomena asked, grinning despite the fact that the subject of Evan's love life was a dangerous one for her to explore with his talkative daughter. ''A princess or a jock?''

''Well, he said he wasn't going to marry Heather. She's very pretty, but I guess that doesn't matter to him.''

Filomena considered steering the conversation in a different direction. That would be the wise thing to do. But she wasn't feeling wise. And she *was* feeling remarkably at home in his house, bathing his daughter. So she said, ''Maybe he doesn't want to be married.''

''I think he does. He was married before, you know. To my mommy.''

''Well, maybe...'' Again she contemplated changing the subject. Again her curiosity overruled her conscience. ''Maybe after getting a divorce, he decided it would be better not to get married again.''

''I don't know,'' Gracie said matter-of-factly. ''My mommy liked sports a lot. I don't know much about her, but I know she liked sports, or athletes, or something. Daddy doesn't talk about her much. I think she made him mad because she left him.''

''I can't believe anyone would leave your father,'' Filomena murmured, fishing Gracie's washcloth out of the tub and wringing the excess water from it. ''He's a very nice man.''

''Cept when he gets angry.''

''What does he do when he gets angry?'' Filomena wondered whether he'd been abusive to his ex-wife. She couldn't imagine it, but she supposed it was possible.

''He says we're in trouble,'' Gracie told her. ''Sometimes he grounds us. Once he caught us jumping up and down on Billy's bed and he got really mad because he said we could have hurt ourselves. He yelled at us a lot that time. He always gets mad when we do something that might hurt us.''

"Like climbing out a window," Filomena reminded her.

"Yeah. He was really mad about that. He told us we did a stupid thing. I was afraid he was going to cry, but he didn't. Daddies aren't supposed to cry. But I think if he was allowed to, he would have cried that time.''

Far from abusive, he sounded like the sweetest, most devoted father in the world. "He gets mad because he loves you," Filomena said in his defense. "I think if you got hurt, it would break his heart.''

Gracie peered up at her, looking surprised and pleased by this explanation. "Maybe that's why he never gets soap in my eyes. Because he knows that stings. You can use that cup to wet my hair—that's how he does it,'' she said, pointing to a plastic cup on the rim of the tub.

Filomena carefully shampooed Gracie's hair, doing her best to keep the lather from touching the little girl's forehead, let alone dripping near her eyes. Gracie babbled about princesses and haunted castles and how the best castles had water all around them and funny ridges along their roofs, and Filomena thought about Evan, about his gentleness and concern, his capacity for love—and about the woman who had walked away from him. Why? Why would anyone leave a family and a home like this one?

She was rinsing the last of the suds from Gracie's hair when she heard footsteps in the hall, too heavy to belong to Billy. She glanced over her shoulder in time to see Evan fill the doorway, his leather jacket unzipped to reveal a cotton sweater and a pair of jeans. He still carried the outdoor chill on his clothes, and it clashed with the humid warmth of the bathroom. "Hey, you didn't have to give her a bath," he said, remaining at the threshold.

"Hi, Daddy!" Gracie chirped, her voice echoing off the hard surfaces of the room. "Fil's doing a great job! She didn't get any soap in my eyes!"

"Great!" He gazed at Filomena, and she wanted to apologize for her presumptuousness in performing an evening ritual that rightly belonged to him. But his eyes were a hushed, sweet gray, and when he said "Thanks," he sounded as if he truly meant it.

Filomena could have stared into his eyes forever—and it might have taken her forever to figure out exactly what he was thanking her for. But she didn't want to respond to him, or to think about the undercurrent that passed between them, dark and relentless. "Well," she said briskly, turning from him, "this bath is hereby officially done."

"You gotta help me out so I don't slip," Gracie instructed her. "Daddy put these no-slip things on the tub, but you still have to help me out."

Filomena had thought perhaps Evan would take over and get his daughter out of the tub, but he only remained in the doorway, watching. She rose on her knees, cushioning them on the fluffy floor mat, and wrapped her arms around Gracie's compact, slippery torso. She clung to Filomena's forearms and hoisted one leg out of the tub, then the other, managing to splash only a quart or so of water on Filomena.

"That's my towel," she said, pointing to one of the two bath towels hanging on the opposite wall. Before Filomena could grab it, Evan reached into the room, lifted it from the towel bar and handed it to her. His fingers brushed hers as he released the towel, and she was shocked by the surge of awareness she felt at that brief accidental contact.

Turning from Evan, she wrapped the towel around Gracie and dried her off. Gracie was prattling about something—she wanted her daddy to brush her hair, because he never yanked at the snarls. But when Filomena looked back toward the door, Evan was gone.

"Do you need help with your nightgown?" she asked Gracie.

The little girl rolled her eyes. "Of course not. I'm not a baby!" She wriggled into the gown and pulled her wet hair through the neck hole. "Daddy, you brush my hair, okay?"

Filomena looked toward the door again. Evan was back, minus his jacket and armed with a pale-blue hairbrush with long white bristles. "Sure, Gracie, I'll brush it." He caught Filomena's eye as she hauled herself to her feet. "Thanks," he said in almost a whisper.

She sensed she was being dismissed, which was just as well. She needed to leave this house, to get away from the children she was growing way too fond of—and away from their father, who could stir too many emotions inside her with one glance, one smile, one simple word, one inadvertent stroke of his hand against hers. She definitely couldn't stick around long enough to watch him brush his daughter's hair. Honestly. A woman could fall in love with a man for no better reason than he didn't yank at the snarls in his daughter's wet tresses.

The hallway seemed cold after the time she'd spent in the steamy bathroom. Her sweater, damp from where Gracie had splattered water on it, felt clammy against her midriff, and she plucked it away from her skin. Downstairs, she found Billy sprawled out on the floor of the den, lying on his stomach with his knees bent, his feet in the air and his chin resting against his fists. The television was off; he was reading.

"Hey, Billy," she called to him. "I'm leaving now."

He twisted around, then pushed himself up to sit. "This book is cool," he said. "Can I hang on to it?"

"Sure."

"I thought I wasn't gonna like it. It's so long. I don't usually like chapter books, 'cause it takes forever to read them. But this is good."

"I'm glad you like it."

"I mean, the way the animals all have different personalities. It's like they're people, only they're animals."

"Exactly." Filomena grinned. That was the gist of her thesis—the use of animals in children's literature as a metaphor for human society.

"So it isn't really like they're magic or anything. I mean, in some books, talking animals are magical. But here it's more like they're just people or something."

"That's right." Her smile expanded. She was proud of Billy for having made the distinction, and pleased that she could share a book she adored with someone who seemed likely to adore it just as much.

"You sure you don't mind if I borrow it for a little while?"

"Not at all. I've got another copy back at home." She heard voices drifting down the stairs, Gracie's and Evan's, and she felt a sudden urgency about leaving. She needed to get out before she saw Evan again, before she thought about him brushing Gracie's hair, or painting the back porch, or kissing her, or being so upset by his children's dangerous behavior that he'd nearly cried. In another day or two, Filomena hoped she'd feel more comfortable around him. But if those few minutes when he'd stood in the bathroom doorway—if that one second when his fingers had grazed her hand—were an indication, she lacked any perspective when it came to him.

She exited into the kitchen to get her jacket and purse. Shrugging her arms through the sleeves, she returned to the den to say goodbye to Billy. Not quick enough. Evan strode into the room from the stairs, saw her in her jacket and stopped. ''You're leaving?''

''I think I'm done here.''

He didn't look as tense as she felt. In fact, he seemed tired but relaxed, his shoes off, his hair endearingly tousled and his smile both sheepish and hopeful. ''I owe you some money,'' he said.

She ought to let him pay her. It would help to remind her of the nature of their relationship. But he was far too appealing to her right now, in his faded jeans and wool socks, his hands in his pockets and one shoulder cocked. ''There's no rush,'' she said, referring to the payment.

''Are you sure?'' He approached her, digging his wallet out of his hip pocket. ''Gracie told me you spent a fortune on the groceries.''

''I didn't spend a fortune,'' she assured him, realizing she didn't want that reminder, that reality check, the concrete evidence that she was working for him. ''Really, Evan, it can wait.''

If he heard tension in her voice, he ignored it. He took her arm and steered her out of the den, down the hall to the front door. At the door, he pulled her to a halt, but his hand remained on her arm, his fingers arching around her elbow. "I wanted to thank you again. You didn't have to give Gracie a bath."

"Well...it seemed like a good idea," she said vaguely. She couldn't tell him she'd wanted to give Gracie a bath because it made her feel that much more like a part of this household.

"I worry sometimes," he confessed, his gaze locked onto her. "She's a girl, and I'm a man, and I worry that maybe I shouldn't be there when she's in the tub."

"You're her father," Filomena assured him.

"I know, but..." He sighed. "I worry, Fil. I worry that I'm not doing things right."

She recalled where he'd just spent his evening. "Did you learn anything useful in the Daddy School?" she asked.

"Yeah. It was good. I'll definitely go back. But..." He sighed again and released her arm. "I appreciate your giving Gracie a bath, that's all."

"It was my pleasure," she said honestly.

"Even though she dumped a ton of water on you?" He ran his fingertips across a damp spot on her sweater. She should have closed her jacket. She should have escaped before he could corner her in the confines of the entry hall. She should have been able to accept his touch without going all tingly and soft inside. "I could run your sweater through the dryer if you want to wait a few minutes."

"No. Really, it's fine." She was already feeling too close to his family. To have her sweater spend five minutes in his drier would be much too intimate.

He seemed on the verge of saying something, then changed his mind and dropped back a step. "One of the things the teacher talked about was that fathers need to learn how to listen. So…I'm listening. Okay?''

She frowned, unsure of what he was getting at.

He smiled crookedly. ''I'll pay you the next time I see you. You want to leave. See? I'm listening.''

She could have told him she *didn't* want to leave. She wanted to stay here, to hold Gracie in her lap and discuss *Freddy the Detective* with Billy and allow herself to admire Evan's angular face, his tall, lean body, his humor, his devotion to his children. If he could listen to her heart, that would be the message he heard. But he could listen only to her words, and they were telling him she wanted to leave.

''You can have tomorrow off. It's my poker night, so I'll be leaving work early. I'll be able to pick up Gracie at preschool.''

She almost protested. She didn't want the evening off. She wanted to pick up Gracie, and then circle over to Billy's school and get him, and drive them here, and putter in Evan's kitchen until he arrived home. But he was listening to her, and if she had half an ounce of sense in her brain she would be grateful for that.

''All right,'' she said. ''I'll see you Wednesday.'' And before she could say anything more, before she could spend another instant staring into his mesmerizing eyes, she swung open the front door and stepped out into the dark, chilly night.

SHE DIDN'T SLAM the door, but she might as well have. He stood in the foyer, the quiet click of the door latch echoing in his mind. Through the sidelight, he watched her bustle down the front walk in her bulky boots, climb into her car and back out of the driveway. Not until the taillights had disappeared did he turn from the door.

He'd wanted her to stay, to talk to him. The Daddy School class had pumped him full of all kinds of ideas, and he'd wanted to discuss them with her, to see if she thought he'd learned the right lessons.

He hadn't realized how desperately he needed adult companionship until he'd had the chance to experience it with her. He had his friends—Murphy, Levi, Brett and Tom—and his colleagues at work, and reliable neighbors. But a true friend, a woman friend, someone not just beautiful but smart and interesting and eager to share her thoughts with him...

He needed Filomena.

He recalled what she'd said at her house on Saturday: she didn't want to become dependent on him. He couldn't let himself become dependent on her, either. She was all set to leave town, and unlike Debbie, she'd given him notice of her impending departure. She wasn't going to abandon him on a whim. He knew exactly how long he could count on her, and it was nowhere near long enough.

But being forewarned that she was planning to leave at the start of the new year didn't make him desire her any less.

Maybe what he needed wasn't Filomena but just a woman in general. He'd been single more than two years. Of course he would enjoy spending an evening with a woman—and without the kids. Just him and a lovely lady dining out, attending a non-kiddy movie, returning to her place or his, and...yeah, sex would be nice. Maybe it didn't have to be Filomena. Maybe any decent, intelligent, reasonably attractive woman would do.

Except that he knew decent, intelligent, reasonably attractive women. He worked with two—Heather and Jennifer. He'd dated a few others. But none of them had ever infiltrated his mind and taken it over the way Filomena had. None of them had ever given his son a book or his daughter a bath.

Damn. What kind of guy had he turned into, judging a woman's appeal by her willingness to shampoo Gracie's hair and expose Billy to a novel about a talking pig? Being a single father definitely skewed a guy's concept of the perfect woman.

He wandered back into the den and flopped onto the couch, feeling the weight of a long, overstuffed day on him. Billy peered up at his father, then closed the book, using a Pokémon card to hold his place. "This book is cool," he told Evan.

"It was nice of Fil to lend it to you."

"Yeah." Billy pushed off the floor and joined Evan on the sofa, evidently buying a few extra minutes before Evan sent him to bed. "She's cool, Dad."

"I know." Even his son was smitten, Evan thought disconsolately. "Did you have fun with her tonight?"

"Well, mostly we just shopped for Thanksgiving. We got four cans of cranberry sauce, so each of us can have our own can."

"That sounds like about three cans too many," Evan said with a laugh. "Did you get your homework done?"

"I did it at the after-school program," Billy said. "Scott said you're supposed to spend Thanksgiving with relatives. Do you think it's okay that we're having it with Fil?"

"Sure. You can spend it with friends, too."

"Scott said only family."

"Scott's wrong. You can share Thanksgiving with anyone you want."

"Good." Billy sighed happily. "'Cuz I really want to spend it with Fil. How was that thing you went to tonight?"

Evan was touched that Billy had thought to ask. "It was very interesting. The teacher is a nurse at Arlington Memorial Hospital. She knew her stuff."

"So…what? She taught you, like, first aid?"

"No. It was a class to help make men better fathers. She taught us how important it is to listen to our children. She said fathers aren't always good at listening. Do you think that's true, Billy? Am I a bad listener?"

Billy considered the question for a minute, which pleased Evan. He didn't want his son blowing him off with an easy answer, one he thought would please his dad. "Sometimes," Billy admitted. "Like when you're rushing to broil something for dinner, you really don't listen to us at all."

"Because I'm rushing. I think it's better if you save the important things to tell me when I'm not rushing. I guess I should communicate that better." That was one of the things Allison Winslow had discussed in class: When it was impossible to listen to your children at a given moment, you had to schedule a time when you could give them your full attention, and then be there and listen.

"Or, like, if something happens at school and I tell you about it, sometimes I feel like you're just sitting there, waiting to lecture me about what I should've done or what I should do next time or something. It's like *you're* telling *me* what happened, instead of listening."

"You're right." Evan curved an arm around Billy and

gave him a hug. "It's because I want to help you. But you're right. I should keep my mouth shut and listen more. If you catch me doing that, I want you to point it out to me, okay?"

"You won't be mad?"

"No. I might be mad if you say you did something you shouldn't have done, but I won't be mad if you ask me to shut up and listen. Just don't say, 'Shut up.'"

"I'll say, 'Put a lid on it, Dad.'"

"I think I can handle that." He gave Billy another hug, then nudged him off the couch. "It's bedtime for you."

"Put a lid on it, Dad," Billy said, then grinned and scampered off before Evan could take a swipe at him.

He leaned back and closed his eyes. In a few minutes, he would go upstairs to tuck Billy in and make sure Gracie was all set for the night. But first he wanted to unwind, to let the tension seep from his shoulders, to assimilate everything he'd endured since his alarm had roused him that morning.

There had been a snafu with one of his suppliers—a train derailment; no injuries, but a whole lot of hockey sticks and pucks destined for his stores had been on that train—and he was going to have to spend the entire day tomorrow making sure trucks picked up all his hockey inventory and delivered it to his stores. He'd told Jennifer that because of the derailment, she'd have to accompany Tank Moody to New London tomorrow, and she'd thrown a fit, although finding out that Tank provided his own stretch limo and was actually a nice guy had mollified her. "He's just an overpaid jock," she'd sniffed, "but the limo might make the whole thing bearable." Evan had come home, broiled hot dogs and then headed out to the YMCA to attend the Daddy School class.

He'd gone expecting it to be a waste of time. What could a neonatal nurse from Arlington Memorial teach him? His kids were long past the days of diapers and strained peas.

But she'd been good. She'd addressed the eleven men in the room not as a nurse but as the mother of a two-and-a-half-year-old girl, as someone who'd observed a father and his child at close range—and as Molly Saunders-Russo's best friend and cofounder of the Daddy School. Most of the other men in the class seemed to be married, but Evan had gotten as much out of it as they had.

He had to learn to listen. Not just to his children, not just to Jennifer and his other colleagues at work, but to everyone else in his life: the staff at Gracie's preschool, Billy's Cub Scout leader, Filomena.

Filomena.

His eyes still closed, he conjured a vision of her leaning over the tub, washing Gracie's hair. Her own hair spilled down her back, held away from her face by a silver clip. He pictured her graceful fingers sifting through Gracie's hair, searching for hidden pockets of shampoo in the waves. He imagined her soft voice, her steady arms propping Gracie as she climbed out of the tub.

He shouldn't be giving his daughter baths anymore. Filomena should be doing it.

But he had to listen to her. He had to pay attention to what she was saying—which was that she didn't want a romance with him. Friendship and a job. Those had been her words on Saturday when he'd kissed her: friendship and a job, and independence. That was what she wanted from him.

He had to listen, even when what he was listening to was the last thing he wanted to hear.

CHAPTER NINE

WELL, AS FAR AS Billy could see, there were a few problems with this Thanksgiving. For one thing, Filomena only had a tiny little television, which she kept in an upstairs bedroom. And the room was kind of cold, and it was hard to watch football on such a small screen. Not that his dad had one of those wide-screen TVs like the one in his friend Scott's family room, but at least it was a reasonable size. Filomena's was pitiful.

When he complained about it, she wasn't sympathetic, either. She told Billy no one had ever watched TV during all the Thanksgivings her parents had hosted in this house, and if he wanted to watch it, he'd just have to make do with the TV she had. He offered to hike through the woods to his house to watch the game there—he promised he'd be back in time for dinner—but his dad said no.

Then she had this music going, Beethoven or somebody like that, a bunch of violins in an orchestra. Dad said it was great music and Billy ought to give it a chance, but it sounded really boring to him.

And then he was stuck playing with Gracie, because Dad insisted on helping Filomena in the kitchen and there was no one else to play with.

But Gracie actually came up with a good idea: "Let's see if we can find the spirits."

The last time they'd been at Filomena's house, on Saturday, he'd been inside for only a few minutes, long enough to eat some cookies and watch Gracie fall asleep on the couch. He'd asked her when they'd gotten home whether she'd bothered looking for a spirit after she'd woken up, but she said she hadn't. She'd probably been afraid to go snooping through the house without him.

They wouldn't really be snooping today. Filomena had given them permission to go upstairs to watch TV on the little set in that cold bedroom, so he figured it was okay to go upstairs and look for spirits. Not that he actually believed in things like that, but for Gracie's sake, he'd pretend he did.

He and Gracie climbed the stairs. It was a long staircase, longer than at home, because Filomena's ceilings were higher. The upstairs hall was drafty and dark, even when he found a light switch and turned it on. There was just one lamp illuminating the entire hall, and it didn't shed much light. But he liked the shadows. If they were going to find any spirits, there would probably have to be shadows.

The first room they came to was the one with the TV in it. There was a big bed, no sheet or blanket on the striped mattress, and heavy wood furniture. The TV seemed out of place sitting on the dresser. Dark-green curtains hung at the window. Gracie immediately crawled under the bed.

Billy checked the closet. He wondered if this was snooping, but it wasn't as if he was poking around in her closet to see what was in it. He was just searching for spirits. If any existed there, though, they were invisible. The closet was empty except for a few boxes on a high shelf that he couldn't reach.

"There's dust under here," Gracie reported, crawling back out from under the bed. Little gray puffballs of lint stuck to her hair. "What do you think the spirit's gonna look like?"

"I don't know. Maybe we won't see it," Billy said. "Maybe we'll *feel* it. Like a cold hand on the back of your neck."

"Yuck," Gracie said, but she obviously wasn't scared. She brushed the dust off her corduroy overalls and headed out of the room.

The next room was more promising. Large white cloths covered the furniture, just like the cloths that used to cover everything downstairs when Billy first found the house and peeked through the windows. Gracie immediately dove under one of the cloths. Billy lifted another. There was all kinds of furniture and stuff here. It was like a storage room. Chairs, small tables and chests of drawers lurked under the cloths.

"What's this?" Gracie asked, standing and pulling back one of the cloths to reveal a machine built into a table.

"I think it's a sewing machine," Billy said. He'd seen something like it at Scott's house.

"How come we don't have one?"

"I think only moms have them."

"Fil isn't a mom."

"Maybe this is her mother's."

That explanation seemed to work for Gracie. She nodded and they moved on to the room across the hall.

This had to be Filomena's bedroom. It was larger than the other two rooms, and it had a nice wide bed made up with linens and a quilt and two fat pillows. The dresser had a strip of lace across it, and on top of that were fancy silver-handled brushes and hair clips and a polished wood box with the lid up, filled with jewelry.

Gracie's eyes got big. "Ooh, look! Here's her moon," she said, lifting Filomena's moon necklace from the box.

"Don't touch that!" Billy yelled, afraid they'd get in trouble if Filomena realized they'd gone through her things.

"But it's so pretty. I think it's magical. I'm not gonna hurt it—I just want to wear it for a minute." Before Billy could stop her, she put it on.

The moon shone silvery-white against her chest. It practically seemed to glow.

"It *is* magic," Gracie murmured, taking it off, her eyes as shiny as the necklace. "You try it, Billy."

"It's a girl's necklace," he muttered—but he wanted to feel the magic, too. Even though he didn't really believe in magic, he wanted to feel it.

Sucking in a breath, he looped the cord around his neck and let the moon fall against his chest. It was surprisingly heavy—yet he felt lit up inside. Just the way he felt when Filomena smiled at him, or when she laughed.

He took it off and placed it carefully back in the box. Then he looked at Gracie. He still didn't believe in magic, but he felt different somehow. Better. Warmer. Even the symphony music drifting up the stairs sounded nicer.

"I think she's a witch," Gracie whispered. "A good witch. I think we should get her to marry Daddy."

Billy snorted. "I don't want Dad marrying a witch." He wasn't even so sure he wanted their dad getting married at all. Dad had been married once, and maybe he forgave their mother for leaving them, but it couldn't have been a happy thing for him to go through. Like when Billy broke his wrist last year after falling the wrong way during a soccer game. He'd survived and his wrist was as good as new, but he sure wouldn't want to break it again. Just because you healed didn't mean you wanted to get hurt a second time.

"But Fil's a good witch. Remember how she read our cards? She said I was stubborn and wonderful."

"You don't need a deck of cards to figure that out. The stubborn part, anyway."

"And she said you were very smart and could do great things in the world if you didn't get distracted."

"Anyone could do great things," he argued. He'd loved what Filomena had said about him as she'd read his cards, but when he was being sensible, he wasn't sure he believed she was actually seeing into his future.

"Hey!" Gracie squealed, moving past the box with the jewelry in it and lifting a bright turquoise silk scarf. Underneath it was a deck of cards. "Maybe she'll read these cards for us."

Billy edged closer, curious in spite of himself. The cards looked big, like the deck of cards his grandparents had given him when he was five, designed bigger so they'd be easier for a kid to handle. He lifted one of the cards and saw that it wasn't a regular card, though. It had a weird picture on it of a queen with a bunch of what appeared to be gold trophies.

"These are magic cards, I bet," Gracie said. "I'm going to read your cards with these."

"You can't. You don't know how."

"If they're magic, I can." She pulled them down from the dresser and plopped onto the rug. It was red and black, green and white, with patterns woven into it that resembled tiny flowers. "Sit down. I'll read your cards."

She had no idea what she was doing, but he figured having her read his cards would be more fun than trying to watch football on that little TV set. He settled onto the rug facing her while she struggled to shuffle the cards. He didn't think big cards were easier for little hands, not after seeing Gracie wrestle with them.

"Here, let me." He took them from her. They were way too stiff, but he did a better job of mixing them up than she could have done. He handed them back to her. "Okay. Go ahead."

Gracie held the cards and stared at the ceiling for a minute. Like the ceiling was going to tell her what to do. "Okay," she said once she lowered her eyes. She set the cards down in a pile on the rug and peeled off the top three. One looked like a pile of sticks with a ten on it. Another looked like a juggler or something, one of those old royal court jesters, wearing a pointy hat with bells on the points. The third was a big smiling sun. "Okay," Gracie said again. "This means you're gonna build a house. In the daylight."

"Well, I sure wouldn't build it at night," Billy said scornfully.

"The sun means the weather will be good. You'll do it in the summer."

"What about the juggler guy?"

"You'll prob'ly drop stuff while you're building it. This means you have to be very careful with your tools and nails. You don't want to drop any nails because you might step on one and it'll stab you in the bottom of your foot and you could die."

He wasn't sure he liked this fortune. "Let's do another

one," he said. "I'll do yours." He took the deck from Gracie, shuffled the cards a bit and turned over the top three. One of them had a bunch of gold coins on it, and the number seven. Another had that woman with the gold trophies. The third showed a guy hanging from a gallows. "Oh, man," Billy said, trying to add drama to his voice. "First you're gonna get rich. Then you're gonna buy a bunch of bowls. Then you're gonna die."

"I don't want to die," Gracie argued.

"Well, check out this card." He jabbed at the picture of the guy hanging. "You tell me, does this look like you're gonna die?"

"That's a man. I'm a girl."

"Hey, don't blame me. I'm just saying, this is a man hanging by a rope. He looks dead to me."

"But I'm a girl. I'll buy the gold bowls. Some other guy will die. He's a robber. He tried to steal the bowls from me, but I caught him and the police came and killed him."

Billy had to admit Gracie's story was better than his. She could be dumb, but she had a good imagination. "Okay. He's the robber. Only, the police didn't come. You bopped him over the head with one of the bowls. Then you strung him up yourself."

"Cool!" Gracie's eyes glowed. Billy was pleased he'd come up with a story at least as imaginative as hers.

"What are you doing in here?" Dad's voice broke in.

"Put the cards down," Filomena said, her voice softer but firmer than Dad's. Billy glanced toward the door and saw them standing there, side by side. Filomena had an apron on over her skirt. Dad had his sleeves rolled up, and his hair was messy. He was frowning.

Billy quickly straightened the cards into a neat pile and

got to his feet. So did Gracie. He felt guilty, but he wasn't going to say anything. Filomena had told them they could go upstairs, right? She hadn't said anything about staying out of certain rooms.

She entered the bedroom, her hand outstretched, and Billy placed the cards in her hand. ''These are called tarot cards,'' she told him and Gracie. ''They're not a regular deck. If you want to play cards, I'll give you a regular deck. But not now, because dinner is ready.''

Wasn't she going to yell at them? Tell them they shouldn't have been in her room, shouldn't have touched her things? Dad would have yelled. He was still frowning.

''Come on, guys—are you hungry? Because we've got at least six tons of food on the table,'' Filomena said calmly. Dad turned his attention to her, as if he wanted to explain that she was supposed to rip into Billy and Gracie. But she didn't seem at all upset. She waved them out the door and down the hall, falling back to talk to Dad for a minute. When Billy glanced behind him, he saw them murmuring to each other, their voices too soft to make out.

He figured he and Gracie had dodged a bullet. He wouldn't press his luck by hanging around in the hall, eavesdropping on them. The way they were huddled together, Filomena's hair so thick and black Dad's looked almost blond when they put their heads together, gave Billy the clear impression that they were talking grown-up stuff, something private that they didn't want him and Gracie to hear, and that he and Gracie wouldn't understand even if they did hear it.

Was Gracie right? Was there something going on between his father and Filomena, something that might make them get married? He honestly didn't think his father wanted to get married again, even if he had forgiven his mom and all. Why bother?

But the way they were whispering, the way Filomena rested her hand on Dad's arm and smiled at him, a smile that made his scowl melt away...well, maybe she *was* a witch, putting him under a spell. Working a little magic on him.

And maybe it wouldn't be such a terrible thing if they got married.

FILOMENA'S WARNINGS to the kids at the supermarket had been right: they'd bought way too much food. And she was delighted.

In her mind, this was what Thanksgiving was supposed to be: a table straining under the weight of abundant food, candles flickering above the holiday linens, light glinting off the silverware and splintering into rainbows when it hit the crystal glasses and serving dishes. And soft, soothing music—she'd chosen a Corelli CD to accompany the meal.

More important than the table settings, the candlesticks, the music and the food was that people she cared for filled the chairs.

She did not want to become dependent on Evan and his children. But that evening, when they'd all joined hands around the table and bowed their heads, and Evan had asked each of them to think about what he or she had to be thankful for, Filomena had been thankful for *them,* for their presence at her table. The past few months of her life had been dreadful. She'd lost her mother and been left with a financial disaster to unravel; she'd been distracted from her studies, worried and grieving. She'd fled the city just to get away, to find a quiet place to heal—and to prepare herself to bid farewell to her childhood home. She should have been a wreck.

But she wasn't, because two scrappy youngsters had trespassed on her property and on her heart. And then she'd met their father. It didn't matter that she would be leaving in little more than a month. What mattered was that they were together now. For that, she was grateful beyond measure.

Billy said he was grateful that he didn't wind up in Mrs. Thompson's class, because everyone said she was mean and she yelled all the time and gave lots of homework. Gracie said she was grateful that Filomena had found her butterfly barrette and that Stuart gave her candy whenever he saw her—Evan interjected, for Filomena's benefit, that Stuart worked with him at Champion Sports. Evan said he was grateful that his children were healthy and happy and that his work enabled him to provide them with a safe, comfortable home, and he was grateful that when they'd done something as boneheaded as climbing out Billy's window, Filomena had brought them back to him.

Filomena said she was grateful that they were all together for this fine feast.

And then they feasted. Gracie and Billy devoured an entire can of cranberry sauce between them. After muttering about how she didn't like whole-wheat bread, Gracie consumed a small mountain of the whole-wheat bread stuffing. Each child polished off a drumstick, and Billy bravely ate a few forkfuls of butternut squash. They made a serious dent in the basket of warm rolls, ignored the steamed beans and avoided spilling their milk, which

Filomena had served in elegant glasses rather than the plastic cups Evan had brought with him.

He'd also brought wine, something white and dry and delicious. She'd been resigned to serving one of her father's Bordeaux, but red wine really didn't go with turkey, and she was delighted that Evan had thought to bring a chardonnay with him. He'd also brought the rolls—one of those cylindrical cardboard boxes that popped open to release precut rounds of dough. He must have known his kids would want to eat them. "Are you sure we're not supposed to broil them?" he'd joked as she'd arranged them on a cookie sheet and slid them into the oven to bake.

The conversation around the table roamed from Tank Moody, the professional football player with whom Evan was doing his big seasonal promotion, to Gracie's having mastered backward somersaults, to Billy's insightful comments about *Freddy the Detective*. The children were not just well-behaved; they were actually pleasant company. Filomena was almost disappointed when they asked to be excused from the table.

"Can we play with those cards?" Gracie asked shamelessly. "They were so pretty."

"They aren't toys," Filomena said with a shake of her head. "If you want a regular deck of cards to play with, look in the drawer in the table next to the couch in the living room. There are several decks inside. Or you can play chess or checkers. The checkerboard's on the coffee table. But the tarot cards aren't for playing with."

"Are they magic?" Gracie asked.

Filomena hesitated before answering. She knew they weren't, but she liked to pretend they were. "Some people think so," she hedged. "They're for telling fortunes. Reading the future is never a game."

"Will you tell us our fortunes?" Billy asked. "Using those cards, I mean."

"Not tonight. Some other time, maybe." She didn't want to tell their fortunes while she had Evan sitting at the far end of the table, facing her, the candlelight rippling gold across his face and his eyes shimmering with the sort of contentment that settled into a person after sharing a filling, tasty meal with loved ones.

She wouldn't want to tell his fortune, either, not tonight and not some other time. It would probably be full of things she'd rather not know: that he would live a long, richly rewarding life, a life she would never be a part of or even witness, because she would have left Arlington and gotten on with her own life, apart from him and his children. That he would fall in love with a wonderful woman. That he would marry again, and spend every night looking as content as he looked right now.

She had definitely grown too dependent on him. For this one night she would indulge herself and not worry about it. Tomorrow she would start pulling back again, erecting her defenses and protecting herself.

"You shouldn't have been so lenient about their messing with those cards," Evan chided once the children were gone from the room. "They had no business going into your room and touching your things."

She shrugged. "They were curious. Curiosity isn't a crime."

"Tampering with other people's property is."

"They didn't 'tamper' with anything," she said, chuckling at the melodramatic term. "Tarot cards are beautiful. I remember the first time I saw a deck. I was enchanted by it.'' She balanced her fork and knife on her plate and nudged it away. "Anyway, no harm was done. It wasn't worth getting upset over.''

"You're so mellow,'' he said, shaking his head in obvious admiration. "Someone else would have thrown a fit and put everyone in a sour mood. *I* probably would have. But you just…'' He shook his head again, apparently amazed. "You just shrugged it off.''

She had never considered herself particularly mellow. She supposed she'd suffered a twinge of irritation when she and Evan had discovered the children in her bedroom. But Thanksgiving was too important a celebration to taint with anger. And the kids had looked so natural seated on the floor beside her bed, as if they belonged there, as if they felt utterly at home.

That was another dangerous thought. She deleted it from her mind. Later, perhaps, when the Myerses had left, she would read her own cards. No doubt they'd tell her to get a grip, to stop lapsing into silly fantasies about Evan's children belonging in her house, about Evan belonging in her life.

"This has been one of the nicest Thanksgivings we've ever had,'' he murmured.

She smiled. It had been one of the nicest for her, too. "How do you usually spend Thanksgiving?''

"Last year my parents were still in New Haven, so we drove down there and had dinner with them. They live in a suburb of Washington, D.C. now. My sister lives near Philadelphia, so they were all going to spend the holiday together.''

"Your sister? I didn't know you had a sister.'' She lifted her wineglass and sipped, wishing she weren't so eager to absorb every detail about him.

"Wendy. She and her husband are lawyers. She got the brains in the family." He said this with a grin so Filomena wouldn't take him too seriously.

She argued, anyway. "She certainly didn't get all the brains. You're a very intelligent man."

"Oh, I'm quite the genius," he said wryly, reaching for the wine bottle. He stood and walked the length of the table so he could refill her glass. He refilled his own, then settled into Billy's empty chair, much closer to her. "She got the school smarts. She's kind of like you, I guess. She actually enjoyed law school. She was always an honors student."

"And you weren't?"

His grin widened. "I was a jock."

The only jocks she'd ever known were girls at her prep school, where everyone was required to participate in sports to some extent. The jocks were more enthusiastic about that requirement than the rest of the girls, but everyone, even the least athletically inclined, had pursued sports. She'd been on the fencing team and president of the Outdoors Club, which organized day hikes and an occasional overnight camping trip.

But *real* jocks, hulking young gladiators in uniforms, big-men-on-campus types who knew the difference between baseball, football and soccer cleats and owned at least one pair of each...she'd never socialized with guys like that.

Until now. But of course, Evan hardly fit the profile of a real jock anymore. He might have been one of those heartthrob athletes in his youth, reeking of testosterone, collecting varsity letters and cheerleader girlfriends. But that description hardly fit him anymore. Today he was a devoted father, a successful business entrepreneur—and a very intelligent man.

She wanted to continue questioning him, but he turned the spotlight on her before she could. "How about you?" he asked. "What did you usually do for Thanksgiving?"

The last few years, Thanksgiving had been low-key. Her mother would fly in from wherever and take a room at the Plaza, and Filomena would meet her there. After Filomena's father had died, she and her mother had lacked the heart for big parties at the house. "When I was a child, my parents used to host Thanksgiving here," she told Evan, staring at the reflection of the candlelight in her wine, as white and brilliant as diamonds. "They'd invite all kinds of guests, cousins, friends from all over the world. People would stay overnight, sometimes several days. There would be heavy philosophical debates, or musical performances—" she motioned with her head toward the side parlor, where the piano was located "—or card games, or Monopoly. My parents had such a huge circle of friends."

"They're both gone now?" he asked gently.

She nodded. "My father died nearly six years ago, my mother three months ago."

"I'm sorry, Fil." He gathered one of her hands in his, closing his fingers snugly around her. There was nothing seductive in the gesture. It was meant to comfort, and it did. "You're way too young to have lost both your parents."

"My father was a lot older than my mother. He was sixty-one when I was born and eighty-three when he died. I was very close to him, though. It doesn't matter how old a person is—if you love him, whenever he dies is too soon.'' She sipped some wine. ''My mother was fifty-five.''

''Was she ill?''

''No. She died in a mountain-climbing accident in the Alps.''

''Mountain climbing? Wow.'' He assessed her thoughtfully. ''The Alps. She must have been a world adventurer.''

''That's exactly what she was. Always off on some new adventure. She was so full of life....'' Filomena sighed to keep her voice from cracking. She managed a feeble smile. ''She died doing something she loved, at least.''

''Still, that must have been a terrible thing for you to go through.'' He squeezed her hand gently. His palms were smooth, his fingers strong and warm. ''And you inherited this house from her?''

She nodded. A month ago, maybe even a week ago, she would have started weeping at this point in the conversation. But Evan's nearness consoled her. The rich aroma of the food, the delicate tartness of the wine, the dancing candlelight and music and the warmth of his hands enveloping hers mixed enough joy in with the sadness to keep her tears at bay.

''It's a fantastic house,'' he said. ''I can understand why my kids fell in love with it. Maybe you ought to keep it.''

She let out a weary breath. ''I can't.'' Her fingers flexed against his palms, but he wouldn't release her. ''When my mother died, I discovered that she'd run up enormous debts. I have to sell the house so I can pay those debts off.''

Evan grimaced, as if her pain was his own. "Ah, Fil. That sucks."

"Actually—" her smile felt stronger "—it doesn't. The house belonged to my mother. If she'd been a bit more organized, maybe she would have sold it herself and financed her adventures with the money from the sale. Instead, I'm doing things a little backward. She had the adventures, and now the house will pay for them." Putting the thought into words almost convinced her of its truth. "I only wish..."

He leaned closer. "You only wish...?"

"I wish she were here. I wish she could help me say goodbye to this place." When he squeezed her hand again, she squeezed back. "Thank you for sharing this Thanksgiving with me, Evan. It's really meant a lot to me, to be able to have one last Thanksgiving here."

He leaned toward her and touched his lips to her forehead. Just a light kiss, not romantic, not erotic, carrying none of the promise of the last kiss he'd given her, none of the risky overtones.

Yet it was just as dangerous in its gentleness. Maybe even more dangerous, because it deepened her affection for him. She would not have wanted to spend Thanksgiving with her friends in New York, or even to have asked them to come here to the house. Before she'd met Evan, perhaps she would have invited her city pals and fellow graduate students, because they were her closest friends.

But now...now she couldn't imagine spending this special evening with anyone but Evan and his children.

They didn't talk anymore. They sipped their wine, holding hands, their fingers woven together. The Corelli concerto drifted through the air and the soft giggles of the children floated in from the living room, and her gaze filled with the sight of a smart, sweet, silver-eyed man sipping wine with her, reminding her that, despite her losses, she had a great deal to be thankful for.

CHAPTER TEN

JENNIFER PEEKED around Evan's partially open office door and sent him a smile that was uncharacteristically kittenish. "Evan? Have you got a minute?"

No, he didn't have a minute. The Friday after Thanksgiving was the biggest retail shopping day in the United States. His phone hadn't stopped ringing since he'd arrived at the office—despite Heather's filtering all the calls and forwarding him only the most imperative ones. Right now, he was on the line with the manager of his Hartford store, he had a supplier from Springfield on hold and he was trying to stave off pandemonium in the Providence store, where a shipment of graphite tennis rackets that was supposed to have been delivered two hours ago was still unaccounted for.

He truly had no time for Jennifer. He also had no time for distracting thoughts of Filomena, but he'd spent far too much of his morning thinking about her. If he could burn so much mental energy on her, he supposed he could spare Jennifer the minute she was asking for.

He beckoned her inside, then resumed his phone conversation. "All right, if you can't move all the ice skates today, you'll sell them tomorrow. Just make sure you don't wind up with only size fourteens and size twos. Call the distributor directly if you've got to. Tomorrow's sales are going to be as important as today's. Okay?

Bye." He clicked to the other line, told the supplier from Springfield to get the damned rackets down to Providence or he'd never do business with him again, slammed down the phone and lifted his weary eyes to Jennifer.

She was still smiling. Something had to be wrong. "I hope you're not going to badger me about the Pep Insoles," he warned her. "Because if you are, I swear I'll fire you."

She shook her head and moved a few steps closer to his desk. "I was just wondering if you'd mind terribly if I accompanied Tank Moody to the Bridgeport store next week."

"You mean, you want to go instead of me?"

"We haven't had a chance to talk about it," she said, shifting her weight from one high-heeled foot to the other, her hips shimmying within the confines of her conservative blue wool suit. "But things went very well with him on Tuesday. I thought, since he and I seem to have developed a certain rapport, we might as well not tamper with a good thing."

"You liked his limo, huh?" Evan teased.

To his surprise, Jennifer blushed. "All I'm saying is, we worked well together."

They worked well together? It wasn't as if they'd been on a mission to parachute behind enemy lines and liberate a double agent being held captive by terrorists. All they'd done was travel to a store, where she'd made Tank comfortable while he'd chatted and flirted with customers. Evan knew exactly what the task had entailed, since he'd done duty as Tank's escort the week before.

More than the high color in Jennifer's cheeks tweaked Evan's curiosity. He noticed a glimmer in her eyes, bright and giddy. She shifted her weight again, as if standing still was impossible for her.

He recognized that restlessness, that oddly frenzied light in her eyes. He'd seen it before—with Debbie. ''Don't tell me you've got the hots for Tank,'' he groaned.

''I don't,'' she said fiercely.

''Because if you run off with him—'' his voice grew gruff, the words rubbing over scar tissue ''—forget about getting fired. I'll kill you both,'' he said, tempering his words with a weak grin.

''Why would I run off with him? I feel nothing for him but rapport.''

''That's a terrific euphemism, Jen.''

''He isn't married, is he?''

''You'd better ask him before this 'rapport' goes any further.''

''I will, when we go down to Bridgeport.'' She paused, assessing Evan. ''So, it's all right with you if I accompany him, then?''

''As long as you don't do anything stupid,'' he warned. She wasn't his wife, after all. She was just his vice president. His conscience, his nag, his nemesis. His right hand.

''Thanks.'' She practically skipped back to the door. ''You and I can talk about Pep Insoles after the new year, all right?''

A silver lining to this new storm cloud, he thought acerbically as she left, closing the door behind her. His phone was ringing, but he ignored it as he tried to assimilate the new situation she'd just presented him with.

Jennifer and Tank. The thin, poised, brilliant executive and the huge, affable football star. The Waspy white woman and the African-American hunk. The Wharton Business School graduate and the Heisman Trophy shortlister from the University of Nebraska.

Evan shuddered. Not that he had anything against Tank, or Jennifer, or a romance between the two. It just kicked up some dust, that was all. It stirred up bad memories.

"Evan?" His door swung open and Heather filled the doorway, glaring at him. "Why aren't you answering your phone?"

"I didn't feel like it," he grunted. "Who was it?"

"Marty in New Haven. He's got extra skates he can send up to Hartford if you want him to."

"Great. Call him back and tell him to work it out directly with Frank. They don't need me approving every little inventory swap."

Heather pursed her lips. "Are you okay?"

"Never been better," he lied, then flipped open one of several folders on his desk and pretended to be engrossed in its contents.

Lips still pursed, Heather pivoted and closed the door, leaving him in solitude.

He sank back in his chair and closed his eyes. The hell with Jennifer and Tank. They were both adults. They could take care of themselves. They could break each other's hearts if they cared to. As long as they couldn't break his, he'd be fine.

His thoughts veered to Filomena. Again.

Unlike Tank and Jennifer, Evan and Filomena didn't have to worry about potential heartbreak. His heart wasn't involved. Friendship was the only thing going for them. Friendship and a job. Right?

Wrong.

She had insisted on staying with Gracie and Billy for the day, since the day after Thanksgiving was a school holiday for them. But she'd refused to accept any compensation from Evan for the day's baby-sitting. She'd told him she would take them to a movie—no, she'd assured him, she wouldn't mind sitting through some nauseatingly cute kid-flick. Billy could invite his friend Scott to join them, if he wanted. And of course, if Billy brought Scott, Gracie could bring a friend, too.

Such generosity went beyond mere friendship. And her refusal to let him pay her implied that it went way beyond her job.

He recalled the packages of leftovers she'd sent him and the kids home with last night, arguing that they had to haul off some of the food because it would spoil before she'd be able to eat it all. He recalled standing next to her at her kitchen sink last night, drying the dishes she washed, toweling off her good silver and seeing it gleam in the overhead light. He recalled what she'd told him about the death of her parents and the botched finances her mother had left behind.

He thought about her having to sell her old family home, and about her scholarly life back in New York City. She had nothing to keep her in town anymore, no reason to stay. Her life was somewhere else.

He should have been focusing on the skate shortage and the delayed shipment of tennis rackets. He should have been worrying about his trusted VP's brain suffering a meltdown over a football star. But all he could think about was Filomena's imminent departure from Arlington, and the loss he would feel once she was gone.

For the first time since Debbie had walked out on him, he wanted a woman to stay.

It was crazy. They weren't madly in love. That one kiss had barely gotten started before she'd brought it to a halt. Passion didn't burn like a wildfire between them. It wasn't as if they couldn't keep their hands off each other.

He'd like to get his hands on her, sure. He'd like to peel off all those layers of apparel she wrapped herself in. He'd like to kiss her deeply, use his tongue, his fingers, his…well, everything. He wanted to see how a woman like Filomena would look naked, climaxing. Would she moan or cry out, or just gasp? Would she clutch his shoulders, close his eyes, wrap her legs around him and whisper his name?

And what kind of idiot was he, torturing himself with images like that? It wasn't going to happen. She'd made that very clear.

He shook his head and forced himself to stare at the budget records in the folder that lay open on his desk. He had work to do—and it was thanks to Filomena that he'd be able to do it without juggling child-care arrangements.

His phone rang again. *Forget about her,* he ordered himself, but even as he reached for the receiver and punched the button to connect him with his caller, he knew he wasn't going to put Filomena out of his mind.

He couldn't.

BY THE TIME he got home, he felt wrung out from the demands the day had placed on him. His earlobe ached from having the phone jammed against it for so much of the day. His head throbbed. His thumb hurt from his having slammed it in a desk drawer while he'd been juggling three calls simultaneously.

His house was empty and dark, and that made him feel even worse.

Only for a minute. Then he realized that if Filomena and the kids weren't at his house, they were probably at hers. Even though he wanted nothing more than to stagger into his den and collapse on the couch, he could handle driving to her house. His reward would be to see her and his kids together.

Thinking that way was trouble. As dangerous as it was to view Filomena as a woman he wanted to make love with, it was even riskier to think of her as someone he wanted his children to bond with.

But he'd been playing it safe ever since Debbie had left. Maybe he'd been playing it safe even before Debbie had left, establishing himself at Champion Sports, assuming the reins, buying a nice house and settling down to raise a family, when all she'd wanted was glamour and thrills.

As he backed out of his driveway and pointed his car in the direction of Filomena's house, he shoved thoughts of Debbie out of his mind. They were replaced by thoughts of the Daddy School class he'd taken. The teacher had discussed the importance of listening to your kids, really listening. It occurred to Evan that it was just as important for him to listen to himself.

He listened, really listened.

What he heard—what he'd been hearing since Thanksgiving, since before Thanksgiving, in fact—what he'd been hearing in a faint whisper ever since the first time he'd seen Filomena, was that he wanted her in his life. He didn't want her to go. Even though that was her plan, even though she intended to sell her house and resume her old life with the new year...

He didn't want her to go. His heart was shouting it at him, and he was listening.

Flurries swirled like talcum powder through the sky as he turned onto Poplar Ridge Road. He cruised along the dark, winding lane, watching for the stone columns that marked her driveway. He felt a surprising surge of energy as he steered onto the gravel path, his senses honed, his posture aggressive and his vision sharp.

He didn't want her to go.

The hell with friendship and a job, he thought. He'd struck out plenty of times during his years playing baseball, but if you were going to strike out, it was always better to go down swinging. And he was going to swing for the stands, for the sky, for the moon.

Her windows were filled with welcoming light as he steered around the circle at the head of the driveway. He got out of his car, turned the collar of his blazer up after a few snowflakes nipped at his neck, and climbed the front steps. He rang the bell, and when the door swung open and he saw Filomena standing on the other side, her hair long and loose past her shoulders, her eyes luminous, her lips widening in a smile, he felt a gust of energy burning from his toes up his legs, up his spine to his brain, spreading heat through him, spreading certainty.

"Did you get my message?" she asked, stepping away from the door and waving him in.

"What message?"

"I left a message on your answering machine that we'd be here."

"I didn't even go inside my house. It looked dark, so I came straight here." Because he'd known she would be here. Because his instincts had told him. Because everything was coming together, like the perfect swing to the perfect pitch, the ball hitting the fat heart of the bat and soaring over the fence.

As he moved farther into her house, he heard Billy and Gracie squabbling. It didn't sound serious. "It's called pointy-something," Billy was saying, "and people think it's for Christmas because it's green and red. It has nothing to do with Christmas trees."

"They're helping me decorate the house," Filomena explained, leading him into the living room. Billy and Gracie shared the space with what appeared to be a small farm's worth of greenery—poinsettias, arrangements of pinecones and branches, clusters of holly tied with red ribbons. The carved mantel was festooned with pine boughs. The windowsills each held a red candle in a candlestick nestled in holly. A sprig of mistletoe dangled in the doorway between the living room and the dining room.

Evan was happy to see his kids—but for one brief, shameless moment all he could think of was how he might be able to maneuver Filomena into that doorway, under the mistletoe.

"I told them I wasn't going to have a tree, so we decided to do this, instead," she explained.

"What do you think, Daddy?" Gracie asked, bounding across the room and leaping into his arms. "Doesn't it smell good?"

"It sure does," he agreed, swinging her high. The room smelled like a forest, clean and tangy. It smelled like life bursting through the first snow. It smelled like Christmas, like home.

"Your hair is wet," Gracie said as he adjusted her against his chest. "Is it raining?"

"As a matter of fact, it's snowing."

"Snowing!" Billy whooped, racing to the nearest window and peering out. Gracie wriggled in Evan's arms until he put her down, and she charged across the room to join her brother at the window.

"Just flurries," Evan whispered to Filomena.

"It doesn't matter," she whispered back. "It's the first snow of the season." Her smile squeezed his heart. Her body—hidden beneath an oversize red sweater and loose-fitting jeans—tempted him. A pine needle was trapped in her hair, and he freed it, letting his hand dawdle for an extra moment, savoring the silky black softness. Just touching her that way, unraveling the stiff green needle and holding it in his palm so she could see it, made him feel unbearably close to her.

It had been so long since he'd felt close to a woman, really close. Close enough to trust her with his children. Close enough to share a holiday meal with her. Close enough to want to share much more with her. "You're probably ready for me to get the kids out of your hair, too," he joked, just to clear his head of romantic mush.

She smiled. "They've been great. We saw a wonderful movie about a talking dog, and then we went to that nursery on the western end of Newcombe and bought all these Christmas plants and decorations, and we've been decorating the house. They might be sick of me, but I'm not sick of them."

His kids would never be sick of Filomena. He couldn't imagine it. "You know," he ventured, keeping his tone casual, "I just happen to have tons of food in my refrigerator. Leftover turkey and cranberry sauce, stuff like that. I could broil it all up and make a meal. Why don't you join us?"

Her eyes flashed. With apprehension or pleasure—or maybe both, he didn't know. "Evan, I—"

"Okay. I won't broil it," he promised, cutting her off before she could decline the invitation. "I'll let you in on a secret—I know how to use a microwave. Don't tell the kids, because if they find out, they'll expect more of me than broiled whatever for dinner every night."

She smiled again, almost in spite of herself. "I'd love to have dinner with you, but—"

"Great."

She glanced toward the children, who were pressed to the window, jabbering about how many inches of snow the trivial flurries might produce. Then she hooked her hand around Evan's elbow and ushered him out of the living room—right under the mistletoe, but she was moving so quickly he couldn't take advantage of that. She dragged him through the dining room and into the kitchen, two rooms removed from the kids, and released his arm. "Evan," she said, then fell silent.

God, she was beautiful. Her complexion had a golden undertone, even this late in autumn, when any lingering summer tan should have faded. Her lashes were as thick as mink, her lips the color of coral. The only thing that kept him from pulling her into his arms was the suspicion that she was trying really hard to keep her distance from him. Anything he did to close that distance would seem like coercion to her.

"Dinner," he said, fighting to keep his hands at his sides. "That's all I asked you for."

"Since I arrived in Arlington, I've had more dinners with you than I've had alone."

"Would you rather be eating alone?"

She offered a hesitant smile. ''No. But that's the problem. I'm afraid...''

''Afraid of what?''

''Becoming attached to you,'' she said bluntly.

Too late, he thought. It was way too late to worry about becoming attached.

He stretched his brain to come up with the right response, one that would reassure her. ''Last night you told me about how your parents had all these friends, lifelong friends from all walks of life who'd come to your Thanksgiving dinners. Right? Well, that's like you and me, Fil. We've become friends. Maybe we'll turn out to be lifelong friends.'' *Maybe more,* he added silently. ''So why shouldn't we eat together while you're in town? What's the harm in it? It beats eating alone.''

Sighing, she studied him pensively.

''Maybe you could bring along some of that leftover pumpkin pie,'' he added, refusing to acknowledge her misgivings. ''I notice you unloaded a lot of turkey on me, but you kept all the pie for yourself.''

''I tried to give you some pie,'' she reminded him with a grin. ''You refused it.''

''Because we only had three pairs of hands. Two,'' he corrected himself. Gracie had fallen asleep when they'd been getting ready to leave. Evan had managed to rouse her so she could walk out to the car herself, but he hadn't trusted her to carry any of the food. ''Come on, Fil. Turkey and the fixings, pumpkin pie and a few more minutes with my little monsters. You said you weren't sick of them yet.''

''All right,'' she said, relenting, her eyes scooting past him as if she didn't want him to read her thoughts. Not that he'd ever had any talent when it came to reading a woman's thoughts. For all he knew, the only reason Filomena had agreed to have dinner with him was so she could spend more time with Gracie and Billy.

And if that was her reason, Evan would accept it. Call it a foul tip. He might not have made it to first base yet, but he was still at the plate, still alive.

"Get the pie," he murmured. "I'll get the kids."

"PATTY? IT'S FIL," she said. The clock on the night table beside her bed read ten, not too late to be calling her closest friend down in New York—especially since the last two times she'd phoned, earlier in the day, Patty hadn't been home.

"Fil! I got your messages, but when I called back, you didn't answer."

"I've been busy, in and out. And I haven't got an answering machine here."

"How are you doing, babe? I feel so bad for you, up there in the sticks all by yourself."

Filomena was hardly all by herself. And that was either a blessing or a profound problem. "I'm okay," she reassured her friend. "How are things in the city?"

"Noisy. Dirty. The usual. Carlos broke up with Julia, and they're both moping, acting very put-upon. It's tedious."

"This is the third time they've broken up," Filomena remarked.

"Like I said. Tedious."

"Which one are we getting custody of this time?"

"Carlos, I think. Julia's being bitchy. He left a couple of CDs at her place, and she's refusing to give them back."

"Why?"

"She says he owes her for the Blue Man Group ticket she bought for him."

"Oh, for God's sake. All right, we'll take custody of him."

"Until they make up again," Patty reminded her.

Filomena smiled and sank back against the pillows. She'd removed her boots, and her socks were as red as her sweater, making her feet feel warm and cheery. Catching up on the city gossip didn't cheer her quite as much. It reminded her of who she was.

Not an Arlington resident. Not a baby-sitter. Not a woman who had just spent yet another evening with Evan, pretending he didn't have the most alluring eyes she'd ever seen, pretending the planes and angles of his face didn't fascinate her, pretending his height, his lean proportions, the length of his legs and the breadth of his shoulders didn't bludgeon her with an almost painful awareness of how masculine he was.

"So, is everything all right with you, Fil?"

"Um…yeah, of course," she said, her voice sounding strangely raspy.

"Are you sure?"

"Listen, Patty—" she swallowed and forced more strength into her tone "—I want to throw a party for New Year's Eve. You can all take the train up. There's a commuter line directly into Arlington. And I've got six bedrooms here. I could put everyone up overnight. It'll be kind of a farewell to the house before I sell it. What do you think?"

"Wait a minute," Patty said. "You're asking me, would I rather risk life and limb in Times Square with a million piss-drunk idiots screaming their heads off while they watch the ball drop, or take the train with a bunch of friends to your country villa for the night? I've got to think long and hard about this.'' She didn't think long or hard. ''Fabulous! You'll invite Carlos and not Julia?''

''Yes.''

''Okay. Who else? Danny and Liz?''

''Sure.''

''Kumiko?''

''Of course. I've got beds, and maybe a few people could bring sleeping bags, just in case.''

''It sounds great, Fil.'' Patty hesitated. ''What's going on?''

Filomena laughed. ''What do you mean, what's going on? I'm planning a party.''

''Something's going on. I can hear it in your voice.''

''Hear what?'' She was still smiling, but wariness mixed with her amusement.

''You don't sound…I don't know. Troubled.''

''I *don't* sound troubled? What does that mean? Am I supposed to be troubled?''

''Well, Fil, you traveled up there to mourn for your mother and close up your old family manse. Now, I'm not saying there's a right way and a wrong way to mourn. I'm just saying you sound happier than I would have expected, under the circumstances.''

''You're criticizing me for sounding happy.'' Filomena laughed again.

''No. I'm being nosy. What's going on?''

''I've made some friends up here,'' Filomena told her, choosing her words carefully.

''Okay.'' Patty sounded as if she knew Filomena had more to tell her. ''Some friends.''

''Some friends,'' Filomena repeated. ''You know what friends are, don't you?''

"What's his name?" Patty asked.

Filomena sighed and decided not to bother trying to conceal anything from Patty. There was nothing to conceal, after all. "Evan," she said. "He's a divorced father of two. He runs a chain of sporting-goods stores. We have nothing in common."

"Are you in love or what?"

"No, I'm not in love! I just said we had nothing in common."

"And I'm saying you sound happy."

"Because he's a nice friend."

"A nice friend." Patty snorted. Filomena had to admit it was an absurdly bland description, especially when applied to Evan. "Is he sexy?"

"Yes. But nothing's going on." She sighed again, feeling a lot less happy than Patty seemed to think she sounded. "Nothing *can* go on. For one thing, as I said, we've got nothing in common. For another thing, I'm leaving in January."

"So, have you slept with him yet?"

"Patty!" She closed her eyes and groaned, aware that her friend was teasing her, but also aware that the teasing cut a little too close to her heart. She still hadn't recovered from the sensation of Evan's fingers in her hair, and all he'd been doing was plucking a pine needle out of it. A simple bit of grooming assistance, probably less meaningful to him than brushing his daughter's hair out after a shampoo, and yet it had left Filomena weak and soft inside, yearning.

She couldn't bring herself to tell Patty she was actually working for him—as a baby-sitter, no less. That was about as unromantic a situation as possible. Admitting that their relationship was held together by money and children would prompt Patty to lecture her on how truly foolish and dim-witted and *wrong* thinking about Evan as anything other than a friend was.

Filomena didn't need Patty to lecture her. She knew it was wrong. That was why she was trying to resist her attraction to him, trying to pretend that having him pull a pine needle out of her hair hadn't been the most erotic experience she'd had in ages.

"I haven't slept with him," she told Patty. "I have no intention of sleeping with him. That's just not going to happen, so you can stop asking."

"Will you invite him to the New Year's Eve party?"

"I don't know. Maybe. If you behave yourself and treat me with respect."

"Great. I want to meet him." Patty chuckled. "A divorced father who sells sporting goods. That's so suburban, Fil. I didn't know suburban guys could be sexy."

Filomena hadn't known that, either. Actually, she'd never thought about it one way or the other. She hadn't been looking for a sexy guy, urban or rural or anything in between.

She certainly hadn't been looking for Evan.

She finished her conversation with Patty and hung up the phone, then settled deep into the pillows propped against her headboard. Closing her eyes, she pictured her crowded, sunless efficiency apartment near the Columbia University campus. She imagined the constant drone of traffic outside her dingy window, the people swarming Upper Broadway at one in the morning, the combative wit and the tumultuous lives of her friends.

It all seemed so far away.

She'd missed that excitement, the clamor and intrigue and the soap-opera melodramas of her pals when she'd first arrived in Arlington. But lately, the only noise that mattered was the high-pitched chatter of Gracie babbling about hair clips and candy, marriage and magic, and the more solid, responsible discussions Billy engaged in, his eyes as dazzling as his father's. The only traffic she thought about was the rush-hour buildup on Dudley Road as she drove to the Children's Garden Preschool to pick up Gracie. The only friend she seemed to need was Evan.

Once again, she recalled his fingers twining through her hair, and something clenched inside her, dark and lush.

She'd grown attached to him only because she was emotionally vulnerable. He'd caught her at a bad time. She'd been bereft over the death of her mother, so she'd turned to him.

A low, helpless laugh escaped her. Yes, she mourned for her mother. But grief wasn't what had made her turn to Evan. Loneliness wasn't what attracted her to him.

He'd asked her to have dinner with him and the kids because he thought it would be preferable to eating alone, but that wasn't why she'd said yes. She'd had dinner with him and the kids because being with them—with *him*— was preferable to a whole lot of things. Being with Evan, basking in his enigmatic smile, observing his bony wrists when he rolled up his sleeves and the contours of his throat when he opened the collar button of his shirt, eyeing the lanky profile of his body and wondering what his chest would look like, what it would feel like, what it would taste like if she pressed her mouth to his skin…

She was in trouble. Big trouble.

Abruptly, she pushed away from the pillows, swung her legs over the side of the bed and crossed the room to her dresser. Her tarot cards sat in a neat stack, wrapped in a silk handkerchief, exactly where she'd left them after taking them away from Billy and Gracie last night. She carried the deck to her bed, sat cross-legged at the center of the mattress and shuffled the cards.

She didn't actually believe the tarot could predict the future, but she saw no harm in using the cards. If they helped a person to think something through, to clarify her wishes, to define her goals, why not?

She pulled the queen of pentacles out to represent herself, then shuffled the rest of the deck, focusing on a question: *What will happen between Evan and me?* Then she dealt out the cards in a Celtic array.

The card representing her current situation—the four of swords—stood for retreat and solitude. Well, that made sense. She'd come to Arlington to collect her wits and figure out how to live the rest of her life as an orphan. Crossing her—the fool. She grinned. The Fool indicated that she was facing a choice. She knew what that choice was. The cards were supposed to tell her how to make it—if she took any of this seriously.

She truly didn't—but she kept going. The cards said she was facing financial struggles—the reversed Ten of Pentacles warned of a lost inheritance. The reversed Ace of Wands predicted that some enterprise might not be realized. The sale of the house? Or her thesis, perhaps? Would she wind up not getting her doctorate, or getting it but not getting a job, not becoming a university scholar like her father?

The Moon card made an appearance. It almost always did for her, although she wasn't sure why. This time it appeared upside down as the final card, the one that supposedly answered her question. According to the cards, her answer was that she would find peace, at a cost. She'd be practical.

The practical thing to do was to take care of Evan's kids and let him pay her for her time—and to stop thinking about him as a desirable man. The practical path would carry her through New Year's Day and straight to the office of a real-estate agent, who would list this house for sale. The practical solution would be to make her last month in Arlington a serene one, devoid of emotional entanglements and upheavals, and then to return to New York City.

The Moon card was telling her to forget about Evan.

She gathered the cards, rewrapped them in the square of blue silk and carried them to her dresser. After setting them down with an angry thump, she turned her back on them.

She didn't believe in that nonsense. She honestly didn't.

But this time, she suspected, the cards were telling her the truth.

CHAPTER ELEVEN

ENTERING THE ROOM at the YMCA where the Daddy School met, Evan spotted a familiar face among the men pushing metal chairs into a circle at the center of the room. He grabbed a chair, carried it with him to the circle and unfolded it next to Dennis Murphy's chair. "Murphy!" he greeted his lawyer and poker buddy. "What are you doing here?"

"Catching a refresher course," Murphy said with a grin. "When you talked about Daddy School last week at the game, it got me to thinking I could benefit from a booster shot."

"Really?" Evan unzipped his battered leather jacket, shrugged out of it and draped it over the back of the chair. "All this time you've been telling me you're the perfect father."

"I am. Only a perfect father would know when it's time for a booster shot." He laughed as he settled into his chair. "The thing is, the kids have been way too wired lately," he explained. "Pre-Christmas excitement, I think. When I tell them to take it down a notch, they drag Gail into it. She doesn't want to play referee between them and me, and she doesn't want to be put in a position of taking sides. So she told me to sit in on a few Daddy School classes and get some fine-tuning."

"So you're doing it because your wife pressured you into it."

"That about sums it up." Murphy shrugged, obviously not perturbed by his wife's pressure tactics. "Anyway, I was curious to see how you were doing."

"You could have waited till tomorrow night to see how I was doing," Evan reminded him. Tomorrow was their poker night.

"I meant, in the context of your kids. I was thinking about you over the Thanksgiving weekend, wondering how the holiday was treating you."

"We did fine," Evan assured him, hoping his smile would deflect more questions. When he was paying Murphy five hundred dollars an hour to handle his or Champion's business, he was pleased by Murphy's tenacity. But when they were pals, sitting side by side in an evening class at the YMCA, he didn't want to be interrogated.

Unfortunately, Murphy was in an interrogating mood. "I would have invited you to have Thanksgiving dinner with us, but we had the whole gang—Gail's sister Molly and her husband, my mother and Gail's parents. It was a huge family bash. Practically unbearable."

"No problem. We had a great Thanksgiving."

"Just you and the kids?"

Evan considered his answer and realized he had nothing to hide. "Fil was also there. Filomena."

"The baby-sitter?"

"Well, she's..." He paused, then decided what the hell. "She's more than a baby-sitter at this point."

"Yeah?" Murphy looked intrigued. "It's about time. It's been, what? Two years since your divorce?"

"You ought to know—your firm handled it."

"And we did an excellent job, too," Murphy recollected. "You got the house, you got full, uncontested custody of the kids, you didn't get hit with any alimony payments and you got to keep every penny of your assets."

"She didn't want my assets. All she wanted was a superstar lover," Evan reminded Murphy. Even though he didn't miss Debbie at all, it hurt to remember why she'd left him—because he wasn't exciting enough, charismatic enough. *Good* enough.

Allison Winslow entered the room, giving him a convenient excuse to push aside that depressing thought. The din of conversation melted away as she sauntered to the circle. "Boy," she said with a chuckle. "Everyone falls silent when I enter. Should I be flattered?"

The Daddy School students laughed, then waited patiently as she removed a colorful down parka, fluffed her curly red hair and smoothed her shirt into the waistband of her pristine white slacks. Her sneakers and her turtleneck were as white as her pants. She must have come to the YMCA straight from her nursing job at Arlington Memorial Hospital, Evan guessed.

As hectic as his day had been, he was glad he'd been able to go home and have dinner with Billy and Gracie before attending the Daddy School. He'd broiled swordfish steaks and immersed himself in the glorious minutiae of his children's lives: Gracie's long-winded description of the snowflakes she and her classmates cut out of folded construction paper, Billy's stellar performance playing a game of dodgeball in gym, Gracie's desperate need for Silly Putty, Billy's heartfelt longing for snow.

How could Debbie have walked away from that? Evan

wondered. Could a superstar lover really be worth sacrificing the joys and challenges of raising one's children?

Evidently, she'd thought so. And Evan thought she was an idiot for having made that choice.

"This evening, I want to talk about the women in your children's lives," Allison announced, startling Evan—and apparently several of the other men in the room. They sat up straighter, shifted in their seats, eyed one another dubiously.

"I know, this is the *Daddy* School," she said. "But some of you have wives, some have ex-wives, some have girlfriends—or even mothers and neighbors who help out with your kids. This class is about improving your fathering skills, and one of the most important ways you can improve those skills is to improve the relationships between your children and the women who are central to their lives."

A couple of fathers grumbled. Evan guessed they were caught up in contentious child-sharing arrangements with ex-wives. In his case, his ex-wife was the exact opposite of central to his children's lives. But there were still women essential to them. Not just their teachers, their friends' mothers or their grandmother, but the woman who'd shown up at his front door five minutes before he'd had to leave for the YMCA.

He swallowed a reluctant laugh. Even at the Daddy School, which ought to have nothing to do with Filomena, there she was, nudging her way back to the front his mind.

"Now, usually I teach Daddy School classes to fathers of newborns," Allison said. "Or sometimes even fathers whose babies haven't been born yet. These fathers are anxious. They feel ignorant or incompetent when it comes to child care. They believe their female partners know much more about child care than they do—and often, they're right,'' she added with an easy smile. ''Then you guys take a class like this, and you learn to be complete experts in father-child relationships—'' this brought rousing guffaws from the men ''—and you forget that one of the most important jobs fathers have is to help your children relate better to the women in their lives. If you don't nurture that relationship, you're failing in your job as a father, just as the women who deal with your children would be failing in their jobs if they didn't nurture the children's relationships with you.''

Evan listened as Allison discussed some of the things men could do to support their children's relationships with mothers and other female caregivers. He agreed with some of her suggestions and disagreed with others—for instance, her assertion that lots of men felt threatened by a strong mother-child relationship. He didn't feel threatened by his kids' affection for Filomena. Quite the opposite—he thought it was wonderful. The only downside to their relationship with her was that the more attached to her they grew, the harder it would be on them when she left.

He couldn't bear to watch his kids lose Filomena. They'd lost the woman in their lives once, and he hated the possibility of their repeating that painful experience. Not that Filomena was their mother, not that she was in any way bound to them as Debbie had been, but...he just couldn't let it happen.

On the other hand, Filomena had been in their lives for only a couple of weeks. She would be in their lives for only a few weeks more. Surely they could survive her departure. If he kept them busy enough, if he started coming home from work earlier—which he would once the holiday-sales season ended—they might not even notice that Filomena wasn't around.

Kids were resilient. And his kids had him, and he was never, ever going to leave them.

"So you need to remember that just as you like to have special time with your kids, those women like to have special time with the kids, too. Men tend to think that because women spend so many hours with the children, they don't need that special time. But if all a woman is doing with her children is feeding them and shopping for them and taking them to the dentist, that's not the same thing as playing go-fish with them, or taking a walk with them, or going to see a special movie with them."

Filomena was free take the kids to as many saccharine-sweet movies as she wanted without any interference from him, Evan thought generously.

"Men have to be unselfish when it comes to special time," Allison lectured. "They have to contribute more to the not-special stuff. If you're married and it's your routine to go off and play with the kids after dinner while your wife cleans the kitchen, think about occasionally volunteering to clean the kitchen so *she* can play with the kids. That's good fathering. Even though you're not with the children, you're being a good father to them. Do you see what I'm getting at?"

The men began speaking up. One was truly hostile toward his ex-wife; Evan was glad he didn't fit into that category. Next to him, Murphy settled back in his chair, his legs stretched out before him and his arms folded across his chest. He'd had a reasonably amicable divorce, Evan recalled, and now he was happily remarried, raising his twins with his new wife. Not a bad outcome.

Evan had no idea what outcome awaited him and his children. Two years after their family had fallen apart, they were still in limbo. If Filomena left—damn, it hurt to consider that possibility, but he'd be a fool to pretend it didn't exist—he was going to have to take steps to socialize more, to try to make his life complete. With or without her.

They weren't in love, after all. Not yet, and maybe they never would be. But as Murphy had pointed out, it was time Evan started building a new life.

Filomena's arrival had forced him to acknowledge that he was ready for a new life. Which alone was reason enough to love her, he thought with a wry smile.

FREDDY THE PIG just wasn't doing it for her.

She'd been neglecting her studies terribly. She knew her graduate adviser would forgive her for falling a bit behind schedule in her thesis work. She'd lost her mother, after all. Her life was in turmoil. She'd be ready to teach a section of the Modern American Literature survey course next spring; the curriculum didn't change much from year to year, and she'd taught the class before. This fall, she'd planned to dedicate the bulk of her time to compiling her research, organizing it and writing the damned thesis.

But the magic was gone.

She used to find excitement in the pages of Walter Brooks's books, his tales of barnyard animals exemplifying the best and worst of humanity. She used to take joy in analyzing the interactions of Freddy and Jinx the cat, and Mrs. Wiggins the cow, and the befuddled but kindly Beans, the humans who foolishly believed they were actually in charge of the farm.

No more. Magic existed in Filomena's life, but it didn't lie in the pages of her books—or, for that matter, in the stack of cards wrapped in silk on her dresser.

The magic was in a house on the other side of the woods. The magic was in her imagination, drawing her to the Myerses, making her want what she most feared: becoming dependent on them.

Bad enough that she depended on them for company, for a purpose and a routine in her daily life, for the spark of energy that fueled her as she continued her room-by-room assault on her own house, preparing it for sale. Far worse was that she depended on Evan and his children for the magic in her life.

Tuesday was her day off. Evan had his poker game that night, and he arranged his workday so he could escape from the office early and pick up the kids himself. Given that she'd spent Monday evening with them so he could attend his Daddy School class, she deserved Tuesday off. She ought to appreciate the tranquillity of an evening without Billy and Gracie.

After finishing a meal of shrimp and herbed rice, a fresh spinach salad and a glass of wine, she lit candles around the living room and put Handel's *Water Music* on her portable stereo, and tried to remember what her life had been like before that night, exactly two weeks ago, when she'd caught those two scamps snooping through her window.

Peaceful. Lonely. Dull.

She wanted to buy them Christmas presents. She probably ought to confer with Evan first, to make sure he wouldn't mind—but she wanted to buy him a Christmas present, too. If she did, would he think she was presumptuous? Would it be embarrassing if she gave him something and he had nothing to give her?

Sitting in her living room, her candles glazing the air with whispers of golden light and Handel's celebratory music embracing her, she took a sip from her refilled glass of wine and found courage in it. The hell with whether Evan considered her presumptuous. The hell with worrying about embarrassing herself. She had been many things in her life, but embarrassed wasn't one of them. When, as a teenager, she'd capsized a kayak in water so shallow she'd actually bumped her head on the river bottom, she hadn't been embarrassed. When she'd started her solo a measure early during the spring glee-club concert at her college, she hadn't been embarrassed. Embarrassment had always seemed to her a waste of emotional energy.

If she gave Evan a gift and he didn't have one for her, who cared? She would be giving him something because she wanted to, because he'd made these past few weeks easier to endure, because he'd made her laugh and smile and dream. As he'd said, this could be the start of a lifelong friendship. Filomena couldn't imagine a time in her life when she wouldn't want to drop in on Evan in Arlington, to see how he and the children were doing, to gaze into his glittering eyes and remember the sensation of his fingers tangled in her hair.

She would definitely buy him a present.

DUDLEY ROAD was all dressed up for Christmas. Store windows had been taken over by elves, Santas and snowmen. Garlands of silver and red tinsel snaked around the displays; candy canes dangled from the showcase ceilings, and white foam shaped to resemble snowdrifts blanketed the showcase floors. In front of the Connecticut Bank and Trust, a fellow in a Santa suit rang a bell and asked for donations for a local homeless shelter.

Filomena stuffed a dollar into his kettle and smiled. She'd spent the entire morning upstairs in the dusty, dingy attic of her house, sorting through cartons of junk. She couldn't begin to guess why her parents had thought it necessary to save plastic egg cups, old aprons, a cracked orange juicer and a percolator missing its basket, although she supposed they deserved a point or two for having assembled all those items in one carton and labeled it "kitchen." The carton labeled "living room," however, was filled with items that must have come from the garage: a hand spade and a gardening claw, a hose nozzle, an unopened plastic bottle of motor oil. Why had anyone carried motor oil upstairs to the attic and stored it in a cardboard box?

She'd lugged the cartons downstairs. Their contents would mostly end up in the trash, but she felt obligated to go through each carton and make sure it contained no treasures worth saving for nostalgia's sake. Still, she deserved a reward for her hours in the attic, and that reward would be a shopping excursion to downtown Arlington.

The chilly air stung her cheeks and swirled under the hem of her skirt as she strolled down the street, pausing to admire each window display. She had to be careful not to spend money like a maniac—but she'd been budgeting her funds carefully ever since she'd begun graduate school five years ago, so frugality was a habit with her.

She'd already picked out presents for Gracie and Billy. Gracie would be getting *Winnie-the-Pooh,* one of the finest talking-animal books in the history of Western literature, and a Piglet doll to hold while someone—Filomena liked to imagine herself in this role—read chapters of the book to the little girl. For Billy, she'd bought a basic chess set, because he'd told her, one late afternoon last week when they'd been waiting for Evan to come home, that he didn't have one. She also found a book that explained the game in language a third grader could understand. And she'd bought another talking-animal classic, *Charlotte's Web,* for both children to share.

Books were her weakness.

The kids' presents were crammed into her leather backpack, slung over one shoulder. She hadn't yet figured out what to get for Evan. She'd considered a book for him, too, but she hadn't found any that seemed right. Did he read adventure novels? Did he like history? She suspected that when he came home from his long, tiring days, all he wanted to do was be with his children. He didn't really have the time to lose himself in the pages of a book.

If he had a wife or a partner, or even a full-time housekeeper, he'd probably read more. Maybe someday he would…and she decided not to think about that.

So. No book for Evan. She wanted to give him something wonderful, something that would make him smile, something perfect—if only she could figure out what.

Digging her hands into the pockets of her coat, she continued down the street. At a department store she paused. A sweater? A scarf? No, too predictable.

She paused again at a shop specializing in kitchenware. A Crock-Pot? If she gave him one, he wouldn't have to serve broiled something for dinner every night.

But she couldn't picture Evan preparing stews. More important, she couldn't picture Gracie and Billy eating stews. They'd struggled with her stuffed peppers, which were really rather basic. In fact, she'd noticed they tended to avoid vegetables whenever possible.

Maybe she could give Evan something fun, like an ice-cream maker. But then she noticed the price tag attached to the electric ice-cream maker in the display window. Over one hundred dollars on sale.

Turning from the store, she closed her eyes and visualized Evan. She saw his perpetually tousled hair, the clean sharp lines of his face, the easy way in which he moved his body. She heard his quiet laugh, pictured his hesitant smile, observed the grace of his large, strong hands.

He needed time. More than anything, he needed time.

Grinning, she continued down the street, heading for a gift shop she remembered her mother favoring years ago. It was a boutique on Newcombe, off Dudley, and it specialized in one-of-a-kind items, handcrafted objects, some pieces utter kitsch and others works of art. She hoped the store still existed.

It did. Her grin expanding, she swept into the shop, hearing a bell jingle above the door as it closed behind her. She held herself motionless for a moment, settling her backpack on her shoulders so she wouldn't accidentally swing it and knock some fragile knickknack off a shelf.

To her left stood a display of pottery—planters and plates resonant with a deep-burgundy glaze. One bowl was so beautiful her breath caught. She gingerly lifted it and looked at the price tag underneath. One hundred twenty dollars. She set the bowl down.

She wasn't there to shop for herself, anyway. And somehow, she doubted Evan would be as taken by the magnificent craftsmanship of the wine-colored bowl. She had to focus on finding something he'd need and appreciate and love.

Time.

When a clerk approached her with a smile, Filomena said, "I'm looking for a clock. The most bizarre, wonderful clock you've got."

TWELVE NOON had to be the worst hour to get any shopping done, but Evan didn't have much choice. He'd spent the morning smoothing out distribution problems, as usual, and getting tallies on what merchandise was moving well and what was stagnating on the shelves in each outlet. He'd also spent a few minutes trying to talk to Jennifer, but she seemed to have transformed into a blithering goofball overnight. "What exactly is going on between you and Tank Moody?" he demanded to know.

"Rapport," she said with a dreamy smile.

"I don't want you falling in love with him. He plays for New England. Their stadium is outside Boston. Our headquarters are here in Arlington. Do you see the problem?"

"Don't worry," she replied. "There isn't going to be a problem."

"As long as you don't do anything stupid and run off with him," Evan muttered, not sure exactly what most unnerved him. The possibility of losing his indispensable vice president? The possibility of losing her to a glamorous professional athlete?

Or the strangely nettlesome notion that she was pursuing her heart's desire, while he was debating with himself about how aggressive he ought to be with Filomena, how resolutely he ought to pursue her, how much he ought to hope for.

Over the weekend, he'd convinced himself he had plenty of grounds for hope. After the Daddy School, he'd backed off from that conclusion, convinced that he could jeopardize his children's happiness by becoming involved with Filomena when he knew she was planning to vanish from Arlington in a few short weeks. Tuesday night, as he'd listened to his poker pals trading mild gripes about their significant others, he'd wondered whether he might be better off exactly as he was.

Alone.

He'd been alone too long. That was his problem. The few women he'd dated in the years since Debbie had left had never posed any threat to his heart or his emotional well-being. They hadn't counted.

Filomena did. Day and night, in his thoughts and in his dreams, she was there. Enticing him. Enchanting him. Bewitching him into believing she was the only woman in his life who had ever truly mattered.

If not for Billy and Gracie, he'd go after Filomena without a moment's pause. Why not? All he'd have to lose was his pride, which was replaceable, and his heart, which he knew from experience would heal. But his kids…he couldn't risk their hearts, could he?

He'd put together a decent shopping list with some useful input from Murphy and from his marketing guy at Champion. Stuart had suggested candy, but he'd also suggested a freestanding two-person dome tent, an item selling surprisingly strongly in all the outlets this season. Evan would bet Gracie and Billy would love camping out in the backyard. The dome tent would be easy to pitch and take down. Maybe next summer, he and the kids would go camping.

He didn't want to get all their Christmas gifts from Champion Sports, though. That would be cheating.

He had a few articles of clothing on his list—also cheating, in a way, but they were items the kids needed, and if he wrapped them up and put them under the tree, they would seem more special and make the piles of gifts look bigger. He was also planning on some major toy purchases: a civilization-building computer game for Billy, a computer arithmetic game for Gracie, a couple of heavily advertised board games that the kids had been screeching for, a race-car set with twisting tracks. And a few videos. For their stockings, barrettes and cheap jewelry doodads for Gracie, a few Matchbox cars for Billy, trading cards for both.

Evan was going to have to buy all of it during brief breaks from work. His life would have been easier if he'd been able to slip out of his office at any time other than noon, when Hauser Boulevard and Dudley Road filled to the point of gridlock with shoppers using their lunch hours to shop. But today, this was how his schedule had worked out.

He would buy the toys another day. The discount toy store was a mile down Hauser, and he'd need his car to transport all the stuff he bought. Today, since he had only a midday break, he'd check out the department stores and try to pick up some of the apparel items on his list. Clothing was light; he didn't need his car to carry it.

He wanted this Christmas to be good for the kids. Last year they—and he—had been in kind of a daze, not quite sure how to go about celebrating the holiday without Debbie present. The year before last was the year Debbie had left, and the entire holiday season had been hellish. He'd relinquished all responsibility for the occasion to his parents, who had bought the kids some lovely presents, put up a tree in their house and had Evan bring Billy and Gracie down to New Haven for a few days, just to be away from their sad, sorry home.

But this was the year he had resolved to get on with his life. And part of getting on with it meant creating a normal, cheerful holiday for his children. On Saturday, they would pick out a tall, fragrant tree and set it up in the living room. Maybe he'd buy one of those gingerbread-house kits—he wondered if they could broil gingerbread—and he and the kids would construct a gingerbread house.

Maybe Filomena would help them.

He had to stop obsessing about her. Cripes. There he was, caught up in the midday stampede of frenzied shoppers, and suddenly his vision was filled with her. He saw her magnificent hair, her dark eyes, a long skirt swaying around her boots. Filomena, radiating beauty and warmth amid a crowd of frantic, package-toting consumers on Dudley.

He glanced toward the Santa Claus clanging a bell and collecting charitable donations near the bank, and then looked back to the spot where he thought he'd seen Filomena, expecting that she'd disappeared. But she hadn't. Not only did he see her again, but she was walking toward him, waving and smiling as if thrilled to see him.

He was thrilled to see her, too.

He nudged his way through the crowd until he reached her. Her cheeks and the tip of her nose were pink from the cold, and her eyes danced. "Wow! What a mob scene!"

"What are you doing here?" he asked. She could shop

any time she wanted. Why would she pick the worst hour of the day?

"I needed some fresh air." She had a leather knapsack slung over one shoulder; her gloved hands curled around the strap. "What about you? Don't you have a business to run?"

He would gladly have abandoned his business for the chance to spend the rest of the day gazing into her eyes. He was going to have to get her a Christmas present, too. Even if she was nothing more than his kids' baby-sitter, he'd give her a present, just as he gave presents to his business colleagues and sales staff.

But she wasn't just a baby-sitter, and he wanted to give her more. He wanted to give her something as beautiful as her eyes, as lovely as her smile. He wanted to give her a kiss.

Standing beneath an overcast sky on the cold sidewalk, being brushed and poked on both sides by people swarming past, he bowed slightly and touched her lips with his. He didn't care if anyone noticed. He didn't care if Filomena was shocked.

He was definitely obsessed, and kissing her seemed like the sanest, wisest thing he could do.

It wasn't a passionate kiss, and she clearly wasn't overwhelmed by it. Neither was he—but he hadn't kissed her to overwhelm either of them. He'd kissed her because he was happy to see her, because he was getting on with his life, and getting on with it meant kissing a woman who meant a lot to him.

In any case, she didn't seem to mind. When he straightened, he found her smiling quizzically at him. "So," she said, her voice just a shade deeper than usual.

No one else would have noticed the change, but Evan did. "What are *you* doing here?"

"I have to buy some clothes for the kids. For Christmas."

"You're giving them clothes for Christmas?" She looked appalled.

"Along with a lot of shamelessly impractical stuff. Do you have a minute? Maybe you could help me pick out some sweaters for them."

"I'd love to help you pick out some sweaters for them," she said, sliding one hand from her backpack and hooking it around his elbow. As if they were an actual couple, a man and a woman who'd arranged to meet, who'd planned this shopping outing. Partners for whom shopping together was a common occurrence. Lovers for whom sharing this chore was a precious opportunity.

Yes. This was his new life, and at least for now Filomena seemed willing to be part of it. Smiling with renewed confidence, he steered her into the nearest store, out of the wintry afternoon.

CHAPTER TWELVE

SHE WAS AROUND a lot now. Not that Billy was complaining—he liked having her around. It was just…well, different. Not just that she was with him and Gracie so much of the time, but that she didn't exactly feel like a baby-sitter anymore.

He knew she was a baby-sitter. He knew his dad paid her; he'd seen his dad hand her a check once, which reminded Billy that she was with him and Gracie because it was a job. But still, there was something different about the whole thing.

She was giving Gracie a bath now. He and Dad were in the kitchen, Dad cleaning the broiling pan while he stacked the dinner plates in the dishwasher. Filomena had had dinner with them. She did that most days now. Sometimes she even fixed the dinner herself—and it wasn't "broiled something." Last night she'd made spaghetti and meatballs with real meatballs, not the already-made kind you could buy in the supermarket, but prepared from scratch, and a big salad, and garlic bread with grated cheese on top. "I'll broil this to melt the cheese," she'd said, "and then we can say it's broiled something, okay?"

It was the *way* she was around. Like she belonged here. Like she was a part of the family.

He swung the dishwasher door shut and leaned against

the counter, watching as his father rinsed the soapsuds from the pan. They skidded along the wet metal in little clusters, like skaters gliding over smooth ice. He couldn't wait to go skating, but he'd outgrown his skates and Dad had said he didn't have enough time to buy him a new pair. Billy guessed that meant he was getting new skates for Christmas.

"Is Fil gonna have Christmas with us?" he asked.

Dad shook the excess water from the pan and set it on the drying rack. Then he wiped his hands on a dish towel and turned to Billy. "Would you like that?"

Billy scowled. He hated it when Dad turned a question around on him—especially when he didn't have a simple answer.

He liked Filomena, liked her a lot. But the way she and his dad kept…well, looking at each other and laughing with each other and being so comfortable with each other… It unsettled him. He wasn't sure why, but it did.

His dad was waiting for him to say something. He shrugged. "I don't know. I guess it would be okay."

"If you don't want her to, Billy, you can tell me."

Would Dad be mad at him if he said he didn't want Filomena to share Christmas Day with them? The fact was, he wasn't sure he *didn't* want her to share it with them. "I like her, Dad. She's really nice."

Dad grinned. "But?"

"But it's not like she's our mother or something."

"No," Dad said. "She's not your mother."

Billy felt better. "Next year, can I go out for county-league basketball?" he asked.

His dad frowned. "Sure. But what does that have to do with Christmas?"

"I don't know. I was just thinking about it." And he

was hoping maybe they could get off the subject of Filomena.

His dad planted a hand on Billy's shoulder and steered him into the den. He nudged him down onto the couch, then sank into the cushions next to him. "Billy, if something's bothering you about Fil, you need to tell me."

"Nothing's bothering me about her."

"So, what's going on?"

Billy didn't know what to say. He noticed a thread dangling from the side pocket on his cargo pants and twiddled it with his thumb.

"Has Filomena been mean to you? Or cold?"

"No. I like her," Billy said honestly. "She bakes great cookies."

"Yes, she does," Dad agreed. A few days ago, she, Billy and Gracie had baked oatmeal cookies with butterscotch chips in them. And she'd promised to help them bake and assemble the gingerbread-house kit Dad had brought home from the store. They were going to do that this weekend—which just proved that she wasn't really a baby-sitter, because if she was, she wouldn't be with them on a weekend when Dad was home.

"So what's the problem?"

"Well, it's just..." Billy curled the thread around his thumb, but it wasn't really long enough to go all the way around. It kept slipping off his finger, and he had to pluck at it and get it free so he could try curling it again. "I mean, if she spends Christmas with us, it's kind of like saying Mom isn't here anymore." He didn't dare to look at Dad, just in case his observation made Dad angry or upset.

Dad didn't say anything right away. He propped his feet up on the coffee table. Billy remembered that his

mother never let anyone put their feet up. He'd been remembering more about her lately, and he thought Filomena might have something to do with that. Like, he
hadn't had to think about his mother when no one was
around to block her from view, but now that Filomena
was, Billy kept feeling the need to peek around her to
see if Mom was still hiding back there.

He didn't think Gracie had any real memories of their
mother, but Billy kept flashing on moments with her: the
way she'd look filling his doorway while he got into bed,
the light from the hall glowing behind her so he couldn't
see her face, only her outline, with her hip pushed out a
little and her arms crossed. Or the way she used to stand
by the sliding glass door across the den from where he
and Dad were sitting right now, and she'd holler out into
the backyard, "Billy Myers, get in here *now!*" and he
knew he was in trouble. Or the way she'd always yell at
Dad—and at Billy, too—when they put their feet up on
the coffee table.

It was a sturdy coffee table, though, and neither of
them was wearing shoes. Billy propped his feet up next
to Dad's and wondered if that meant he was taking
Filomena's side, if a person could actually take sides in
all this.

"You miss your mother, don't you," Dad said.

Another tough question. His teacher's math tests were
easier than this. "I don't know," he answered, shrugging
again.

"It's okay to miss her."

"I think actually I don't," Billy said. Hearing himself
say it convinced him he didn't. "It's just that if Fil stays
for Christmas, it's like giving up or something."

"Giving up what?"

"Giving up that Mom will ever come home."

Dad sighed deeply. "She's not going to come home, Billy. Maybe someday she'll realize she misses you and Gracie so much she'll return to Arlington to see you. But she'll never be living here, not in this house. Not even for Christmas. And that has nothing to do with Fil."

"Fil was reading my cards the other day," Billy said, remembering an evening when Dad had called and said he would be getting home late because the store in town had gotten in a shipment of something—skis, maybe— and the staff was a little thin, so he was going to help unload and shelf the new stock. So Filomena had grabbed an old deck of cards and read Gracie's and Billy's fortunes for them. Gracie's was the usual stuff, about how she was wonderful and creative and a princess and all that, but Billy's had been different from what he'd expected, which made him believe Filomena was actually *reading* the cards, instead of just making up a story she thought he might want to hear.

"What did your cards say?" Dad asked.

"That I dreamed about things that could never be. But then she said I shouldn't ever stop dreaming, anyway. She said the cards said I couldn't stop even if I wanted, so I was just...*destined*—" that was the word she'd used "—to keep on dreaming, and I was going to have to learn how to figure out which dreams were possible and which were only just dreams."

"That sounds pretty serious," Dad observed.

"Well, yeah."

"Is there something you dream about that's not going to come true? Something about your mother, maybe?"

Billy nodded. "I used to dream she'd come home and

say she was sorry, like, she did a stupid thing and she wanted us to forgive her.''

His dad smiled crookedly. ''I don't think that's a possible dream.''

''Is that why you want to have Fil spend time with us? And give Gracie her bath? Because Mom's never coming home?''

''I want Fil to give Gracie her bath because I think sometimes it's better if a girl gets a bath from a woman, instead of a man. And I want Fil spend time with us because she's a smart, funny, generous woman and I enjoy her company.''

''So you're gonna invite her to spend Christmas with us, too,'' Billy guessed.

''I think so. If you wouldn't mind.''

If Mom wasn't coming home, what difference did it make? Anyway, when Billy thought about it, he realized that what he minded wasn't Filomena spending Christmas with them but the idea that his mother wasn't. They were going to have Christmas in this house, his home, and his mother would never be a part of it again.

''Are you in love with Fil?'' he asked.

''No,'' his father said, then paused. He grinned and raked his hand through Billy's hair, messing it. ''I like her a lot, though. I think she's a very special woman. I'm glad she's in our lives.''

''So am I. She does make great cookies.''

''She does indeed.''

''Daddy!'' Gracie bellowed from upstairs. ''Time to brush my hair!''

''Her Majesty has summoned me,'' Dad whispered to Billy with a wink before hoisting himself off the sofa. Billy remained where he was. Next to his feet on the coffee table was the book Filomena had lent him, about Freddy the Pig. It was a cool book.

He couldn't remember if his mother ever gave him a book. She probably had, but he honestly couldn't remember.

"I WANT YOU to spend Christmas with us," Evan said as he walked Filomena to the front hall to get her jacket from the closet.

He didn't think the suggestion would shock her, and it didn't. She stood inches from him, facing him, her hair rippling black over her shoulders and her hand falling away from the closet doorknob as she contemplated his invitation. In the dim light of the front hall, the hollows of her cheeks seemed more defined, her lashes thicker.

He'd grown used to seeing her face, admiring it, memorizing it. She'd become a constant presence in his family's life, a healthy, welcome addition. Obviously she'd been around enough that Billy was making certain connections. *Are you in love with Fil?* he'd asked, and while Evan hadn't lied in his answer, he'd asked himself that question more than once and answered it more than one way.

If he *did* love her, he wasn't sure what kind of love it was. Except for the occasional light kiss on her cheek, he'd kept his hands to himself and his mind sealed off from erotic thoughts about her, at least while she was with him. He wanted her—hell, he wanted her the way his kids wanted snow, the way they wanted magic, the way they wanted lots of toys on Christmas morning. But he wouldn't push, couldn't rush. If he actually went and fell in love with her and then she left—as she was bound to—he'd feel pretty damned lousy. Been there, done that and all.

So he was taking his time, letting the friendship develop, letting her grow more and more comfortable in his world. She enjoyed giving Gracie baths, so he gratefully allowed her to give Gracie baths. When he'd taken the kids to pick out a tree, he'd invited Filomena to join them, and she had. She'd helped them stand the thing up in the living room and decorate it with tinsel and popcorn and unbreakable ribbon-wrapped balls, and she'd promised to oversee the construction of the gingerbread house. Having her spend Christmas Day with them seemed almost obvious.

Still, she didn't say yes. "That's a special family time," she murmured.

"So is Thanksgiving, and we all spent that day together. And you've invited me to your New Year's Eve bash." She'd even suggested that he invite a few of his friends to it, so he wouldn't feel like an outsider among her New York City buddies. He'd invited Murphy and his wife, Gail, and Jennifer—who'd immediately said yes and informed him that she would be bringing Tank Moody as her guest. When he'd asked Filomena if she'd mind having a professional football player at her party, she'd laughed and said, "As long as he's nice, I don't mind. Some of my friends might even be impressed. They think Arlington is a remote backwoods outpost."

She probably thought that, too. But she was here. And he wanted her to be here, in his house, on Christmas Day.

She remained silent.

"Fil," he murmured, "what's the hang-up? What's so different about Christmas?"

"Everything," she said, then smiled pensively. "It's a

day when children miss their mothers. I know I'll be missing mine. And I bet your children will be missing theirs.''

He should have known she'd pick up on Billy's complicated emotional state. She was so attuned to his kids she could read their fortunes in an old deck of poker cards—and he bet she didn't need the cards at all. Her knowledge of them was intuitive. Ace of spades or deuce of clubs, she could read them.

''Billy's working some things through,'' Evan conceded, ''but that doesn't mean we can't all spend the day together.''

''What happened with their mother?'' she asked. ''I know it's not my business, and if you don't want to talk about it, I'll understand. But I just can't believe...'' She trailed off.

''You can't believe what?''

''I can't believe a woman would have walked out on them. And on you,'' she added quietly.

He let out a long breath. No, he didn't want to talk about it, but whether or not it was her business was irrelevant. He was going to lose her anyway. So why not tell her? It wasn't as if he had to protect his ego or project himself as some sort of irresistible stud no woman could turn her back on. He might as well tell Filomena the truth.

''You have a minute?'' he asked, smiling wryly. ''Or maybe an hour?''

Her smile looked warmer than his felt. ''I've got time.''

He slid his hand around hers and led her into the kitchen. Through the doorway to the den he heard the rumble of the TV. ''Bedtime, Billy,'' he shouted.

"Can I just watch the end of this show?"

He glanced at the wall clock. Three minutes past eight—which meant that the show wouldn't end until eight-thirty at the earliest. "No," he insisted. "Bedtime now. I'll be upstairs to tuck you in in fifteen minutes."

"Okay," Billy grumbled. After a moment the TV went silent and Evan heard the clomp of footsteps up the stairs.

He motioned toward the table. Filomena sat, her long skirt billowing and then settling onto her legs. He saw the slope of her thighs beneath the fabric, the angle of her knees. Deliberately, he turned away. "Would you like something to drink?"

"No, thanks."

He pulled a beer from the fridge for himself, wrenched off the cap and returned to the table, where he planted himself in a chair facing her. He took a swig of beer, let the sour bubbles lubricate his throat and then began. "She left more than two years ago. Almost two and a half now."

"Why?"

This was the hard part—admitting why. Admitting that he had disappointed Debbie, failed to satisfy her, come in second in a two-man race. "She fell for someone else," he said, keeping his tone as even and neutral as he could.

Filomena laughed. He set down his bottle with a sharp thump, wounded that she could find the miserable story of his divorce amusing. She must have sensed his hurt, because she choked back her laughter and shook her head. "I'm sorry. It's just that…it's so hard to believe."

"What's hard to believe about it?"

Her smile lingered, softening as she gazed at him. "I don't know. If you were to stand side by side with another man, it would have to be a pretty spectacular other man to make a woman choose him over you.''

He appreciated the compliment imbedded in her words, but the fact remained that Debbie had chosen the other man. ''He was pretty spectacular,'' he confirmed. He might have added that *spectacular* was a relative term, that every woman had her own definition of it and that when Debbie had walked out on him, he'd understood, deep in his soul, that she'd left because she didn't consider him the least bit spectacular. His ego had healed since then, but the scar tissue still ached every now and then, like a touch of arthritis at the site of an old injury.

''And her leaving the kids, too,'' Filomena continued. ''It boggles the mind.''

He shrugged. Obviously, Mr. Spectacular had been *so* spectacular Debbie had been willing to sacrifice her children for him. ''He was a baseball star. I'd brought him in to do a promotion for Champion Sports, and she fell for him.''

''A jock?'' Filomena shook her head again. ''She left you and the kids for a jock?''

''She liked jocks,'' Evan said, almost as if he were defending Debbie. ''I was a jock when she fell for me. That was clearly what she was looking for—a jock.''

''I can't picture you as a jock,'' Filomena argued. ''You're too...'' She struggled to find the right word.

''Too what?''

''Smart?'' she suggested, then grinned.

He could have taken offense, as an erstwhile jock, that she was generalizing about the intellectual limitations of jocks. But her smile was so good-natured he didn't. ''Some jocks are smart. Some are stupid.'' He took a swallow of beer and leaned back in his chair, amazed that even plodding through this unpleasant conversation, he was glad to be with Filomena, soothed by her company and stirred by her beauty. "My senior year of college I was scouted by a couple of professional baseball teams. But a pro-ball career wasn't what I wanted. I was good, but I wasn't superstar material. I'd have wound up playing minor league for a few years, traveling around on buses and earning next to nothing. Maybe I'd have made it to triple-A. Maybe even a major-league team for a season or two. But it wasn't what I wanted. I wanted to put down roots, create a home, have kids."

"Much more worthwhile goals than playing baseball," Filomena said. Well, of course she'd say that. She had a pretty low opinion of sports and jocks.

"I was very clear with Debbie about what I wanted to do, and she went ahead and married me anyway. Maybe she shouldn't have. But she did, so I assumed that she wanted the same things I wanted. Maybe at first she *did* want those things, or else she just buried her own feelings and accepted what she had. I don't know."

"Maybe she married you because she loved you," Filomena suggested.

"Maybe." He allowed himself a faint smile. "I was sure she loved the kids, at least. She went through some postpartum stuff—mood swings, depression. I urged her to see a professional to help her work through that. She didn't want to, though. She said she wasn't crazy—she was just sick and tired of changing diapers and cleaning up spills. I did as much of the child care as I could, but I had to support us, too. I couldn't do everything."

Damn it, he sounded as though he was blaming himself. Intellectually, he knew better than to bear the blame for Debbie's change of heart. But he couldn't help feeling that it was at least partly his fault.

Filomena looked as if she was going to say something comforting. He didn't want her to comfort him, to tell him everything had been Debbie's fault. He didn't want her to feel sorry for him. When he saw her extending her hand across the table, he pulled his own hands back and linked them around the bottle of beer, balancing it on his knee.

"She left because this golden boy came along, this jock idol, the kind of guy she'd always dreamed about, and he opened his arms to her," Evan said crisply, determined to communicate to Filomena that he had no use for comforting. "She left us and went off with him. And that was that."

A shadow of concern darkened Filomena's eyes. "Does she keep in touch with the children at all?"

"No. That's the part I'll never forgive her for—abandoning them like that."

"You forgive her for abandoning you?"

"I can take it."

"I think your kids can take it, too," Filomena observed calmly. "They seem to be doing wonderfully. Maybe because they have such a wonderful father."

He wasn't so sure about that. Hadn't Gracie's preschool teacher urged him to take classes in how to be a better father? Hadn't he been sitting in those classes the past few Monday evenings, listening to Allison Winslow and trying to learn what was lacking in his fathering skills?

If the kids seemed to be doing wonderfully, it was probably because of Filomena. They needed a woman in their lives, one who was loving and caring, patient and dependable. And except for the fact that she would be leaving in January, she was all those things.

He took another pull of beer, studying her as he swallowed. Why was it that, no matter how often he reminded himself of her plans to leave town in a few short weeks, he still wanted her? Caution—call it self-preservation—held him back, but his heart wanted her anyway. His body wanted her. Sometimes he believed even his soul wanted her.

He just couldn't bear to come in second again. With Filomena, he'd be coming in second to her life, her goals, her career, her home in New York, her friends there— hell, he was coming in sixth or seventh by that calculation.

But he still wanted her.

She probably wouldn't want him at this point. All her kind, sympathetic words notwithstanding, she knew what he was: a decent, solid, responsible guy. The sort women chose second, if at all.

"So that's what happened with their mother," he concluded, doing his best to keep his voice uninflected. No anger, no resentment. No yearning.

"Thank you for telling me," she said, and offered a dubious smile. "I still find it hard to believe."

He reminded himself, yet again, that as hard as she found it to believe, she, too, would be leaving him. But she would be here for a little while longer, and he could continue to tantalize himself with the possibility that something might occur between them. "So, will you spend Christmas Day with us?" he asked.

Her smile widened. "I'd love to."

"Okay." He set down his beer and turned to stare at the window. If he gazed into her face for another minute, he'd wind up circling the table, hauling her out of her chair and yelling at her for pitying him—if, indeed, she pitied him. Or he'd wind up kissing her, because she exuded so much warmth and womanliness, so much spirit. The first choice would be wrongheaded, the second choice just plain wrong.

She pushed away from the table and stood. "I really should be going," she said. "It's getting late."

"And I've got to tuck in Billy," he remembered, shoving to his feet. He stifled the instinct to touch her arm as they walked back out to the hall. She opened the closet and pulled her jacket off its hanger. He took it from her and held it so she could slide her arms into the sleeves. And then, because it was part of the same motion, he smoothed the jacket over her shoulders. Through the thick suede he felt her, and a pain tugged at him in his gut, below his belt, in his brain. He wanted her. In spite of everything.

He forced himself to lift his hands, and she rotated to face him. She peered up, her eyes locking onto his, and murmured, "Your wife was a very foolish woman." Then, as if she could read everything in his gaze—his thoughts and his wants and his future, like the future she read for his children in the cards—she rose on tiptoe and touched her mouth to his.

His willpower crumbled; his self-protectiveness evaporated. He returned his hands to her shoulders and pulled her closer. Her hair was caught inside the collar of her jacket and he eased it out, just for the pleasure of having it spill against his skin. Then he kissed her, brushing her lips with his, stroking, nipping, coaxing, taking everything she would give.

She gave plenty, her body softening against him, her

mouth opening to him. His tongue found hers and he groaned.

She tasted so good. She felt even better. She felt like friendship and warmth, like hunger and lust. He wanted to yank off her jacket so he could feel her body closer to his own, but she'd just put the jacket on, and he knew that sooner or later—*sooner*—she was going to ease out of this kiss and say good-night. What she'd started in the front hall wasn't going to end in his bed.

And that was probably just as well. No matter how perfectly she fit in his arms, no matter how erotically her tongue moved against his, no matter how much the warm scent of her, the faint sighs trembling in her throat and the tentative motions of her fingers against his arms unleashed his own long-simmering desire, he wasn't going to make love with her. Not tonight.

Maybe—if he came to his senses—never.

But he didn't want to come to his senses, not quite yet. He wanted to hold her for just a moment longer, to stroke the breadth of her lips with his tongue, to twine his fingers into her hair and savor its weight and texture. Just one precious moment longer.

She was the one to break away, turning her face and resting her head against his shoulder. He ran his hands gently through her hair as she struggled to catch her breath. After a while she was no longer panting, and he lowered his arms to circle her waist, just to hug her.

"I don't know where we're going with this, Evan," she whispered. "I really don't."

"Don't worry about it," he said, to himself as much as her. "Just let it be."

She leaned back and angled her head to look at him. A hesitant smile played across her mouth. Her lips were damp from kissing him, and that sheen of moisture turned him on even more. He wondered if she could feel his arousal through all the layers of clothing she had on. "I should go," she said, which led him to conclude that she could.

"Okay." He would see her tomorrow. He would see her that weekend, when she and the kids would create their gingerbread house. He would see her on Christmas Day and New Year's Eve and as many other days as she would let him.

Maybe they would kiss again. Maybe one of those kisses would end in his bed. Maybe she would revamp her entire life so she could be with him for a long, long time. Maybe she would decide staying in Arlington seemed like a much better idea than leaving.

Or else maybe this kiss would be as intimate as they'd ever get. She would come to her senses and resume her position as his children's baby-sitter and his friend. And maybe that would be for the best.

Maybe he should do exactly what he'd told her to do. Just let it be.

CHAPTER THIRTEEN

EVERYONE AROUND the conference table seemed distracted. Stuart was popping mints into his mouth, one after another, and jiggling his foot. Heather kept rattling papers and fussing with her perfect blond hair. Jennifer had the appearance of someone who'd been abducted by aliens and deposited back on earth with a mutated personality—glassy eyes, moony smile, none of her familiar abrasiveness.

Evan didn't want to be there any more than the rest of them. He'd finished his shopping except for one last gift, which was sitting in a showcase at Arlington Jewelers on Dudley, waiting for him to decide whether he was brave enough to give it to Filomena. He'd phoned and found out the store would be open until midnight tonight, and was assured that no one had bought the one-of-a-kind piece yet. As soon as he and his senior staff finished this meeting, he could head over to the jewelry store, study the thing a bit more and hope that, if he made up his mind to buy it, Filomena would like it—or at least wouldn't think he was nuts for giving it to her.

"Okay, guys," he said, flipping a page in his binder. They all flipped pages in their binders, as well, as synchronized as the Rockettes. "Here are the numbers for the New London store. They're underperforming compared with the other stores. What's the problem there? Can we figure it out?''

"Military salaries," Stuart suggested.

"Hmm?"

"Well, New London is a navy town, isn't it?"

"Coast guard," Heather corrected him.

"Coast guard, Navy—either way it's boats, right? Anyway, there's all this talk about how the military doesn't pay its people enough. So maybe they can't afford to splurge on racquetball equipment or in-line skates at holiday time.''

Evan glanced at Jennifer. Ordinarily, she would have jumped all over Stuart, spewing statistics to counter his assumption. But she only nodded and grinned. "I wouldn't want to have to support myself on a military salary," she said.

Of course she wouldn't. Coast-guard employees risked their lives on every mission, but they never got to ride around in limos. "Jennifer, give me an analysis," he said sharply, hoping to snap her out of her reverie. "It's Christmas Eve and we all want to get out of here."

"'Twas the night before Christmas,'" she quoted dreamily.

"So help us figure out what's going on in the New London store. I don't buy Stuart's explanation."

"I don't really buy it, either," Stuart interjected. "I just thought I had to say something so we could go home.''

"Every outlet except for New London is breaking the bank this year," Evan reminded his staff. "We're way above projections. This year's bonuses are big—" Heather perked up when he said that "—but New London is dragging its butt. Jennifer, you were down at that store last week with Tank. Was the place comatose? Any traffic at all?''

"It wasn't as crowded as Hartford or Bridgeport," she said. "But I didn't notice any significant problems."

"Was the staff cheerful? The displays neat? It's a great store with great inventory, but things aren't moving there."

"It's not as if they're losing money," Jennifer pointed out. "They're just not as profitable as the other stores."

Evan rolled his eyes. He knew that. They all knew that. The issue was *why* that store wasn't as profitable.

"We'll have to talk to Peter about it," Stuart suggested. Peter Blanchette was the manager of the New London store.

"I think you need to put a woman in charge of that store," Heather announced.

"Don't give me an equal-rights lecture," Evan warned her. "We've got women managing Seekonk, Bridgeport and Providence. And I've got women at the top, right in this room—"

"—who'd love to get out of here and finish their Christmas shopping," Jennifer finished.

Evan was tempted to remind her of how many times she'd held him prisoner in this room. The Pep Insoles presentation came to mind. Had *he* sulked about being stuck in the conference room?

Well, yes. But he was allowed to sulk. He was the boss.

"All right," he relented, because he wanted this meeting to be over as badly as the rest of them. New London's numbers were troubling, but every other outlet was performing phenomenally. Champion Sports was going to have a superlative year. And now it was time for them to all go home and have a superlative holiday. "We'll figure out New London later. Let's get out of here."

Stuart cheered. Jennifer flung her arms around Evan's neck and thanked him for the leather portfolio he'd given her that morning. He'd given one to Heather, too, and she'd thanked him much less effusively. Heather was extremely particular about whom she hugged. He shook hands with Stuart, who'd received a more masculine-style leather portfolio. The rest of the staff had received boxes of Swiss chocolates, Champion pens—and bonus checks that had put everyone in a remarkably festive mood.

He glanced at his watch. Three-thirty. After leaving the conference room, he marched up and down the hall, bellowing, "Go home, everyone! Have a good holiday!" Then he ducked into his own office, dropped off his binders of sales figures, locked up his desk and donned his wool coat.

A light snow was sifting through gray clouds when he exited the building. Arlington's downtown looked almost absurdly Christmasy as the soft powder turned rooftops white and dusted the sidewalks. The store decorations, the wreaths and lights, the extra energy with which everyone moved lent the world a special aura. People ought to have been frantic—and maybe they were, hurrying to buy one last present, one final treat—but everyone Evan saw seemed to be smiling. They all had crystals of snow glistening on their hats or in their hair, which made them look magical.

Did he look magical, too? Was he grinning like that silver-haired woman with the bulging tote bag, like that skinny young man with the waist-long ponytail and the bounce in his gait?

Probably. He was pleased that Champion had performed so well this season, that he had nearly all his shopping done, that he would get to spend all day tomorrow with his children.

And Filomena.

He turned the corner onto Dudley and wove among the crowds until he reached the jewelry store. The windows had fake snow painted onto them, and multicarat diamonds glittered in velvet perches behind every pane of glass. He wasn't looking for a diamond, though. Not for Fil. Not for a woman who was going to be gone once the old year rolled into the new.

He pushed the door open—and simultaneously pushed all thoughts of Filomena's departure out of his mind. He and she would be together tomorrow. They'd share the holiday. She had promised to help him cook a ham, which, as best he could figure, was already cooked but still needed something other than broiling done to it. She and the kids had constructed the gingerbread house and baked butter cookies shaped like snowmen over the weekend. The entire house smelled like an evergreen forest, thanks to the tree.

Tomorrow would be wonderful, and he wasn't going to think beyond that.

As the door swung shut behind him, he dusted the snow from his shoulders and headed over to the glass showcase. There it was. Utterly impractical, grossly overpriced—and perfect for Filomena. He beckoned a clerk with a wave and pointed to it. "I want this," he said. "Gift-wrapped, please."

"For someone special?" the clerk guessed, unlocking the showcase.

"Yeah," Evan murmured, promising himself that giving it to the most magnificent woman he knew wouldn't be a huge mistake. "Someone special."

FILOMENA LEANED BACK into the embracing cushions of the sofa. The floor of Evan's living room was a mess of wrapping-paper scraps and scattered ribbons. A few piles of gifts—articles of clothing, pairs of ice skates and the books she'd given the children—lay amid the debris, not neglected so much as reserved for a later time, when the initial flood of Christmas adrenaline dried up. She could hear the kids shrieking in the den, and the electric hum of the race-car set Evan had given them. Without a doubt, race cars were cooler than books.

She didn't mind that the kids had tossed aside the books she'd given them. Eventually, they would get tired, and then they'd want to sit quietly and read. In the meantime, Gracie was carrying her Piglet doll everywhere with her.

The living room was surprisingly cozy and not too formal. The two chairs facing the couch looked a bit rigid, but the couch, a gentle blue brocade, was plush and comfortable, and Filomena felt almost decadent lounging on it by herself, the skirt of her velvet jumper tucked around her legs, the sleeves of her burgundy turtleneck pushed up and her hair falling loose down her back. Across the room stood the tree, its branches still wide and fresh, its silver garlands and ornaments glinting in the lamplight.

She couldn't exactly say this was the best Christmas she'd ever had. She recalled a Christmas when she was eight and she received a stained-glass ornament to hang in her window. It was a crescent moon, her first moon, and she'd brought it back to her prep school and fastened it to her window with a clear plastic suction cup. The light would spill through its pale-blue glass and cast mysterious shadows on the opposite wall. Not an expensive gift, but she'd adored it. That Christmas had been marvelous. So had the Christmas her family had celebrated in Hawaii when she was sixteen. She and her parents had hiked to the center of a dormant volcano and eaten a picnic lunch on the grass growing inside the crater. What an amazing way to spend Christmas!

But this year's Christmas definitely merited placement in the top three or four Christmases of Filomena's life. From the moment she'd arrived at the Myers house at noon, she'd felt a part of this home, this family. The kids had given her a detailed tour of every single gift they'd received: "Grandma and Grandpa sent this," they'd said, showing her some complicated Lego sets, "and our aunt and uncle sent these" —some Disney videos. They'd let her take a turn racing a car around the track Evan had set up in the den. Her car had skidded off the track three times, but Billy had assured her that was supposed to happen, sort of, and it was awesome when the cars fishtailed and stuff.

And Evan. Evan in a soft flannel shirt and even softer-looking jeans, demonstrating surprising culinary flair by marinating the ham in orange juice and brown sugar and cooking it in the microwave—a recipe he told Filomena he'd gotten via a panic-stricken phone call to his mother last night. Evan smiling, beaming at the children, relating funny stories about his colleagues, filling Filomena's glass with wine and whispering, "I have something for you, but we'll do that later." His words kept echoing inside her, even as she watched part of a video with the kids, let them demonstrate their new computer games to her, helped Evan to prepare a salad and oversaw the children's efforts at setting the table. *I have something for you,* he'd said, and for some reason, she couldn't exactly think of it as the sort of something that would come in a gift-wrapped box. He had something and they would do it later.

If only his eyes didn't glow so seductively when he gazed at her; if only his smile didn't make her breath catch. If only he didn't touch her so casually, arching an arm around her to reach into the silverware drawer, brushing a strand of her hair back from her face, resting his hands on her shoulders as he stood behind her at the computer terminal, giving her pointers on how to play the game Billy had loaded onto the machine.

If only he hadn't returned her kiss the way he had the night he'd invited her to spend Christmas with him, maybe she wouldn't keep thinking about what they were going to do later.

Exchange presents—that was what they were going to do. And she was pretty sure later had arrived. She'd set her gift for him under the tree, next to a box wrapped in shiny silver foil and adorned with a white-and-silver bow. Obviously it wasn't a gift for the children, or that beautiful wrapping paper would have been torn to shreds hours ago and the contents of the box exposed, scrutinized, played with or ignored, depending on whether the gift was a toy or a book.

Was that box something for her? She didn't want to guess what was inside it, because she didn't want to be disappointed. Yet she couldn't imagine being disappointed by anything Evan gave her.

She heard his voice drift in from the den, quietly reminding the kids not to play rough with the race cars.

Then his footsteps in the hall, past the stairway and through the arched doorway into the living room, a balloon-shaped glass of brandy in each hand. "Hi," he said. His smile melted something inside her.

"Hi."

He set the two glasses on the table in front of the sofa, then crossed to the tree and pulled the two remaining packages out from under the low boughs. He eyed her gift to him curiously, pretending to weigh it in his hand, scowling and shaking it. "Don't!" she warned him when the click of marbles inside the package deepened his frown.

"Is it fragile?"

"Not really, but if you shake it like maracas, it could break."

"It doesn't sound like maracas," he said, placing both packages on the table. "I'm bummed out. I was really hoping for maracas this year." He sent her a wicked grin.

"Well, go ahead and open it," she suggested. "Get bummed out."

He settled onto the sofa next to her, his weight causing the cushions to sink slightly, drawing her closer to him. The children's squeals and the whine of the toy cars zipping around the track sounded far away. They seemed even farther away when he lifted the two glasses, handed her one and tapped it with his. "Merry Christmas," he murmured.

"Merry Christmas." She sipped. The brandy was smooth and tart, sliding down her throat and leaving warmth in its wake. Her father hadn't taught her much about brandy, but she didn't need his expertise to know this was delicious. "Now, open your maracas."

He lifted the box, held it as if about to shake it again

and then tore at the gift wrap. He didn't tatter it as mercilessly as his kids might have, but he wasn't exactly fastidious about getting the paper off the box. Once he'd accomplished that, he removed the lid and studied the contents. Although his smile remained, a line etched across his forehead. "What is it?"

He hated it. She'd aimed for whimsy, creativity, something he would never buy for himself or even think about. She had known she was taking a risk, but everything she did with Evan carried a risk, so this hadn't been much different.

"It's a clock," she told him, trying to keep her tone positive. She eased the contraption out of the box so he could see it better. "See, this column marks the minutes. The small silver balls drop into the column, one per minute." She pointed to the tube down which the balls were supposed to fall when the clock was plugged in. It was marked in increments of five. "Then, when there are sixty balls in the column, it empties and a bigger ball drops into the hours column." She pointed to the wider tube, which was marked from one to twelve. "There are instructions on how to set it. The back is clear, so you can see the mechanism while it's working." She rotated the contraption so he could view the back, which was constructed of clear plastic to display all the gears and levers and the motor.

"It's a clock?" He was still frowning slightly, but she detected an edge of excitement in his voice. "Let's get it running." The instruction pamphlet in hand, he carried the clock to an outlet near the door and plugged it in. She heard repeated *thunks* as the balls dropped into place. "Wow! This is cool!" he exclaimed, a boyish eagerness charging his voice. "This is the most amazing clock I've ever seen!"

"You like it?"

"It's great! Where in the world did you find it?"

"At a little specialty-gift shop I remembered from when I was a child." She began to relax.

"This is really cool." He turned the clock around so he could watch the gears turn and a wide screw rotate, lifting the minute balls up to the top of their tube. "I'm not going to get any work done ever again. I'm just going to stare at this all day."

"I got it for you because I thought if there's anything you need, it's time."

He left it on the floor, facing the couch, and rejoined her, his gaze lingering on his new toy. "I love it," he murmured, scrutinizing it from that distance. He let out a hoot when another minute ball dropped down the tube. "The kids are going to want to play with it, but I won't let them. It's *mine*," he said with exaggerated greediness. After a long moment—she wondered if he was waiting for the next ball to drop—he turned and planted a sweet kiss on her lips. "It's perfect," he whispered.

The kiss? she wondered. Or the clock?

"I love it that you wanted to give me time," he added, punctuating the statement with another brief kiss. "That clock comes pretty damned close."

"It was the best I could do."

"It's wonderful." From across the room came the tap of a ball falling into place. His lips were so close to hers she could feel their movement as he grinned. "I wish I'd found something as wonderful for you, Fil, but I hope…" His voice trailed off as he turned from her and reached for the silver-wrapped box. His humor seemed to fade, and she realized he was nervous about the gift he'd gotten for her. She vowed to herself that whatever it was, she would swear she loved it. Since it came from Evan, she *would* love it, no matter what.

The box was heavy. She rested it on her knees and meticulously lifted the taped corners. Unlike him and his children, she wasn't going to destroy the paper in her eagerness to get to the gift inside.

He leaned back into the upholstery, glancing at the clock when another ball rolled down the tube. She smoothed the folds of the paper and set it on the table, then studied the heavy white box. Taking a deep breath, she opened the lid and removed a layer of protective tissue. Below it was what appeared to be a crystal ball.

She suppressed the urge to laugh. Did he think that because she read cards she could divine the future in a crystal ball? Did he think she actually believed in the tarot and all that? If she did believe it, she wouldn't be here with him right now. Her cards had told her to play it safe and not get involved with him.

Yet sitting next to him on the sofa, their glasses of brandy side by side before them and the taste of his kiss still on her lips, she felt more involved with him than she'd ever felt with a man before. They hadn't known each other long, yet their lives had become intimately linked, and the hell with the tarot reading.

Cautiously, she lifted the crystal ball from the box—and realized it wasn't really a crystal ball. It was a sphere of crystal, all right, but suspended inside it was a silver crescent moon and three small, elegant silver stars. She gasped at its beauty.

He looked hopeful. "You like it?"

"Oh, yes." She sighed, utterly transfixed. She would

take it back to New York with her and display it on her dinette table. No, on the shelf in front of the window, so what little sunlight seeped through the narrow glass would shine on it and make it shimmer.

No, she would keep it on her nightstand, so it would be the last thing she saw before she fell asleep, the first thing she saw when she opened her eyes.

A waxing moon. From Evan.

"It's wonderful," she murmured, then set it carefully on the coffee table, freeing her hands so she could wrap her arms around him. The kiss she gave him was slower and deeper than the one he'd given her, but he didn't object. Quite the opposite—he opened his mouth to her, invited her in and then followed her back, his tongue dancing with hers, his mouth devouring hers. His hands moved restlessly through her hair, and when she brushed her teeth against his lower lip, he groaned and went still. Deliberately, he extricated his hands from her hair and leaned back. She saw his chest rise with each breath.

"I guess you like it, huh?" he joked, although he was hardly smiling.

"Not only because it's beautiful but because it's gloriously impractical. Maybe even more impractical than the clock."

"I don't get to be impractical very often," he admitted, sliding one hand down her arm until he could lace his fingers through hers. "I like being impractical with you."

He kept her hand snugly in his as they lifted their glasses and drank. The tree sparkled. The clock dropped another ball. Filomena's gaze alighted on her moon and she smiled. Evan's shoulder felt solid against hers.

Impractical. Yes. Everything about this was impractical, and she savored it. What else was Christmas for, if not to be impractical, to forget about the cold reality waiting outside the door and revel in the magic, believe in it, let it triumph for just this one night? What better way to celebrate Christmas than with a gift of time, time spent with a loved one, a night lit by an enchanted moon?

She wasn't sure how many balls dropped before their brandy was gone and they stirred from their companionable silence. Evan stretched and stood, his hand still clasping hers so he could pull her to her feet. Without a word, he led her out of the living room and down the hall to the den. "Bedtime, guys," he announced.

"Daddy, you've just got to see one thing—" Billy began.

"Daddy, you should see how he made his car wiggle back and forth!" Gracie chimed in.

"Tomorrow," Evan insisted. "You can show me tomorrow."

"You don't have to go to work tomorrow?" Billy asked.

"Nope. The stores will be open, but I don't have to be there. So let's tidy up a bit and then it's upstairs time."

They didn't protest too much about having to part temporarily with their new toys, although they did seem to spend longer than usual picking up their things and straightening out the room. When Gracie asked Filomena if she would read some of *Winnie-the-Pooh* to her, Filomena couldn't say no.

The evening rituals felt so normal to her, so familiar: bathing Gracie and then leaving her hairdressing to Evan. Sitting with Billy and discussing something profound and solemn. Tonight their conversation dealt with the logistics of Santa's visiting so many houses in one night.

"That's why Christmas always seems like the longest night of the year," Billy reasoned. Then a few minutes in Gracie's room, where Filomena read the first chapter of *Winnie-the-Pooh* while Gracie clutched her Piglet doll and fought to keep her eyes open. By the time Filomena reached the end of the chapter, Gracie's eyelids had won the battle. Filomena tucked her blanket around her and tiptoed out of her room.

Evan was in Billy's room, talking about Billy's new skates. "This weekend," he was promising, "I'll take both you kids to the rink and you can break them in, okay?"

"As long as I don't have to stay with Gracie. She goes too slow."

"I'll skate with Gracie," Evan promised, then glanced over his shoulder at Filomena, standing in the doorway. "Or maybe Fil will skate with her."

She shouldn't let such suggestions invade her heart. She shouldn't allow herself to believe she was a part of this family.

"I don't mind skating slowly," she said.

Evan kissed Billy's forehead, then backed out of the room, switching off the light. He closed the door and turned to face Filomena. His hair, as always, was adorably mussed. His shirt was slightly rumpled, his grin slightly crooked. Gazing at him, she felt a rush of emotion that wasn't quite like what she'd felt when she'd unwrapped the crystal moon, when he'd kissed her, when he'd said he liked being impractical with her. It was a combination of all those feelings and more, a soul-deep yearning to give in to the magic, just for this one magical night.

"Please don't go," he whispered, and she understood

that he was thinking what she was thinking, feeling what she was feeling. Wanting what she was wanting.

She looped her arms around his neck and rose on tiptoe to kiss him. The only place she would go tonight was wherever Evan wanted to take her.

HIS BEDROOM was at the other end of the hall. It boasted a broad window overlooking the backyard, which was covered with a creamy layer of snow that glowed in the moonlight. Beyond the yard the forest that connected his house with hers stood dark and still, all shadow and silhouette.

Filomena had glimpsed his room once or twice but never been inside it. The children never went in there while she was baby-sitting, so she'd never had a reason to enter it.

She had a reason now, and her heart pounded in the knowledge of what that reason was. She'd thought about this moment for so long, dreamed of it, warned herself against it. She was no femme fatale, no love-'em-and-leave-'em vixen who took such things lightly. But Evan...

For one night with him, she would forget who she was and what her life was about.

He edged up behind her, sharing the view she was admiring. She felt his mouth touch the crown of her head. "I've wanted you from the first moment I saw you," he confessed.

She spun around, both flattered and unnerved. "You did?"

He nodded. "That first time, when you came tramping out of the woods with Billy and Gracie and I didn't even know who you were."

"Is that why you hired me?"

"God, no. Hiring you ruined everything. You were my kids' baby-sitter. How could I even think about making love to you?"

"Maybe you should have thought about it, anyway," she teased. She'd certainly thought about it. Plenty of times.

"Making a pass at you, Fil…" He offered a lopsided, stunningly sexy grin. "I mean, it's not as if I'm some kind of smooth operator. I'm just an ordinary suburban dad."

"Ordinary?" She laughed, letting her hands come to rest on his shoulders. "Evan, you are the most extraordinary man I've ever met."

He kissed her then, a fierce, devouring kiss. Not the sort of kiss a smooth operator might give, but a kiss that communicated all his need, all his longing, the kiss of a man who had what he wanted and wasn't going to let it get away. He ran his hands along her back, as low as her hips and up again, his palms skimming the velvet of her jumper, his body radiating heat into her chest and hips as he drew her close. Then he broke from her and sighed. "Is there a zipper on this thing?" he asked.

She laughed. "No. You have to pull it over my head."

"Oh." He gathered handfuls of the plush fabric, catching her turtleneck on his way. Her moon necklace got tangled in the mess, and before she knew it he'd tugged everything off her in one pull. Her hair crackled with static electricity before settling back against her shoulders.

Stripped to her bra and tights, she felt a sudden chill—until Evan's gaze swept the length of her. Then she felt warm. Hot. She had never been ashamed of her body—

she wasn't stylishly thin, but she was healthy, with broad shoulders and firm muscles. The intensity burning in Evan's eyes, the motion in his neck as he swallowed, the nearly imperceptible tremor in his hands as he reached around her to unfasten her bra told her he was thrilled by what he saw.

He had her stripped naked in less time than it would have taken for a ball to slide down the minute column of his new clock. He had himself stripped naked in even less time—with some assistance from her. Two people could unbutton a shirt faster than one. Two people could shove down a pair of slacks much, much faster.

His body was a wonder of sleek surfaces—taut muscles stretching across his chest and back, sinewy arms and legs, not a hint of fat anywhere on him. It was an athlete's body, lithe and limber. Sparse swirls of gold-tinged hair spread across his upper chest, his shoulders appeared to have been carved out of rock, and his arousal...

She curved her fingers around the swollen flesh. He groaned and peeled her hand away. "Don't do that unless you want this over very quickly," he pleaded in a hoarse whisper.

Somehow they made it across the room to the bed. He switched off the bedside lamp, letting the room fill with the silver moonlight that spilled in through the windows. And then they lost themselves to each other, hands sliding, gliding, legs twining and flexing, lips grazing over skin. He kissed her throat, her breasts, the soft curve of her belly. He caressed her sides, her thighs, wedged his hand between her legs and found her damp, so ready for him.

She touched him, as well, at first avoiding his erection

while she learned the warm expanse of his back, the tense flesh of his buttocks, the ridges of rib and muscle shaping his chest. But eventually she sneaked back down to trace his penis with her fingers. He was damp, too, as ready for her as she was for him. "Evan," she whispered.

"I know." Barely a breath of sound. "I know, Fil..." He rolled away from her and yanked open a drawer in his night table. She heard the sound of foil tearing, and then he came back to her. In one smooth, graceful motion he was on top of her, his legs spreading hers, his body finding hers. He entered her with a thrust so deep and certain she nearly came just from the acute pleasure of having him inside her.

For a moment they remained motionless. It took all her concentration just to breathe, just to keep her eyes focused on his beautiful face, the tension in his jaw, the helpless hunger in his eyes. And then he moved, and she moved with him, their bodies rocking, dancing, meeting again and again in such perfect harmony she felt tears gather in her eyes. He paused for a moment, then drew a shaky breath and started again, closing his eyes, gathering her hands in his and squeezing.

His thrusts came faster, harder, lifting her higher. She followed him, then surged ahead of him, feeling her body coil tight, needing, needing more, until her soul burst in a blissful, throbbing release. Above her he shuddered, overtaken by his own climax.

After an eternity, he sank onto her. His mouth found her cheek, planted a kiss there, and then he settled onto his side, breathing raggedly. She watched him, wishing he would open his eyes. When at last he did, they were shaded with worry.

"I'm sorry," he murmured.

"Sorry?" For what? Making love with her?

"I went so fast, I—"

"Shh." She touched her fingers to his mouth to silence him. "You were wonderful."

His lips moved against her fingertips and she pulled her hand away. "Really?"

"Yes, Evan. Really."

He studied her face in the moonlight, as if searching for a sign that she was lying. Why on earth should he be so doubtful? She hadn't had sex all that many times, but she could honestly say that none of those other times had come close to satisfying her the way this had. The way *he* had.

"Really," she said again, because he seemed so desperately in need of convincing.

He traced her cheek with his thumb, tucked her hair behind her ear and sighed. "I haven't…" he began, then halted, his gaze skittering away.

She cupped her hand to his cheek and guided his face back to hers. "You haven't what?"

"I haven't—" he swallowed "—been with a woman since my wife left."

That stunned her into silence. Two years? He was such a strong, virile man. Surely he must have known women, had urges, acted on them.

But he was more than a virile man. He was a father who had no time. He was a solid businessman who'd been abandoned for a hotshot famous athlete. He was a gentleman whose ex-wife had done quite a number on him. He was someone who would never have been with a woman just to have sex.

"I am honored," she said, the words rising from her heart, "that you saved all that passion for me."

He closed his eyes again, but this time she saw relief wash across his features, soothing him, rinsing the strain from his mouth and erasing the lines in his forehead. "That passion belongs to you, Fil. It's all yours."

"Good." She kissed his tender smile. "I want it all."

CHAPTER FOURTEEN

FROM SOMEWHERE behind Evan came the sound of the kids' voices. As his mind sluggishly groped toward full consciousness, he realized the kids were far away. Their voices were drifting up the stairs from the den. They sounded as if they were behind him because he had his back to the door.

He had his front to Filomena. She slept in his arms, her shoulder blades pressed to his chest, her tush nestled snugly against his groin. One long strand of her hair snagged in the stubble of his beard.

A wave of heat swelled in his brain and rolled down his spine to his hips, lurching him from pleasantly to ferociously aroused. He couldn't believe he wanted her again. They'd gone at it all night long like horny adolescents, like sex-starved fiends, like a man and a woman wildly, insatiably, in love. Hadn't they done it enough?

No, they hadn't. He could have made love to Filomena a million times, and it wouldn't have been enough.

He skimmed his hand along her side, following the slope down to her narrow waist and up to her hip. She made a soft sound, half a yawn and half a sigh, and arched her back. He was so hard it hurt.

He couldn't make love to her now, not with the kids up and about. He wasn't worried about them barging into his bedroom—not with a Santa sackload of new toys to occupy them downstairs—but he wouldn't be able to give himself fully to Filomena, knowing they were on the loose. A part of his mind would remain with them. He couldn't help it. He was a father.

Filomena arched again, shifted onto her back and blinked awake. She gazed up at him, her eyes so stunningly pretty he wanted to kiss them.

He kissed her mouth, instead. He kissed her so deeply, so thoroughly, so blissfully, that for a few scattered seconds he actually lost his awareness of the kids. For those few seconds, when his hand moved to her breast and circled it, and she covered his hand with hers, holding him against her, and she hooked her foot around his leg and drew him nearly on top of her, he forgot that he had a son and a daughter.

"Good morning," he murmured when he came up for air.

"Good morning."

He was unused to the sound of a woman's voice in the morning. Unused to the warmth of one in his bed. He could get used to it really quickly, if the woman happened to be Filomena.

A gale of Gracie's laughter blew up the stairs, cooling off his body. He eased out of Filomena's arms and settled on his back next to her, staring at the ceiling until the fog cleared from his brain. Once he could think again, he realized he had a big problem.

"What about the kids?" he asked.

"What about them?"

"You're going to go downstairs wearing what you wore yesterday. They'll know you spent the night."

"I think we can deal with that. Don't you?"

He didn't know. He'd never been in this situation before.

Gracie was probably young enough not to understand the implications of Filomena's emerging from his bedroom dressed in yesterday's outfit. But Billy... He already knew something was going on between his father and his baby-sitter. He knew it related to the fact that his mother was gone. He might not have all the mechanics down, all the anatomical configurations worked out, but he knew that when a woman spent a night in a man's bedroom, something was definitely going on.

"Relax," she whispered, propping herself up on one elbow and placing a light kiss on his cheek. "I'll handle it."

"We need to do this right," he warned. "Because..." He fell silent, afraid of saying the wrong thing, pressuring her, laying on the table cards she didn't want to play.

"Because what?"

He couldn't lie to her. "Because I'd like you to spend more nights in my bed."

"Relax," she said again, brushing another breezy kiss against his cheek before she swung out of bed.

Trying not to ogle her, he got out of bed, too. He loved the ease she seemed to have about her body, the strong muscles in her arms and legs, the generous curves of her breasts and hips. He loved the long black tumble of her hair and the golden undertone of her skin, which was as smooth and soft as the velvet dress she'd worn yesterday.

She lifted that dress from the floor, unraveled her top and necklace from it and shook the wrinkles out of the garments. He didn't want her to put them on. He didn't want her to leave this room. He wanted to spend the entire day behind the closed door with her, making love to her the way he had all night, touching her everywhere, kissing her everywhere, drowning in the sound of her hushed moans and broken sighs. He wanted to make her come the way he had last night, make her cling to his back and bite her lip and pulse around him as if her heart were beating between her legs. He wanted to make her crazy with ecstasy.

For the first time since Billy's birth, he wished he weren't a father.

He opened the door to the master bathroom. "Let me get you a towel," he said, preceding her into the small room and pulling a clean bath towel from the shelf. She might think she could handle breakfast with his kids, but he still wasn't sure it was going to be that simple. Not with Billy wondering, putting it together, sitting in judgment of him.

"You can have the shower," she said generously. "I'll just wash at the sink. I'll shower when I go home."

He didn't want her to go home, but if he begged her to stay, she'd feel smothered. Forcing a smile, he yanked the shower lever until the water sprayed hot.

The shower failed to help him unwind. The steaming water slid over his skin, making him wish Filomena's hands and lips were sliding over his skin. And her hair. God, her hair had turned him on. It had tickled and teased, sensuously soft. At one point, when she'd been on top of him and her hair had cascaded down around his face...

He adjusted the water to a cooler temperature and murmured, "Billy and Gracie, Billy and Gracie," until his body subsided.

When he turned off the water and swung open the frosted glass door, Filomena was gone from the bathroom, although her scent lingered in the steamy air. He wrapped a towel around his waist and opened the door into the bedroom. She wasn't there, either.

For a strange, disorienting moment he wondered if he'd dreamed last night. But no, his bed was an absolute mess. No way could he have left the sheets so rumpled by himself.

Remembering how those sheets had become rumpled practically nullified the therapy of the cool shower and the chant of his children's names. He turned away from the bed, heading back to the bathroom to shave.

Ten minutes later, dressed and groomed, he mustered his courage and left the bedroom. Perhaps Filomena wasn't nervous about facing his children because they weren't hers. Perhaps she figured she'd be gone from their lives in a matter of days, so any embarrassment she might feel would be as transient as she was.

What a depressing thought. Shrugging it off, he strode down the hall to the stairs. Cheerful voices and an appetizing aroma emerged from the kitchen.

"Fil's making French toast!" were the first words from Gracie's mouth. Not "How come Fil's here for breakfast?" Not "How come Fil's wearing the same outfit as yesterday?" Not "How come you look like you didn't get more than a half hour of sleep last night?"

French toast was clearly the answer to all Gracie's questions.

She was kneeling on one of the kitchen chairs, her elbows on the table and her chin resting on her hands as she studied the crystal moon Evan had given Filomena. Billy stood by the counter, where Filomena must have plugged in the clock she'd given him. Evan couldn't catch the boy's eye—and maybe that was just as well.

Filomena herself was at the stove, arranging slices of egg-and-milk-soaked bread in a skillet he vaguely recalled using a year ago to make scrambled eggs, which neither of the children had eaten. One of his few forays away from the wonderful world of broiling. He'd learned his lesson.

But the French toast smelled great, and at least Gracie seemed ready to accept Filomena's presence. "This thing is so pretty," she said, gazing at the moon inside the ball. "Fil says you gave it to her for Christmas."

"That's right." Evan wandered farther into the room, wishing Billy would turn around and acknowledge him.

"It's beautiful. Did you spend lots of money on it?"

From the stove came the sound of Filomena's laughter. "Gazillions of dollars," Evan deadpanned. "Fil's worth it, don't you think?"

"I think this moon is worth it," Gracie said reasonably.

Evan sidled up beside Billy. "Fil gave me the clock. What do you think?"

"It's cool," Billy said, his gaze sliding toward Evan for a second and then turning back to the clock.

"You okay?"

"Yeah. I'm fine." Billy pushed away from the counter and gave his father a solemn smile. "Fil's making French toast."

"I know. And she doesn't have to do that," Evan said, addressing Filomena as much as Billy. "She shouldn't be making breakfast. She's our guest."

"Well, I told her that," Billy said indignantly, "but she said she *wanted* to make breakfast. I told her we could just have cereal or bagels or something, but—"

"It's true," Filomena confessed, forking the browned

slabs of toast onto a plate. "I had a craving for French toast, and you're all going to have to suffer for it."

By the time they were seated around the table, coffee and milk and orange juice poured, maple syrup passed around and plates heaped with French toast, Evan realized that Billy wasn't upset about Filomena's having spent the night. He was upset about Filomena's having made breakfast. Several times he'd explained that he'd offered to put bagels and cream cheese out on the table and that would have been a great breakfast, but Filomena had denied him the opportunity to act like a proper host. Despite his resentment, he managed to wolf down more slices of French toast than anyone else, including Evan.

He asked whether they could go to the skating rink that day, and when Evan said it was a possibility, Billy asked Filomena if she'd join them. Obviously, he didn't mind her appearing in his kitchen in the morning, clad in the same clothes she'd had on yesterday. Whether or not he understood all the implications, he didn't seem the least bit troubled by her having spent the night with his father. When she said she needed to go home and take care of some things, he actually looked disappointed.

Evan felt as disappointed as his son looked. He didn't want her to go home and take care of things.

But if he'd learned anything in his life, it was that no matter how tightly he held something, it could still slip away. As much as he loved his children, he couldn't keep them safe inside his house forever. As much as he loved Filomena, he couldn't make her stay. He could only be here, where she could find him if she decided he was what she wanted.

"I really do have to go," she said, once she'd set down her fork and drained her cup of coffee.

Evan pushed his chair back, stood and detoured to the living room to find the box the crystal moon had come in. Filomena carefully wedged the glass globe into the protective cardboard. Then she said goodbye to the children—Gracie raced to her for a hug and also demanded a hug for the little stuffed pig Filomena had given her—and Evan walked her to the front door.

The wind had blown some of the powdery snow over the front walk. He glanced down at her shoes and thought about ordering her to stay in the house until he could sweep the walk clear for her. Exercising restraint, he only asked if she'd prefer to leave by the garage, so she'd have less snow to walk through.

"Oh, that's nothing," she said, peering through the window next to the door and waving a hand dismissively. "Hardly any snow at all."

She was right. It certainly wasn't enough snow to convince her stay. "Can I see you tonight?" he asked.

She turned to him and smiled. "For dinner?"

"Dinner and after."

Her smile widened. "Twist my arm. I'll say yes."

"Consider it twisted." He could bear her leaving if he knew she'd return. He opened his mouth again, wanting to tell her he loved her—but discretion held him back. No pressure. No grasping for what he couldn't have.

So he kissed her, pouring all his love into the kiss, hoping it would tell her what he didn't dare to put into words. She kissed him back, sweetly, softly, one arm wrapped around him while the other hugged her crystal moon.

And then she was gone.

FOR THE FIRST TIME in too long, she plugged her laptop into the phone jack and checked her e-mail.

She had to. In the past few days—in the past few hours—she had drifted so far off course she was in danger of never finding her way back to shore. Seated in the piano room with the sun bouncing off the new snow and glaring white through the windows, she had only to close her eyes to find herself back in Evan's bed, in his arms.

Or in his kitchen, fixing breakfast for his kids.

Good Lord, what was she turning into? A suburban hausfrau? A soccer mom? A woman so drunk on love she no longer knew who she was?

The e-mails helped to remind her. One was from Patty, crammed with information concerning the train everyone would be taking out of the city on December 31. If Filomena couldn't pick them up, Patty wrote, they'd share cabs to her house. "I can't wait to see you!" Patty concluded.

Two e-mails were from real-estate brokers Filomena had spoken with over the phone, both pitching their skills and services, mentioning the sale prices of other properties they'd recently represented and asking for the privilege of listing her house. One e-mail was from her thesis adviser at Columbia, saying he hoped she was faring well and getting her mother's estate in order and reminding her that the section of Modern American Literature she would be teaching during spring semester would be meeting Mondays, Wednesdays and Fridays at 10 a.m.

The final e-mail was from her mother's lawyer. "I'm aware that the real-estate market is usually rather sluggish at this time of year," he wrote. "If you can't sell the house quickly, you might consider taking a home-equity loan to settle your mother's debts quickly. The house might be easier to sell in the spring, and you can pay off the home-equity loan at that time."

In other words, she thought grimly, Leila Albright's creditors were growing impatient. Leila had died more than three months ago, and they were tired of waiting for their money.

She closed her eyes again, wishing she could transport herself back to Evan's house, away from all her obligations, her mother's debts, her mother's death, away from the world lying in wait beyond Arlington's borders. But she couldn't. The messages in her e-mail in-box were her reality. She had to sell this house. She had to teach her section of Modern American Lit.

And Evan had hired her to baby-sit only through the end of the year.

She set aside her laptop, rose to her feet and wandered into the living room. She'd placed the crystal moon on the mantel—a lousy location for it, half-lost amid the pine boughs and holly sprigs she'd arranged there. She removed the moon from its perch and trudged up the stairs to her bedroom. The shower she'd taken when she'd arrived home hadn't roused her. She was feeling the aftereffects of a long, wondrous night that had included pitifully little sleep.

In her bedroom, she set the moon on her night table, next to her neatly made bed. The blue silk scarf on her dresser snagged her attention.

"It doesn't mean anything," she muttered, even as she scooped up the cloth and its contents—her tarot deck. "But what the hell."

She shuffled the cards, cut the deck three times and dealt out five cards, from right to left, all the while pondering the question *Is my life back in New York City?*

The first card was the Lovers—which didn't necessarily have anything to do with lovers, Filomena remembered with a wry smile. The Lovers represented a choice. Between her passion for Evan and her passion for scholarship? Between New York and Arlington? Between using her brain and heeding her heart?

The second card was the Three of Swords, a sad card. It stood for losing her mother, she decided.

The third card was the Knight of Cups. Evan, obviously—a man with light hair and pale eyes, thoughtful and loving. The third card dealt was supposed to represent her present circumstance. She had to laugh at its appropriateness, even though she reminded herself she didn't believe in any of this tarot nonsense.

Next, the Seven of Pentacles—hard work and ingenuity. "My thesis," she reasoned. "My doctorate."

The final card was Death. "Swell," she grunted, even though she knew the Death card didn't really represent death, any more than the Lovers card represented lovers. The Death card symbolized transformation.

All the cards faced right side up, none reversed, which meant the answer to her question was yes. Her life was back in New York City.

If she believed in the tarot.

Which she didn't.

Yet she'd done the reading, hadn't she? And if she didn't believe in it, if she didn't believe in magic, if she didn't believe there were forces that sometimes contrived to turn a person's fate inside out, then how could she explain what had happened to her in the past few weeks? What had brought Evan's children through the woods into her life and brought her into theirs, into his? Why had her mother died while climbing Mont Blanc? Why had she left Filomena a crushing debt, but also this house—which she herself could have sold to pay off her debts?

Wasn't it possible that everything had happened in some sort of miraculous conspiracy to bring Filomena to Arlington so she could meet a man who just happened to be in desperate need of a baby-sitter at the exact moment she was in desperate need of something to do? Wasn't it possible that magic had something to do with it?

"What a crock," she snorted, rewrapping the cards inside the cloth and tossing the deck onto her dresser. Spinning away, she saw the moon Evan had given her, silver-white as it caught a shaft of sunlight.

How could he have known to give her the most beautiful moon in the world? How could he have made such magnificent love to her?

How could she ever explain the past few weeks of her life if she didn't believe in magic?

"My life is in New York City," she whispered, then let out a long, dreary sigh. She had never imagined herself the sort of woman who made love with a man all night and grilled French toast for his children in the morning. She was half her mother—an adventurer—and half her father—a scholar. She didn't belong in Evan's domestic world. She knew that.

And yet...

And yet. If the real sun could light up a lustrous moon encased in crystal, anything was possible.

THE DOORBELL RANG and Evan told himself, for the umpteenth time, to calm down. He was going to a party. Having fun was the main idea.

Sighing, he swung open the door to find Murphy and his wife, Gail, standing on the stoop. "All set?" Murphy asked. The collar of his coat was turned up against the winter night, and Gail was bundled in wool, her face half-hidden by a scarf. They'd asked if they could follow him to Filomena's house so they'd all arrive together.

It occurred to Evan that the Murphys were attired more formally than he was. He couldn't see Gail's dress, but he could see her ankles and feet. She had on stockings and elegant high-heeled shoes. Below the hem of Murphy's coat, Evan saw tailored trouser legs. He himself had chosen dark slacks, a pale-blue shirt and a crewneck sweater featuring an abstract pattern of bright colors. He'd worn it to work once last year, and Heather had told him it looked fabulous on him, but it was weird enough that he couldn't bring himself to wear it on a regular basis.

If Murphy was wearing a suit, so be it. Filomena hadn't specified the fanciness level of the party, which probably meant that everything from tuxedos to blue jeans was acceptable. Evan wasn't going to let himself get tied in knots over his outfit or anything else about the party. For all he knew, this might be his and Filomena's grand farewell. He'd damned well better enjoy himself.

"Let me grab my coat," he said, swinging open the closet door and pulling his bomber jacket from its hanger.

"Where are the kids? Did you get a sitter?" Murphy asked.

Evan shook his head. "I farmed them out." Billy was spending the night at his friend Scott's house, and Evan had managed to make an overnight plan for Gracie at the home of a classmate from her preschool. If he wanted— and if Filomena wanted—he could spend the night with her, as long as he woke up early enough to collect his kids before they drove their hosts insane.

"Smart move. You wouldn't believe what we're paying some fourteen-year-old twit to stay with Erin and Sean tonight."

"She's not a twit," Gail said, the words slightly garbled by her scarf.

"You're right. She's a shark. Five bucks an hour—and it's not like she gave up a hot date to sit for us. She's a high-school freshman. She'll probably be able to pay her entire college tuition if she invests tonight's earnings wisely."

"She's an enterprising young lady," Gail defended the sitter.

Evan zipped his jacket. "Well, given what you're paying her, we ought to get on over to Fil's and start partying." He pulled his keys from the pocket of his slacks, then said, "I'll meet you around by the garage, okay?"

He wanted tonight to go well. He wanted Filomena's party to be a success, and afterward, when her guests had settled down to sleep, he wanted to take her to bed and spend all night with her. Barring disaster, that was how things would go. When they woke up, it would be a new year. He could worry about losing her then.

He backed out of the garage and drove down the street, monitoring Murphy's headlights in his rearview mirror. This week had gone well, he reminded himself. Every night Filomena had been in his bed. Every night he'd learned a little more about her—that the inside of her elbow was an erogenous zone. That she'd once hiked to the bottom of the Grand Canyon with her parents, slept in a lean-to beside the Colorado River and climbed back up the next day. That her father took up scuba diving at the age of seventy. That she loved books about animals that acted like humans because she wanted to believe in magic, even though she didn't *really* believe in it. That she liked to cuddle with him after making love, breathing into the hollow of his neck, clinging to him, weaving her legs through his. That when she climaxed, she sometimes whispered his name—and when she did, it was all he could do not to tell her he loved her.

He loved her. He knew it and accepted it, and reminded himself that once she left he would be all right. He'd survived worse.

But he wasn't going to think about that tonight.

Only a couple of cars were parked in the circular drive in front of her door. But the windows were bright, and when he climbed out of his car, he heard the muffled din of voices and music emerging from the house. He remembered that most of her guests had taken the train up from Manhattan and so wouldn't have crammed her driveway with cars. He also remembered that all those guests would be sleeping at her house. It would not be the quiet, romantic night he would have wished for.

He met up with the Murphys on the front steps and rang the bell, wondering if Filomena would even hear it through the chatter and music.

She heard. She opened the door, and he felt all his emotions rise like the head on a glass of beer, bubbling, frothy, light yet dense. She wore a long, slim-fitting black skirt and a black tunic with gold threads running through it. Gold earrings dangled from her ears, a gold chain linking crystal beads circled her throat and gold bangles adorned her wrists. She shimmered.

The hell with the party. He wanted to race to her bedroom with her now and kiss the insides of her elbows until she was gasping and moaning and whispering his name.

"Hi, come in!" she said before Evan could introduce her to Murphy and Gail. As soon as he did, she said to Murphy, "I remember you from the poker game," then smiled warmly at Gail and took her coat. "Drinks are in the kitchen and food is everywhere else," she informed them, gesturing toward the living room with a sweep of her arm. "I'll go put these coats upstairs. Make yourselves at home."

Evan wanted to make himself at home, but he couldn't. Even though he knew his way around her house well enough to lead the way to the kitchen, he couldn't feel at home. Not when her house was filled with so many strangers.

Strangers to him. Not to her. These were her friends, from the other world she lived in.

She rejoined him in the kitchen, where he was pouring Gail a glass of wine. Looping her arm easily around his waist, she said, "Get yourself a drink, and then you can meet everyone."

He helped himself to a bottle of beer and let her tuck her hand through the bend in his elbow. He appreciated that she was publicly linking herself to him, but he still felt a bit daunted as she meandered through the living room with him, presenting him to a brilliant poet, an aspiring actor, a skinny, goateed gentleman with dreadlocks who owned a gallery, a plump, rosy-cheeked woman whose hobby was skydiving. Everyone seemed bright and glittery and fascinating.

And who was he? A daddy. An Arlington father of two who worked damned hard so he could make a good life for his kids.

What could he talk to these people about? Billy's prospects as a basketball player in the county league? Gracie's puppet show at preschool? Behind him, two people were discussing a Bertolucci retrospective at some art theater in Greenwich Village. The last four movies he'd seen had all been G-rated, filled with cutesy songs and gross-out humor.

Filomena left his side to answer the door, and the crowd swallowed her up. He leaned against the wall near the doorway to the dining room, sipping his beer and surveying his surroundings. Decorative candles burned on tables and windowsills—he hoped none got knocked over—and through the speakers of a portable stereo spilled the sweet sounds of Christmas music performed on a harp.

This was her life, he reminded himself. This group of intellectual, eclectic, multifaceted people, sky divers and artists, students and urban warriors, was her social circle. This was who she was.

He spotted Jennifer and Tank Moody entering the room. Tank might not have been the tallest person present, but he projected size, dominance, power. Clad in a fashionable suit and beaming a megawatt smile, he radiated charisma. Jennifer looked slightly overwhelmed, hanging off his arm.

Overwhelmed had never before been a word he associated with Jennifer.

He wove a path through the throng, sidestepping a table filled with platters of exotic snacks and cinnamon-scented candles, until he reached Jennifer and Tank. Tank immediately gave him a crushing handshake. "Evan! Great seeing you, man! This party seems interesting. Where'd you find that beer?"

"Through that door," Evan said, pointing in the direction of the kitchen.

"You want something, baby?" he asked Jennifer.

"I'm fine for now," she murmured, smiling up at him.

Baby? Evan couldn't believe his tough, determined second-in-command would let any man call her that.

"Look at him," she whispered, watching in awe as Tank moved through the room, pausing to introduce himself to someone, winking and circling an arm around the shoulders of a pretty young woman. "He's so smooth."

"He's got you under his spell," Evan warned her.

"I know. I don't care." Jennifer smiled bravely at Evan. "The football season is just about over. During the off-season, he lives near his mother in Cincinnati. So..." she concluded with a shrug.

"And you don't care?"

"These few weeks were worth it, Evan. I promise I'll be back to my old self in a week or two, okay? I'll be the bitch you know and love. But this time I've spent with Tank...definitely worth it."

And his time with Filomena was definitely worth it, too, he assured himself. Every minute he'd spent with her had been a blessing. Every hour she'd cared for his children had been wonderful for them and essential for his peace of mind.

She floated toward him through the crowd, and her approach transformed everyone else in the room into a meaningless blur. He almost forgot to introduce her to Jennifer. "I've heard so much about you," Filomena said graciously, laying a hand lightly on Evan's arm. "Evan says you keep him sane at work."

"If Evan said that, he was lying through his teeth," Jennifer argued with a laugh.

"And Tank—he's absolutely charming." Filomena glanced his way. He was smiling flirtatiously at the sky diver. Evan remembered how easily he'd melted the hearts of grandmothers at the Champion store in New Haven. Yes, Tank was a charmer. He could probably even charm a sophisticated New Yorker who didn't follow football—like Filomena.

Evan sucked in a deep breath. He didn't like the route his thoughts were traveling. He didn't like worrying that a sports hero could beguile the woman he loved. It had happened before.

When Debbie had left, he'd been too shocked to fight it. When Filomena left, Evan would not be shocked—but in the meantime, he was going to fight for her, to make sure she wasn't charmed blind by Tank Moody and all her colorful, sophisticated friends. Maybe Evan was just a father and a businessman, but damn it, he could be charming, too.

"How about a dance?" he asked Filomena.

She frowned, obviously puzzled. "To 'Greensleeves'?" she asked, naming the tune emerging from the speakers of her stereo.

"Of course to 'Greensleeves.'" Actually, dancing wasn't his long suit, but if it would get Filomena into his arms, why not?

He planted his beer on the nearest table, slid his right hand around her waist and folded his left around her fingers. Pulling her close, he nuzzled her long, loose hair. "You are so beautiful tonight," he whispered.

She drew back and peered up at him, surprised but obviously pleased. "Why, Evan! You romantic fool!"

"That's me," he agreed. "A romantic fool." And then he pulled her close again, guiding her head to his shoulder. The harp plucked the sentimental ballad, and the party guests ignored them, engrossed as they were in their scintillating arguments about whether sushi was preferable to sashimi or whether Tom Stoppard was a more seminal playwright than Harold Pinter. The majority of them probably had their Ph.D.s or, like Filomena, were close to getting them. The majority could probably identify a play by Harold Pinter after hearing one line and could discourse on sashimi in Japanese.

But Evan was the one holding Filomena. He was the one she was dancing with. And as soon as he steered her into the dining-room doorway, under the mistletoe, he was the one she was kissing.

CHAPTER FIFTEEN

BY ONE O'CLOCK, everyone who wasn't staying the night had left and everyone who was had succumbed to fatigue and vanished up the stairs to sack out in the various guest bedrooms Filomena had set up. She roamed around the living room in her stocking feet—her shoes were someplace, but she couldn't remember where—blowing out candles and gathering dirty glasses and wrinkled napkins from the tables.

She carried the glasses to the kitchen, where Evan was filling the sink with hot water and dish detergent. Bubbles foamed in the basin, and lemon-scented steam rose from it.

What a glorious sight he was, tall and lean, his hair disheveled but his posture alert, as if it were the middle of the afternoon and he was brimming with energy. Maybe he was. Maybe the bright slashes of color in his sweater fueled him. Maybe parties stimulated him.

This party had stimulated her. It had been an unqualified success. Everyone had mingled well, the food had been enthusiastically consumed and that football player, Tank Whatever, had added a dash of star quality to the proceedings. Her mother wasn't the only one who could meld a disparate group of people into a mass of collective good cheer. Filomena had inherited the hostess gene. She ought to be delighted.

But it was late, and the house was quiet, and she was fading.

"You don't have to do that," she said when Evan lifted an empty platter from the counter and swirled it in the soapy water.

He glanced over his shoulder at her. "How many times have you taken care of business in my kitchen? I owe you big. This is the least I could do."

"I was just going to leave everything for tomorrow." She placed the glasses carefully on the counter.

"If we do some tonight, there'll be less to do tomorrow."

"How practical." She sidled up next to him and rested her head on his shoulder. Actually, she didn't quite rest it, since scrubbing of the platter made his arm move back and forth, giving her head a bumpy ride. "I hope you enjoyed the party," she said.

"I did."

"My friends thought you were cool."

"Cool? Me?" He chuckled. "Yeah, right." He rinsed the suds off the platter. It was one of her mother's Lenox dishes, a perfect circle of creamy porcelain.

"My mother always used to serve hors d'oeuvres on that plate. Toast points with caviar, or smoked salmon. Or pâté."

He shook the excess moisture from the dish and reached to put it into the drying rack. She intercepted him, taking the heavy plate in her hands. It was still warm from the water.

"What am I going to do, Evan?" she asked, the last of the party's giddiness seeping from her like air from a balloon, leaving her flat and empty.

He shut off the water and turned to her, his face etched

with concern. He must have heard the pain in her voice, the sorrow. He took the plate from her and put it in the rack, then enveloped her hands in his. Like the plate, they were warm and familiar. "Maybe you're right," he said. "Let's leave the rest and get some sleep. It's late."

She shook her head. She was so sad all of a sudden, so weary. "That was my mother's favorite serving dish. She's dead, Evan. She's gone."

He gave her hands a gentle squeeze. "I know."

"It's finally sinking in. This party and all my friends—and now I have to sell the house. I'll have to sell all these things—my mother's platters, her dishes, most of the candlesticks. I have no place to store all her stuff and I can't afford to rent storage space. I can't save them."

"Don't think about it now," he urged her.

"I've avoided thinking about it for too long," she confessed. He didn't deserve to have her unload all her grief on him, but she trusted no one else with it. Not even her good friends, all sound asleep in their makeshift beds and sleeping bags upstairs.

Only Evan. He was the only one she could talk to about this.

"I have to sell the house. I have to raise the money to pay off her debts—"

"Fil."

"She's dead, Evan. I'll never see her again. She'll never serve pâté on that platter again...." Her voice broke. Maybe it was fatigue, maybe the final crash after she'd exhausted her supply of energy, but tears filled her eyes and overflowed, and a deep sob seized her chest, wringing her heart.

Evan wrapped his arms around her and held her while she cried. He was so strong, so solid, absorbing her misery. He was a man, someone she could lean on. Someone who had given her the moon.

She was too heavy for him to lift, but he swept her into his arms, anyway, cradling her against his chest as he carried her through the kitchen. He nudged the light switch with his elbow to extinguish the light on his way through the door, then moved through the living room to the stairs.

"Where are we going?" she asked, her vision blurred with tears and her voice watery.

"Upstairs. You're dead on your feet, Fil. I'm going to put you to bed."

"Don't let me go," she pleaded. She'd lost her mother. She was about to lose her childhood home. She couldn't bear to lose Evan, too. Not tonight.

"I won't," he promised.

He carried her into her bedroom, relying on the faint light seeping in from the hall to find his way to her bed. Once he'd lowered her onto the plush down comforter, he turned on the bedside lamp. Next to it sat the moon he'd given her.

She loved it. She would never part with Evan's gift to her, even if she had to get rid of everything else she owned.

So many decisions loomed ahead of her in the new year. So much change. She didn't want to face it. She wanted the earth to stop spinning so she could stay where she was right now, lying on her bed with Evan seated beside her, gazing down at her, brushing her hair back from her damp cheeks.

"Make love to me," she pleaded in a ragged whisper. So what if she only wanted to fend off reality for a little longer? It would arrive soon enough. All she wanted was one more night with him, one more chance to stop the world, to remain in this safe place for a little while longer.

He leaned down to kiss her, kicked off his loafers and swung his legs up onto the bed. Within minutes, their clothing was gone. All that existed was Evan and Filomena and their passion, the demands of their bodies, the need in their souls. He was slow, patient, resisting his own urges until she pulled him on top of her, no longer willing to wait. Every touch made her want him more; every sigh and groan resonated in her heart. When at last he sank into her, she felt transformed, redeemed, as far from her sadness as she could be.

It was all a deception, she knew. Evan's potent body, his sleek motions, his grace and hunger and unabashed lust could distract her only for a while. Once she turned off the lamp and nestled into the circle of his arms, once he drew the blanket over them, kissed her forehead and drifted off to sleep, reality tiptoed back. It hovered close by, waiting for her, reminding her that the magic that had carried her through these past few weeks was about to run out.

The holidays were over; the new year had come. Soon she would be following all her friends back to Manhattan and resuming her life there.

Without her mother. Without her Arlington home.

Without Evan and his wonderful children.

She snuggled closer to him, determined not to think about it for just a tiny bit longer.

FIVE DAYS LATER she was gone.

It didn't matter how well he'd prepared himself for the inevitable. Kissing Filomena goodbye had been the worst moment of his life. Worse than the day Debbie had left him. Worse than the time Gracie had spiked a fever and he'd rushed with her to Arlington Memorial Hospital—where her pediatrician, Dr. Cole, had assured him that she had roseola and would be fine. Worse than the day his father had lost his job. Worse than the evening in mid-November when he'd left the poker table to check on his children and discovered them missing.

This was worse, because if Filomena loved him half as much as he loved her, she wouldn't have left.

They'd talked about her departure. She'd told him she had signed a contract with a real-estate broker who had suggested she leave everything in the house for now so it would appear warmer and more appealing to prospective buyers. She'd told him her adviser at Columbia was eager to plan her schedule for the time she had remaining in her doctoral program. She'd told him New York City wasn't much more than ninety minutes away by train, and even less time by car, and they could visit each other once she'd returned to the city.

He didn't want to visit her. He didn't want to be her weekend boyfriend. For the past month she'd been an integral part of his life, his family. She'd spent time with the kids. Eaten dinner with them. Given Gracie her baths. Slept in Evan's bed.

He was thirty-one years old. For God's sake, he didn't want to date a student! He wanted...

He wanted what they'd had during those few precious weeks.

He could have asked her to stay. Maybe he should have. But what would have been the point? She knew what she could have had in Arlington, and she'd walked away from it.

The kids were subdued. Molly Saunders-Russo praised Evan for picking Gracie up on time every day, but she remarked that Gracie seemed a little melancholy lately. "She isn't as bubbly as usual, Evan. Is something going on?"

"A friend of ours moved away," he explained. Calling Filomena a "friend" was a ridiculous understatement— yet it was apt. She'd been not just a baby-sitter but a genuine friend to his children, someone who listened to them, talked to them, respected them. Someone who read their cards and read their books to them. Someone they'd been able to trust.

She phoned him twice from the city. Both times, she sounded busy, almost frenetic. "I can't believe the size of the class I'll be teaching, Evan! They jacked up the enrollment. I'm going to have my hands full. I'd hoped for only fifteen kids in my section, but it's more like twenty-five. Did I tell you the Budapest String Quartet is going to be playing on campus? Oh, and remember Carlos? You met him at my New Year's party. He works at a gallery, remember? They're having a special exhibit of works by new artists, and my friend Suzanne is going to have a painting of hers exhibited there. You met Suzanne, too, the tall blond woman with the pierced eyebrow..."

This was Filomena, he reminded himself: dynamic, adventurous, preparing to teach undergraduates by day and gallivanting to concerts and gallery shows by night. She had returned to the life she wanted, a life more glamorous and exciting than anything he could offer her.

He'd survive. He swore to himself that he would.

"Do you have a minute?" Jennifer asked him one Monday morning, two weeks after Filomena had left town. She stood in his office doorway, dressed in a severe brown suit and her favorite shin-kicking shoes, her hair pulled back to display stern pearl earrings and a single pearl on a narrow gold chain around her neck.

Evan waved her inside. "What's up?"

She strode into his office, took the chair across the desk from him and rested a folder of papers in her lap. She looked offensively brisk and bustling. "It's time for us to make our move with Pep Insoles."

He didn't give a rat's ass about Pep Insoles. But that was a bad attitude for the head of Champion Sports to have, so he decided to pretend he cared about the product. Far more fascinating than Pep Insoles was Jennifer's miraculous transformation back into the hardheaded vice president she'd been before Tank Moody had crossed her path. "How are you doing?" he asked.

"I'm fine." She tapped her folder with a neatly polished nail. "I think we should give this deal the green light, Evan. Pep Insoles is offering us exclusive rights to distribute their product in the Northeast. This is a great opportunity for Champion."

"Okay, but how are you *really* doing?" he persisted. He knew Tank Moody had returned to Ohio at the conclusion of the football season. Surely Jennifer must be suffering a little in his absence.

She angled her head to study him. "I'm fine, Evan. How are you?"

"Don't you miss him?"

"Who? Tank?" She sighed. "Well, I'm not going to make myself crazy about it. We both knew going in that it would be one of those things."

"One of what things?"

"A one-night stand, only slightly longer." She smiled. "He was wonderful, Evan. I'll never forget him. But we

both knew it wasn't the sort of love that would last forever. It was what it was. Magic as long as it lasted, but
it didn't last very long.''

"You thought it was magic, huh?''

"Of course. But that's just it—magic isn't for real.
You enjoy it, you let it dazzle you, but you never forget
it's just an illusion.'' She tapped her file again. "So,
where are we with Pep Insoles? Are we ready to go to
contract with them?''

"Sure,'' he said, because he saw no reason not to.
"But I want us to keep close tabs on their labor practices,
okay? I don't want to stock anything that's manufactured
by underpaid kids.''

"We can write that into the contract,'' Jennifer pointed
out.

"Great. Go ahead and call your buddies in Atlanta.
Tell them we're ready to nail things down.''

The smile Jennifer gave him wasn't gooey and gushy
like the smiles she'd been giving Tank at Filomena's
party. It was a cool, satisfied smile, the smile of a woman
in complete control of her life. There wasn't an iota of
magic in it.

Jennifer was right. Magic was just an illusion. He
ought to accept reality the way she had, square his shoulders and get back to life as he once knew it.

He picked Gracie up early that afternoon at the Children's Garden. Molly was in the front office, her young
daughter seated in a baby swing beside her desk, gurgling
happily as the chair rocked to and fro. "Hi, Evan,'' she
greeted him. "Gracie's washing up. They were finger-
painting. She'll be just a minute.''

"No rush,'' he said. It was a novelty arriving so early

for Gracie that she wasn't ready for him. "How was her day?"

"Good. She didn't nap during rest time, so she might be ready for bed early tonight. I think she's beginning to outgrow her need for a nap—which is a good thing, since she'll be starting kindergarten next fall. Most kindergartens don't schedule in nap time."

He eyed Molly's baby and realized how old Gracie had become. He used to think of her enrollment in kindergarten as a means of improving his work schedule; he'd be able to put her in the same after-school program as Billy and pick them both up at the same time.

But now he thought of kindergarten in terms of Gracie's maturity. She was evolving into an entirely new person. She wasn't the kid she'd been just weeks ago. She didn't need naps anymore.

"I can't make the Daddy School tonight," he said, abruptly aware that with his children changing, he was going to need Daddy School classes more than before. He no longer saw the Daddy School as proof of his own shortcomings as a father. It was, rather, a way of improving himself, a way of opening his mind to new ideas and approaches. A way of thinking about what was going on in his life and his kids'. A way of addressing his needs as a human being.

"Oh?"

"I don't have a baby-sitter." He would to have to find a new one. If he was ever going to come to terms with Filomena's absence, he ought to begin by finding and training a new sitter for the kids.

"I'm going to be starting a series of Saturday-morning classes," Molly informed him. "Before the baby, I used to teach classes here at the school Saturdays at 10 a.m.

Fathers could bring their children with them. Sometimes one of the teachers would take the kids upstairs or outdoors to play while I worked with the fathers, and sometimes we'd have joint classes with the dads and kids together. I'll be resuming those classes in a few weeks. They're a lot of fun—and you don't have to worry about baby-sitters.''

"Sounds great," he said. Daddy School and playtime for Gracie and Billy rolled into one. "Let me know when those classes start. I'll be there."

Molly smiled gently. "You're a wonderful father, Evan. You know that, don't you?"

He shrugged. "Just doing my best."

A few minutes later, he and Gracie left the building. She thumped her boots against the pavement and counted the early stars. "I love the winter 'cuz I get to stay up later," she announced.

"Actually, you don't," he argued. "It just gets late earlier."

"That's silly, Daddy!"

He scooted down to the Elm Street School to pick up Billy, then headed for home. He was feeling better. Not about being a father, not about his wonderful kids, but...about magic.

Jennifer had been right. Magic was an illusion. It was dazzling, it was fun—but it wasn't real.

What he'd had with Filomena wasn't magic. It was as real as anything had ever been in his life. His children had once believed Filomena was a ghost or a witch or some such thing, but she wasn't. She was a woman, and everything he'd ever felt for her was real. His world in Arlington was as real as hers in Manhattan. And damn it, he wanted her to be a part of his reality. As big a part as possible.

"Listen, kids," he said, suddenly energized, "we're not going straight home, okay? We're going to stop at McDonald's, grab some burgers and fries, then take a little trip."

"Now?" Gracie squealed.

"Where?" Billy asked.

"New York City."

"Can we get milk shakes, too?"

"Sure."

"I want chocolate!" Gracie bellowed.

"You want chocolate?" Evan steered toward the fast-food outlet right by the entrance ramp to the highway. "Then chocolate it is."

BILLY HAD BEEN to New York City once before that he could remember. Dad had taken him and Gracie to Madison Square Garden to see the circus. He remembered the smell of sawdust and animal poop, the clowns, some lady who rode a unicycle balanced on a tightrope, and cotton candy. He'd never eaten cotton candy before. Actually, you couldn't really eat it. You'd take a chunk into your mouth and it would melt away, leaving sweetness behind on your tongue.

But he'd never been in New York at night. And he'd never gone on any trip that his dad hadn't planned in advance and told him about. This was a real adventure.

Next to him, Gracie was asleep in her booster seat. Leave it to her to sleep through the most exciting thing they'd ever done. She hadn't even finished her milk shake. Dad had put the lid back on it and wedged it into the cup holder between the two front seats.

"What are we going to do in the city?" Billy asked. On either side of the highway were boxy apartment buildings filled with rows of bright, square windows. Streetlights arched over the highway, making it almost as bright as day.

"See Fil."

"Really?" He missed her. He hadn't wanted to say anything to Dad about it, because he kind of suspected that Dad missed her, too. Yesterday afternoon, while Dad was reading the Sunday newspaper and Gracie was playing with her new computer game, Billy had hiked through the woods—even with snow on the ground, he could follow the path easily—to Filomena's house. The fresh green paint on the back porch looked awfully bright in contrast to the snow. The front drive was plowed, and down at the street end of it, near the stone pillars, he could see a For Sale sign with a real-estate company's name printed on it.

He'd peeked into the windows, just the way he had when he used to visit the house, before Filomena came. The furniture wasn't covered with sheets anymore, but the place was haunted, for sure.

Her spirit haunted it. Closing his eyes, he could hear her laughter. He could smell cookies baking and turkey roasting. He could picture her long skirts and her jangly earrings, and he could feel her arm around his shoulders while they discussed whether Freddy the Pig and the other animals were smarter than Mr. and Mrs. Bean, who owned the farm where they all lived. He could remember her reading his cards, telling him he was a dreamer.

He had dreamed of going to New York City to see her. And now his dream was coming true.

His father steered off the highway onto a street lined

with towering buildings. "Do you know where we're going?" Billy asked.

"I have her address."

The sidewalks were filled with people, more people than he ever saw crowding the sidewalks in downtown Arlington. Most of them walked like soldiers, facing straight ahead, carrying shopping bags and briefcases and backpacks and swinging their arms. But some were just hanging out, dressed in colorful parkas and hats, kidding and shoving each other and lingering in the pools of light in front of restaurants and delis. Someone roller-skated smoothly through the throng, weaving back and forth and avoiding all the pedestrians. Billy was a pretty good skater, but he didn't think he could skate through a crowd like the one on the sidewalk, not without crashing into someone.

"Does she know we're coming?" he asked his father.

"Um...not exactly."

Well, that was okay. It made this trip more of an adventure. They'd surprise Filomena, and she'd be so happy to see them, and the surprise of it would make her even happier. Like a surprise birthday party or something.

They drove across a really wide street with train tracks running down the middle of it, and then they were on a quieter street of apartment buildings. Dad cruised slowly along the street, looking for a parking space. He turned the corner, drove around the block and cruised even more slowly. Up ahead, a car engine spurted to life. The car pulled away from the curb and Dad grabbed the space.

"Gracie's sleeping," Billy warned his father.

"I can carry her." He waited for Billy to climb out of the car, then leaned in, unfastened Gracie's seat belt and lifted her out of her booster seat. She made a whiny sound, then settled against his shoulder as he arranged her in his arms.

Dad led Billy to one of the brick buildings. "This is her address," he said. "Let's hope she's home."

"What are we gonna do if she isn't?" Billy asked.

"I don't know. We'll think of something. Finding a parking space is almost impossible in Manhattan, and we did that, didn't we? The rest should be easy."

The rest of what? Billy wanted to ask. But he only followed his father into the entry of the building. There was an inside door that was locked, and on the wall a metal panel with buttons on it. Next to each button was a name. "F. Albright" was near the top, because the names were listed alphabetically.

His father pressed the button next to "F. Albright." Nothing happened.

He pressed it again. Nothing.

He hoisted Gracie higher in his arms. Her head bobbled and then sank back onto his shoulder. She started to snore.

"What are we gonna do?" Billy asked.

His father looked frustrated. Maybe worried, too. "See, Billy, the problem is, I decided this wasn't about magic. But I guess we did need some magic to make sure Fil would be home. And we didn't get any magic. That's the whole problem, Billy—we don't need a lot of magic. Just a little."

"I don't believe in magic," Billy said, although he wasn't exactly sure what his father was talking about.

"I don't, either. But I think we could have used a little right about now."

"So, like, what should we do? Chant a magic spell or something? Like abracadabra hocus-pocus?"

"Maybe we should walk over to the campus. She works at the university."

"Where is it?"

"A couple of blocks away," he said. "Maybe she's at her office there, or in the library studying."

Why would she be in the library studying? She was a grown-up. It wasn't as if she had to do homework or anything. Once Billy was her age, he sure wouldn't be going to the library and studying.

Sighing, Dad leaned against the outer door, using his hip to open it. He paused, half in and half out of the building. "Say your magic chant again," he whispered.

"What? Abracadabra or hocus-pocus?"

"Both. Say them again," Dad ordered him.

Dad was acting weird, but Billy supposed that was part of the adventure. "Abracadabra hocus-pocus."

"One more time." Dad was smiling now.

Billy smiled, too. "Abracadabra hocus-pocus."

Then he heard the footsteps on the pavement. Someone was approaching the building. The footsteps grew faster, and he heard Filomena's voice. "Evan? Oh, my God, is that you?"

She rushed to the building and swept inside, bringing the cold night air in with her. She had a purple knit cap pulled down over her forehead, and matching purple mittens, and a long skirt and her familiar boots and a canvas tote bag in one hand, bulging with books and papers. She dropped the tote bag, tried to hug Dad, realized he had his hands full with Gracie and hugged Billy, instead.

Ordinarily Billy didn't like being hugged by ladies. But this was different. This was Filomena.

"Oh, my God!" she said again, and sighed. "I can't believe you're here! When did you get here? Have you been waiting long? Why didn't you tell me you were coming?''

"It's a surprise," Billy said before his father could answer.

She peered up at Dad. He grinned. "It's a surprise," he repeated.

Gracie stirred in his arms, rubbed her eyes and scowled at Filomena. "What's the surprise?" she mumbled.

"We missed you," Dad said to Fil.

It suddenly got very quiet in the entry. And warm. The air grew still, yet Billy sensed something rippling in it, like an invisible current. Filomena and Dad were staring at each other. Billy and Gracie could have been back home in Arlington for all Filomena and Dad noticed them.

"What's the surprise?" Gracie said again.

"I love you, Fil," Dad said. "And that's probably not a surprise."

She bit her lip. "You never even called me. I called you twice, but I thought...I thought maybe you didn't want to talk to me anymore."

"Oh, Fil..." He sighed, bent down and lowered Gracie to the floor. "Sorry, sweets—I need both hands for this," he explained, straightening back up and gathering Filomena's purple-mittened hands in his. "When you called and talked about all the exotic things you were doing, I figured you were lost to me. I can't offer you excitement. I can't offer you an Ivy League Ph.D., or Budapest concerts, or gallery openings. I'm the kind of man a woman leaves when she wants glamour and excitement in her life.''

"You may be right," Filomena murmured. "You're

more the kind of man a woman looks for when she wants a home and a family and all the things that matter.''

''Is that what you want?''

''If you're the man, that's what I want. I've missed you so much, Evan.'' She rose up and kissed him. Not a mushy icky kiss like actors did on TV, but a pretty big kiss anyway.

''What's the surprise?'' Gracie asked Billy.

''Shh.'' She could be such a pest sometimes.

''I came back to New York,'' Filomena said, ''because it's the only home I have.''

''Could you ever think of my house as your home?''

Her eyes twinkled. Billy thought he saw tears in them. ''Your house is a wonderful home.''

''But could you think of it as *yours?*''

She nodded, and Billy definitely saw some tears sliding down her cheeks. ''I always felt at home there.''

''Then come home.''

''I love you, Evan,'' she whispered, and kissed him again.

''Is that the surprise?'' Gracie asked.

''I guess I could commute,'' Filomena murmured. ''I'm teaching only three days a week, and the train isn't bad. And I'm sure I could sublet this apartment. Patty's sharing a one-bedroom place with two other grad students. I bet she'd love to take over my lease. Oh, Evan…why did you let me leave? Why didn't you ask me to stay?''

''I was afraid you'd say no. I thought it would be easier to lose you if I hadn't asked than if I had.'' He made a sound that was half a sigh and half a laugh. ''It wasn't easier. All that mattered was that I lost you. And all that matters now is that I've got you back.''

"I'm not going anywhere," she promised, then grinned. "Except home."

"What's the surprise?" Gracie asked Billy.

To shut her up, he said, "The surprise is that Dad and Fil got together because of me."

The grown-ups turned to stare at him. "Because of *you?*" Dad blurted out.

"I said abracadabra hocus-pocus. Three times. And it worked, didn't it?"

Dad laughed. Filomena looked confused, but she laughed, too. "Yeah," Dad admitted. "All we needed was a little magic. And it worked."

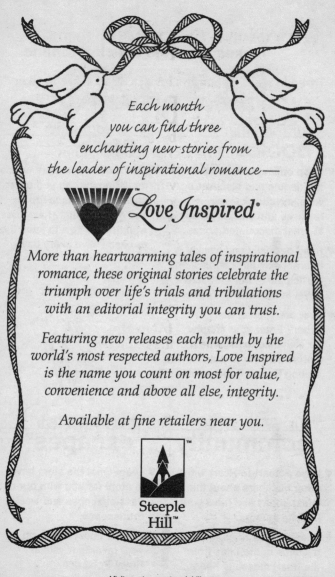

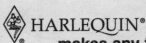

MAITLAND MATERNITY

Where the luckiest babies are born!

Join Harlequin® and Silhouette® for a special 12-book series about the world-renowned Maitland Maternity Clinic, owned and operated by the prominent Maitland family of Austin, Texas, where romances are born, secrets are revealed…and bundles of joy are delivered!

Look for

MAITLAND MATERNITY

titles at your favorite retail outlet, starting in August 2000

HARLEQUIN®
Makes any time special™

Silhouette®
Where love comes alive™

Visit us at www.eHarlequin.com   PHMMGEN